HANS ANDERSEN'S FAIRY TALES

HANS ANDERSEN'S
FAIRY TALES

Retold by E. Jean Roberton from the original
English version by Caroline Peachey

ILLUSTRATED BY SHIRLEY HUGHES

SCHOCKEN BOOKS • NEW YORK

First published by Schocken Books 1979

10 9 8 7 6 5 4 3 2   81 82

Library of Congress Cataloging in Publication Data

Andersen, Hans Christian, 1805–1875.
  Hans Andersen's fairy tales.

  Reprint of the 1961 ed. published by Blackie, Glasgow.
  SUMMARY: A collection of 25 tales including such lesser-
known titles as "The Leaping Match," "The Shepherdess and
the Chimney Sweep," and "The Garden of Happiness."
  1. Fairy tales, Danish. [1. Fairy tales]
I. Roberton, E. Jean.   II. Peachey, Caroline.
III. Hughes, Shirley.   IV. Title.
PZ8.A54Hao   1979   [Fic]   79-64120

Manufactured in the United States of America

ISBN 0-8052-3719-4 hardback
ISBN 0-8052-0632-9 paperback

Contents

CONTENTS

HANS ANDERSEN'S FAIRY TALES

The Tinder-Box

A soldier came marching along the highroad—left, right! left, right! He had his knapsack on his back and a sword by his side, for he had been to the wars and was now returning home. On the road he met an old witch and a horrid-looking creature she was.

'Good evening, soldier,' she said. 'What a bright sword and what a large knapsack you have, my fine fellow! You're a proper soldier. So I'll tell you how you could have as much money as you want.'

'Thanks, old witch,' cried the soldier.

'Do you see that large tree?' said the witch, pointing to a tree that stood close by the wayside. 'It's quite hollow. Climb up to the top, and you will find a hole large enough for you to creep through and you can get down into the tree. I will tie a rope round your waist, so that I can pull you up again when you call me.'

'But what am I to do down in the tree?' asked the soldier.

'What are you to do?' repeated the witch; 'why, bring back lots of money, to be sure! As soon as you get to the bottom, you'll find yourself in a wide passage; it is quite light—more than a hundred lamps are burning there. Then you will see three doors, which you can open, for the keys are in the locks. In the middle of the first room is a large chest with a dog sitting on it—

his eyes are as large as saucers but don't you worry about that. I will lend you my blue apron which you must spread out on the floor. Then go briskly up to the dog, seize him and set him down on it. When you've done that you can open the chest and take as much money out of it as you please. That chest contains nothing but copper coins. If you like silver better, you have only to go into the next room; there you will find a dog with eyes as large as mill-wheels. Don't be afraid of him; you have only to set him down on my apron and then rifle the chest at your leisure. But if you would rather have gold, you can have as much of it as you can carry by going into the third chamber. The dog that sits on this third money-chest has eyes as large as the Round Tower. But don't be alarmed; if you set him down on my apron he will do you no harm, and you can take as much golden treasure from the chest as you like.'

'Upon my word! that's not a bad plan,' said the soldier. 'But how much of the money am I to give you, old woman?'

'Not a penny of it,' replied the witch. 'The only thing I want you to bring me is an old tinder-box which my grandmother left there by mistake last time she was down in the tree.'

'Well, then, give me the rope and I'll get going,' said the soldier.

'Here it is,' said the witch, 'and here is my blue apron.'

So the soldier climbed the tree, let himself down through the hole in the trunk and suddenly found himself in the wide passage lit by many lamps, as the witch had described.

He opened the first door. Good! There sat the dog with eyes as large as tea-cups, staring at him as though in utter amazement.

'There's a good dog!' said the soldier, as he spread the witch's apron on the floor and lifted the animal on to it. He then filled his pockets with the copper coins in the chest, shut the lid, put the dog back in his place and went on into the second apartment.

Hurrah! There sat the dog with eyes as large as mill-wheels.

'You had really better not stare at me like that,' remarked the soldier; 'you'll hurt your eyes,' and with that he set the dog down on the witch's apron. But when he beheld the vast quantity of silver the chest contained, he threw all his pennies away in disgust and hastened to fill up his pockets and his knapsack with it. Then he passed on into the third chamber. The dog in this chamber really did have eyes as large as the Round Tower, and kept rolling round and round in his head like wheels.

'Good evening,' said the soldier, and he lifted his cap respectfully, for such a monster of a dog had never been seen or heard of before. He stood for a minute or two, looking at him. Then thinking, 'The sooner it's done the better!' he took hold of the immense creature, lifted him down, and raised the lid of the chest. Oh, what a lot of gold there was! Enough to buy not only all Copenhagen but all the cakes and sugar-plums, all the tin soldiers, whips, and rocking-horses in the world! Hastily the soldier threw out all the silver money he had stuffed into his pockets and knapsack and took the gold instead. He crammed not only his pockets and knapsack but his soldier's cap and boots too until he could hardly walk for the weight he carried. He lifted the dog on to the chest again, banged the door of the room behind him, and called out: 'Hallo, you old witch, pull me up again!'

'Have you got the tinder-box?' asked the witch.

'Gracious me, I'd quite forgotten it!' shouted the soldier, and he went back to fetch it. The witch then drew him up through the tree and soon he stood in the high road again, his pockets, boots, knapsack, and cap stuffed with gold pieces.

'What are you going to do with the tinder-box?' asked the soldier.

'That's no business of yours,' returned the witch. 'You've got your money; give me my tinder-box at once!'

'Well, take your choice,' said the soldier. 'Tell me at once what you want with the tinder-box, or I'll cut off your head.'

'I won't tell you,' screamed the witch.

So the soldier drew his sword and cut off her head. Then he knotted all his money securely in her blue apron, slung it across his back, put the tinder-box into his pocket and set off for the nearest town.

It was a large and handsome city. He walked into the first hotel in the place, called for the best rooms and ordered the choicest dishes for his supper—for he was a rich man with plenty of gold to spend.

The servant who cleaned his boots could not help thinking they were disgracefully shabby and worn to belong to such a grand gentleman. However, next day, the soldier provided himself with new boots and very gay clothes besides. He was now a great man, and the people of the hotel were called in to give him information about all the places of amusement in the city, and about their King and the beautiful Princess, his daughter.

'I would rather like to see her,' said the soldier.

'No one can see her,' was the reply; 'she dwells in a great copper palace, with many walls and towers round about it. No one but the King may go and visit her because it has been prophesied that she will marry a common soldier and our King wouldn't like that at all.'

'I should like to see her just once, though,' thought the soldier.

Well, he lived a gay life; he went continually to the theatre, drove out in the Royal Gardens and gave much money in alms to the poor. He knew by past experience how miserable it was not to have a shilling in one's pocket. He was always gaily dressed and had a crowd of friends who all declared he was an excellent fellow and a real gentleman, which pleased our soldier very much. But, as he was giving and spending every day and never received anything in return, his money began to dwindle away. At last he had only twopence left and was forced to remove from his splendid apartments and take refuge in an attic, where he had to brush his boots and darn his clothes himself, and where none of his friends ever came to see him because it was quite exhausting to go up so many stairs.

One evening it was very dark and he could not afford to buy himself a candle; however, he remembered all at once that there were a few matches lying in the tinder-box that the old witch had bade him fetch out of the hollow tree. So he brought out this tinder-box and began to strike a light. No sooner had he rubbed the flint-stone and made the sparks fly out, than the door burst suddenly open and the dog with eyes as large as tea-cups, which he had seen in the cavern beneath the tree, stood before him and said, 'What commands has my master for his slave?'

'What's this?' cried the soldier; 'this is a wonderful tinder-box if it will really provide me with whatever I want. Fetch me some money this instant!' said he to the dog. The creature vanished and in half-a-minute he was back again, holding in his mouth a large bag full of pence.

So now the soldier understood the virtue of this marvellous tinder-box. If he struck the flint once the dog that sat on the chest full of copper came to him; if he struck it twice, the dog that watched over the silver answered him; and if he struck it three times the monstrous guardian of the golden treasure appeared.

The soldier could now go back to his princely apartments. He bought himself an entirely new suit of clothes, and all his friends remembered him again and loved him as much as ever. But one evening he thought: 'How truly ridiculous it is that no one should be allowed to see this Princess! They all say she is so very beautiful: what a shame it is that she should be shut up in that great copper palace! And I do so want to see her—where's my tinder-box, by the bye?' He struck the flint, and lo! before him stood the dog with eyes as large as tea-cups.

'It is rather late, I'm afraid,' began the soldier; 'but I want to see the Princess so much; only for a minute, you know.'

The dog was out of the door and, before the soldier had time to think of what he should say or do, he was back again with the Princess sitting asleep on his back.

You could see she was a real Princess—so beautiful, so enchantingly beautiful was she—and the soldier could not refrain from kissing her, for he was a real soldier. Then the dog ran back again to the palace with the Princess. But the next morning, while she was at breakfast with the King and Queen, the Princess said that she had had a very strange dream. She had dreamt that she was riding on a dog, an enormously large dog, and that a soldier had knelt and kissed her.

'A pretty sort of dream, indeed!' exclaimed the Queen. And she insisted that one of the ladies of the court should watch by the Princess's bedside on the following night, in case she should be disturbed again by dreams.

Next evening the soldier summoned the dog to fetch the Princess a second time. So he did, and he ran as fast as he could; however, he wasn't quick enough to prevent the ancient dame who was watching at the Princess's bedside from following them. She saw the dog vanish into a large house and saying to herself, 'I know what I'll do,' she took out a piece of chalk and made a great white cross on the door. But on the way back the dog happened to notice the white cross on the door, and he immediately took another piece of chalk and put crosses on every door throughout the town.

Early in the morning the King, the Queen, the old court dame, and all the officers of the royal household all came out, every one of them curious to see where the Princess had been. 'Here it is!' exclaimed the King, as soon as he saw the first street-door with a cross chalked on it. 'My dear, where are your eyes?—this is the house,' cried the Queen, seeing the second door which bore a cross. 'No, this is it, surely—why, here's a cross too!' cried all of them together, on discovering that there were crosses on all the doors. It was obvious that their search would be in vain, and they gave it up.

But the Queen was an exceedingly wise and prudent woman. She took her gold scissors, cut a large piece of silk stuff into strips, and sewed these strips together so they made a pretty, neat little bag. She filled this bag with the finest white flour, tied it to the Princess's waist and then took up her golden scissors and cut a little hole in the bag, just large enough to let the flour drop out gradually all the time the Princess was moving.

That evening the dog came again and took the Princess on his back. He ran away with her to the soldier (who was getting very fond of her and would gladly have been a prince so he could have married her). He never saw how the flour went drip, drip, dripping, all the way from the palace to his master's room, and from his master's room back to the palace. So next morning the King and Queen easily found where their daughter had been and they took the soldier and cast him into prison.

So he sat in the prison and, oh! how dark it was, and how wearisome! The turnkey kept coming in to remind him that tomorrow he was to be hanged. This piece of news was far from agreeable, and the tinder-box had been left in his lodgings at the hotel.

When morning came, he peered through his narrow iron

grating and saw the people all hurrying out of the town to watch him hanged; he could hear the drums beating and presently, too, he saw the soldiers marching to the place of execution. What a crowd there was rushing by! Among the rest was a shoemaker's apprentice; he bustled on with such speed that one of his slippers flew off and struck the bars of the soldier's prison window.

'Hey, there, shoemaker's boy!' cried the soldier; 'it's no use you hurrying, for none of the fun will begin till I come; but if you'll oblige me by running to my lodgings and fetching me my tinder-box, I'll give you sixpence. But you must run like the wind.' The boy liked the idea of earning sixpence, so he raced off and brought the tinder-box to the soldier. And then— ah, yes, now we shall hear what happened!

Outside the city a gibbet had been built and the soldiers were gathered round it with many thousands of people. The King and Queen were seated on a magnificent throne opposite the judges and the whole council. The soldier was brought out and the executioner was on the point of fitting the rope round his neck, when, turning to their Majesties, he asked them to let him smoke a pipe of tobacco before he died. The King could not refuse this harmless request, so the soldier took out his tinder-box and struck the flint—once he struck it, twice he struck it, three times he struck it—and lo! the three magic dogs stood before him.

'Help me; don't let me be hanged,' cried the soldier. And straightway the three terrible dogs fell on the judges and councillors and tossed them high into the air—so high that in falling down again they were broken to pieces.

'We will not——' began the King. But the monster dog with eyes as large as the Round Tower did not wait to hear what his Majesty would not; he seized both him and the Queen and flung them up into the air after the councillors. And the soldiers were all desperately frightened and the people shouted out with one voice: 'Good soldier, you shall be our King and the beautiful Princess shall be your wife and our Queen.'

So they put the soldier into the King's couch and the three dogs raced before it, while all the boys whistled through their fingers and the soldiers presented arms. They took him to the palace and made the Princess his wife, which she liked much better than being a prisoner in a copper castle. The wedding lasted a week and the three dogs came to the feast and opened their eyes wider than ever at all they saw there.

The Swineherd

There was once a poor Prince who had only a small kingdom. However it was large enough to support a wife and he decided he would marry.

His name was renowned far and wide and there were a hundred princesses who would have said 'Yes, thank you,' if he had asked them. But he wanted to marry the Emperor's daughter.

It so happened that a rose-tree grew where the Prince's father was buried—a most beautiful rose-tree, which blossomed only once in every five years and even then bore only one flower— but what a wonderful rose it was! It was so sweet that whoever smelled it forgot all his cares and sorrows. Furthermore, the Prince had a nightingale who could sing so beautifully it seemed that all the loveliest melodies in the world lived in her little throat. He put the rose and the nightingale into two large silver caskets and sent them to the princess.

The emperor had them brought into a large hall where the Princess was playing at 'visiting' with her ladies-in-waiting, and when she saw the caskets with the presents she clapped her hands for joy.

'Oh, I do hope he has sent me a little kitten,' she said—but out came the rose-tree with its beautiful rose. 'Oh, how prettily it's made!' said all the ladies-in-waiting. 'It is more than pretty,' said the Emperor, 'It is really charming.'

The princess touched it and was almost ready to cry. 'Nonsense, father,' she said. 'It's not a work of art at all, it's real!'

'How horrid,' said all the ladies together. 'It's a real one.'

'Let's see what's in the other casket before we get bad-tempered about it,' said the Emperor. So the nightingale flew out, and sang so delightfully that no one could say anything ill-humoured about her.

'*Superbe, charmant!*' exclaimed the ladies, for they all used to chatter in French, each one worse than the last.

'The bird reminds me of the musical box that belonged to our blessed Empress,' said an old knight. 'It has the same tone, the same skill.'

'Yes, yes,' said the Emperor, and he wept at the thought of it.

'I still hope it's *not* a real bird,' said the Princess.

'Of course it's real,' said the messenger who had brought it.

'Well, then, let it go free,' said the Princess, and she refused to see the Prince.

However, this didn't discourage him. He stained his face brown and black, pulled his cap over his ears, and knocked at the door. 'Good day to my lord the Emperor,' said he. 'Can I have work at the Palace?'

'Yes, certainly,' said the Emperor. 'We have a great many pigs, and I need somebody to look after them.'

So the prince was appointed Imperial Swineherd. He was given a dirty little room close by the pigsty and there he sat and worked for the rest of the day. By the evening he had made a pretty little cooking-pot and hung tiny bells round it, so when the pot boiled they tinkled in the most charming manner and played the old tune:

> '*Ah, my dearest Augustine,*
> *All is lost, all is lost.*'

But the cleverest thing about the whole arrangement was that whoever held his finger in the steam from the pot could smell all the dishes that were cooking in every kitchen in the city.

Now the Princess happened to walk that way and when she

heard the tune she stood quite still. She was pleased, for it was the only piece she knew and she played it with one finger. 'Why, that's my piece,' said the Princess. 'That swineherd must have been well educated. Go and ask him the price of the instrument.' So one of the ladies ran in, but she was careful to put wooden slippers on first because of the dirt.

'What price would you take for the new cooking-pot?' she asked.

'Ten kisses from the Princess,' said the swineherd.

'Whatever next!' said the lady.

'Well, I won't sell it for less,' said the swineherd.

'What did he say?' said the Princess.

'I don't really like to repeat it,' said the lady.

'Well, you can whisper it in my ear. He is a most impudent fellow,' said the Princess when she heard and she walked on. She had only gone a little way when the bells tinkled so prettily she had to stop.

'Wait a minute,' said the Princess. 'Ask him if he will have ten kisses from the ladies-in-waiting.'

'No, thank you,' said the swineherd. 'Ten kisses from the Princess or I keep the pot myself.'

'How tiresome he is,' said the Princess. 'You will all have to stand round me so that nobody sees us.'

So the ladies-in-waiting gathered round her and spread out their dresses. The swineherd got his kisses and the Princess got the pot.

There was great jubilation. The pot was kept boiling the whole evening and the whole of the following day. They found out what was cooking on every stove throughout the city, from the Prime Minister's to the cobbler's, and the ladies of the court danced round it and clapped their hands.

The swineherd never let a day pass without making something. At last he constructed a rattle which, when it was swung round, played all the waltzes and jig tunes that had ever been heard of.

'Ah, that is *superbe*,' said the Princess when she passed by. 'I

have never heard prettier music. Go and ask how much it costs;
but mind, no more kisses.'

'He demands a hundred kisses from the Princess,' said the lady
who had been to ask.

'I think he must be mad,' said the Princess, and walked on, but
when she had gone a little way she stopped again. 'One must
encourage art,' said she, 'and I am the Emperor's daughter. Tell
him he can have ten kisses from me and the rest from my ladies-
in-waiting.'

'Oh, but we shouldn't like that at all,' they murmured.

'What are you muttering about?' asked the Princess. 'If I
can kiss him, surely you can!'

So the lady went back to the swineherd, but he said, 'A
hundred kisses from the Princess herself.'

'Stand round,' she said, and all the ladies stood round her
again while the kissing was going on.

'I wonder why there's such a crowd by the pigsty?' said the
Emperor, who happened just then to step out on his balcony. He

rubbed his eyes and put on his spectacles. 'It's the ladies-in-waiting! I'd better go down and see what they're doing.'

They were so busy counting the kisses that they did not notice the Emperor. He stood on tip-toe to see. 'What's all this?' he said. And when he saw what was happening he boxed the Princess's ears, just when the swineherd was taking the eighty-sixth kiss.

'Clear out,' said the Emperor, for he was very angry, and both the Princess and the swineherd were thrust out of the city. The Princess wept, the swineherd scolded and the rain came pouring down.

'Alas, unhappy girl that I am,' said the Princess. 'If only I had married that handsome young Prince! Oh, how unlucky I am.'

The swineherd went behind a tree, washed the dirt from his face, threw off his rags and stepped out again in his most princely attire. He looked so noble that the Princess could not help courtseying to him.

'I have learnt to despise you,' he said. 'You wouldn't have anything to do with an honourable Prince. You didn't set any store by the rose and the nightingale. But you were ready to kiss the swineherd for the sake of a trumpery plaything. You have got your deserts.' Then he went back to his own little kingdom and shut his palace door in her face. Now indeed she had good reason to sing:

'Ah, my dearest Augustine,
All is lost, all is lost.'

The Princess and the Pea

There was once a Prince who wished to marry a Princess, but she had to be a *real* Princess. He travelled all over the world hoping to find such a lady, but there was always something wrong. Princesses he found in plenty but it was impossible for him to decide whether they were real princesses, for first one thing and then another seemed to him not quite right about them. At last he returned to his palace quite depressed, because he wanted so badly to have a real Princess for his wife.

One evening a fearful tempest arose. It thundered and lightened, and the rain poured down in torrents and the night was as black as pitch. All at once a violent knocking was heard at the door, and the old King, the Prince's father, went to open it.

A Princess was standing outside the door. What with the rain and the wind, she was in a sorry state. The rain trickled down from her hair and her clothes clung to her body. She said she was a real Princess.

'Ah, we'll soon see about that!' thought the old Queen-mother. She said nothing about what she was going to do, but went quietly into the bedroom where the Princess was to spend the night, took off the bed-clothes and put a pea on the bottom of the bed. Then she laid twenty feather mattresses one on top of the other and put twenty eiderdowns over the mattresses.

The next morning they asked her how she had slept. 'Oh, very badly,' she replied. 'I scarcely closed my eyes the whole night. I do not know what was in my bed, but I had something hard under me, and I am black and blue all over. It has hurt me so much!'

Now it was obvious that the lady must be a real Princess, since she had been able to feel the one pea through twenty feather mattresses and twenty eiderdowns. None but a real Princess could have had such a delicate sense of feeling.

So the Prince made her his wife, and the pea was put into a glass cabinet where it can still be seen unless somebody has carried it off.

That's a fine story, isn't it?

The Wild Swans

Far, far away, in the country where the swallows go in winter-time, there dwelt a King who had eleven sons and one daughter, the beautiful Elise. The eleven brothers went to school with stars on their breasts and swords by their sides; they wrote on golden slates with diamond pens, and could read either with a book or without one. In short, it was easy to see they were princes. Their sister Elise used to sit on a little glass stool, and had a picture-book which had cost the half of a kingdom. Oh, the children were very happy! But they weren't to stay happy for ever.

Their mother was dead and their father the King married a very wicked Queen, who was not at all kind to the poor children. They found this out on the first day after the wedding when there was a grand gala at the palace, for when the children played at receiving company, instead of letting them have as many cakes and sweetmeats as they liked, the Queen gave them only some sand in a little dish and told them to imagine that it was something nice.

The following week she sent the little Elise into the country to be brought up by some peasants, and it was not long before she told the King so many falsehoods about the poor Princes that he would have nothing more to do with them.

'Away out into the world, and fend for yourselves,' said the

wicked Queen; 'fly away like big dull birds.' But she could not make their transformation so disagreeable as she wished, and the Princes were changed into eleven white swans. With a strange cry they flew out of the palace windows, over the park and over the wood.

It was still early in the morning when they passed by the place where Elise lay sleeping in the peasant's cottage. They flew several times round the roof, stretched out their long necks, and flapped their wings, but no one either heard or saw them. They were forced to fly on, up to the clouds and into the wide world, so on they went towards the forest which reached as far as the seashore.

The poor little Elise stood in the peasant's cottage amusing herself with a green leaf, for she had no other plaything. She pricked a hole in the leaf and peeped through it at the sun and she thought she saw her brothers' bright eyes, and whenever the warm sunbeams shone on her cheeks, she thought of her brothers' kisses.

One day passed exactly like another. When the wind blew through the thick hedge of rose-trees in front of the house, she would whisper to the roses, 'Who is more beautiful than you? No one.' But the roses would shake their heads and say, 'Elise.' And when the peasant's wife sat on Sundays at the door of her cottage reading her hymn-book, the wind would rustle in the

leaves and say to the book, 'Who is sweeter and more gentle than you?' 'Elise,' replied the hymn-book. And what the roses and the hymn-book said was no more than the truth.

When Elise was fifteen years old her father sent some of his servants to bring her home. Now when the Queen saw how beautiful she was, she hated her more than ever and would willingly have transformed her into a wild swan like her brothers, but she dared not do so because the King wanted to see his daughter.

So the next morning the Queen went to the bath which was made of marble and fitted up with soft pillows and the gayest carpets. She took three toads, kissed them and said to one, 'Seat yourself on Elise's head so she becomes as dull and sleepy as you. Sit on her forehead,' said she to another, 'and let her become so ugly that her father doesn't recognize her again.' And 'Place yourself on her bosom,' she whispered to the third, 'that her heart may become corrupt and evil and a torment to her.' Then she put the toads into the clear water which immediately took on a sort of greenish colour, and having called Elise, undressed her and made her get into the bath. As she sank under the water, one toad settled among her hair, another on her forehead and the third upon her bosom. But Elise seemed unaware of it. She climbed out and left three poppies floating on the water. If the animals hadn't been poisonous and kissed by a witch, they might even have been changed into roses while they were on her head and heart—she was too good for magic to have any power over her.

When the Queen saw this, she rubbed walnut juice all over the maiden's skin so that it became quite swarthy and smeared a nasty salve over her lovely face. Then she tangled up her long thick hair until it was impossible to recognize the beautiful Elise. When her father saw her, he was shocked and said she could not be his daughter. No one would have anything to do with her but the mastiff at the palace gates and the swallows— and they, poor things, could not speak up for her.

Poor Elise wept and thought of her eleven brothers, none of whom she had seen at the palace. In great distress she stole away and wandered the whole day over fields and moors till she reached the forest. She did not know where to go, but she was so sad and longed to see her brothers so much that she made up her mind to find them.

She had not been long in the forest when night came on and she lost her way in the darkness. So she lay down on the soft moss, said her evening prayer, and leaned her head against the trunk of a tree. It was very still, the air was mild, and the green lights of many hundred glow-worms gleamed from the grass and moss around. And when Elise touched one of the branches hanging over her, bright insects fell down upon her like falling stars. She dreamed of her brothers all the night long. It seemed to her that they were all children again playing together and that they wrote with diamond pens upon golden slates, and looked at the pictures in the beautiful book which had cost half of a kingdom. But they did not just make letters and numbers as they had done formerly. No; they wrote of the bold deeds they had done and the strange adventures with which they had met. In the picture-book, too, everything seemed alive. The birds sang and men and women stepped from the pages and talked to Elise and her brothers, jumping back into their places when she turned over the leaves so that the pictures did not get confused.

When Elise awoke, the sun was already high in the heavens. She could not see it for the tall trees of the forest entwined their thickly-leaved branches closely together, but as the sunbeams played upon them they looked like a golden veil waving to and fro.

The air was fragrant and the birds perched upon Elise's shoulders. She heard the noise of water and when she went towards it she found a pool, formed by several springs, with the prettiest pebbles in the bottom. The bushes were thick but the deer had trodden a broad path through them and she went down to the water's edge. The water was so clear that if the boughs and bushes around hadn't been moved to and fro by the wind she might have thought they were painted upon the smooth surface.

As soon as Elise saw her face reflected in the water she was quite startled for it looked so brown and ugly. However, when she wet her little hand and rubbed her brow and eyes the white skin appeared again. So she took off her clothes, stepped into the fresh water and bathed herself, and afterwards there was not a king's daughter more beautiful than she in the whole world.

After she dressed herself again and braided her long hair, she went to the bubbling spring, caught some water in the hollow of her hand and drank it, and then wandered farther into the forest. She didn't know where she was going but she thought of her brothers and of the good God who, she felt, would never forsake her. He it was who made the wild apples grow in order to feed the hungry and who showed her a tree whose boughs bent under the weight of their fruit. She ate her noon-day meal under the shade of this tree, then propped up the boughs and walked on amid the dark twilight of the forest. It was so still that she could hear her own footsteps and the rustling of each little withered leaf that was crushed beneath her feet. Not a bird was to be seen here, not a single sunbeam penetrated through the thick foliage; and the tall stems of the trees stood so close together that when she looked straight before her she seemed entirely enclosed by trellis-work. Oh, the forest was more lonely than any place she had ever know before, and the night was so dark that not even a single glow-worm was shining. Sadly she lay down to sleep and it seemed to her that the boughs above her opened, and she saw an angel of God smiling down upon her and a thousand little cherubs with him. When she awoke in the morning she could not tell whether this was a dream, or whether they really had been watching over her.

She walked on a little farther and met an old woman with a basket full of berries. The old woman gave her some of the berries and Elise asked if she had seen eleven Princes ride through the wood.

'No,' said the old woman, 'but yesterday I saw eleven swans with golden crowns on their heads swim down the brook near by.'

So she led Elise on a little farther to a precipice, the base of which was washed by a brook. The trees on each side stretched towards each other, and wherever they could not reach one another the roots had taken themselves out of the earth and hung over the water interlaced with the branches.

Elise bade the old woman farewell and wandered along by the side of the stream till she came to the place where it reached the open sea. The great ocean lay before her, but not a ship was to be seen. How was she to go on? She noticed the numberless little stones on the shore, all polished and rounded by the waves— waves which were softer than Elise's delicate hand.

'The sea is persistent,' said she, 'it conquers everything, no matter how hard. I will be no less persistent. Thank you for the lesson you have given me, bright waves. My heart tells me you shall carry me to my dear brothers some day.'

On the wet sea grass lay eleven white swan feathers. Elise collected them together and saw that drops of water hung about them, but whether of dew or tears she could not tell. She was quite alone on the sea shore, but she did not mind that for the sea was full of interest to her. It was always moving, always changing, always new, and so gave her more pleasure in a few hours than the gentle inland waters could have offered in a whole year. When a black cloud passed over the sky it seemed as if the sea were saying, 'I too can look dark,' and then the wind would blow and the waves fling out their white foam. When the clouds shone red in the sunset and the winds were asleep, the sea turned the colour of a rose-petal. At other times it was green, or white, as it rested peacefully, swelling gently like the bosom of a sleeping child.

At sunset Elise saw eleven wild swans with golden crowns on their heads fly towards the land, one behind the other like a streaming white ribbon. She climbed the precipice and hid herself behind a bush. The swans settled close to her with a rustle of their long white wings.

As the sun sank beneath the water, the swans also disappeared and in their place stood eleven handsome Princes. Elise uttered a loud cry for, although they were very much altered, she knew they were her brothers. Then she ran into their arms, called them by their names—and how happy they were to see and recognize their sister, who was now grown so tall and beautiful! They laughed and wept, and soon told each other how wickedly their step-mother had treated them.

The eldest of the brothers said, 'We fly or swim as long as the sun is above the horizon but when it sinks below it, we appear again in our human form. Therefore we have to look out for a safe resting-place, for if we were flying among the clouds at sunset, we should fall down as soon as the spell broke. We do not live here but in land quite as beautiful as this which lies on the opposite side of the sea, a long way off. We have to cross the deep waters to reach here and there is no island midway on which we may rest at night. One little solitary rock rises from the waves, and we only just find room enough to stand on it side by side. There we spend the night in our human form and when the sea is rough we are sprinkled by its foam, yet we are grateful to this resting-place for without it we should never be able to visit our native country.

Only once a year are we allowed to make this visit to the home of our fathers. We need two of the longest days for our flight and we can only stay here for eleven days, during which time we fly over the great forest where we can see our father's palace and the tower of the church where our mother is buried. Here even the trees and bushes seem kin to us, the wild horses race over the plains as in the days of our childhood, the charcoal-burner still sings the same old tunes we used to dance to and here we have found you, our dear little sister! We have still two days longer to stay here before we fly over the sea to that other land, beautiful indeed, but not our fatherland. How can we take you with us? We have neither ship nor boat.'

'How can I release you from the spell?' said Elise. And so they went on talking most of the night and slept very little.

Elise was awakened by the rustling of wings and saw the swans fluttering above her; her brothers were again transformed. For some time they flew round in large circles but at last they went off, far away. The youngest only remained behind. He laid his head in her lap and she stroked his white wings, and so they stayed the whole day together. Towards evening the others came back, and when the sun was set they stood on the firm ground in their natural form again.

'Tomorrow we shall fly away,' they said, 'and we cannot return for a year, but we must not leave you. Have you courage to come with us? Our arms are strong enough to carry you through the forest; shall we not have sufficient strength in our wings, to take you over the sea?'

'Yes, take me with you,' said Elise.

They spent the whole night weaving a mat of pliant willow bark and tough rushes, and when it was finished it was thick and strong. Elise lay down on it and when the sun had risen and the brothers were again changed into wild swans, they seized it with their beaks and flew up high among the clouds. She slept on and as the sunbeams shone full upon her face, one of the swans flew over her head and shaded her with his broad wings. They were already far from land when she woke. It seemed so strange to be travelling through the air and over the sea that she thought she was still dreaming. By her side lay a cluster of pretty berries and a handful of savoury roots. Her youngest brother had collected and laid them there, and she thanked him with a smile, for she recognized him as the swan who flew over her head and shaded her with his wings.

They soared so high that the first ship they saw beneath them seemed like a white sea-gull hovering over the water. Then Elise saw a large cloud behind her. It looked like a mountain and on it were gigantic shadows of herself and the eleven swans. Soon, however, the sun rose higher, the cloud remained far behind and the floating picture disappeared. They went on flying the whole day, with a whizzing noise like that which an arrow makes as it cuts through the air, but yet they went slower than usual for they had their sister to carry. A heavy tempest was gathering and the evening approached. Elise watched the sun anxiously. It was setting and there was no sign of their ocean rock. The swans flew faster and faster. Alas! it would be her fault if her brothers did not arrive in time. They would become human beings when the sun set and fall into the sea and be drowned. She prayed most fervently. Still there was no rock to be seen. The black clouds drew nearer, violent gusts of wind announced an approaching tempest and lashed up huge waves and one flash of lightning followed another. A sudden glimpse of the sun showed it was on the rim of the sea.

Elise's heart was beating violently. Suddenly the swans shot down so swiftly that she thought she must fall, but in another moment they began to hover. She saw the little rock below her and it looked like a seal's head raised just above the water. The sun was sinking fast—it seemed scarcely larger than a star—her foot touched the hard ground, and the sun vanished altogether—like the last spark on a burnt piece of paper. Arm in arm her brothers stood round her and there was only just room for them all. The sea beat wildly against the rock, flinging a shower of foam over them; the sky seemed in a continual blaze, the lightning flashed across it every moment, and peal after peal of thunder rolled round it; but sister and brothers kept firm hold of each other's hands. They sang a psalm, and their psalm gave them comfort and courage.

By daybreak the air was pure and still and as soon as the sun rose, the swans flew away from the rock. The waves were still high and when they looked down from the clouds on the blackish-green sea, covered as it was with white foam, they might well have thought that millions of swans were swimming on its surface.

As the day advanced, Elise saw a land of mountains and glaciers floating in the air before her. In the centre was a palace a mile in length, with splendid colonnades, surrounded by palm trees and gorgeous-looking flowers as large as mill-wheels. She asked if this was the country to which they were flying but the swans shook their heads, for what she saw was the beautiful airy castle of the fairy Morgana where no human being was admitted. Even as Elise looked at it, mountains, trees, and castle all disappeared, and in their place stood twelve churches with high towers and pointed windows. She thought she heard the organ play, but it was only the murmur of the sea. Soon they were

close to these churches, and behold! they changed into a large
fleet sailing below them, yet when she looked down again she
saw the ships become as a sea-mist passing rapidly over the water.
Many such strange scenes floated before her eyes before the real
land appeared in sight. Beautiful blue mountains, cedar woods,
towns, and castles rose up and before sunset Elise sat down among
the mountains in front of a large cavern where young creepers
grew round so thickly that the ground appeared covered with a
gay embroidered carpet.

'Now we'll see what you dream about tonight!' said her
youngest brother, as he showed her the room where she was to
sleep.

'Oh, if only I dream how you could be released from the spell!'
she said, and she could think of nothing else. She prayed most
earnestly for God's assistance and even in her dreams she went
on praying. Suddenly she felt she was flying up high in the air
towards the castle of the fairy Morgana. The fairy came forward
to meet her, radiant and beautiful, and yet somehow she looked
like the old woman who had given her berries in the forest and
told her about the swans with golden crowns.

'You can release your brothers,' said she, 'but have you courage
and patience enough? The water is softer than your delicate
hands, and it can mould the hard stones to its will, but then it
cannot feel the pain which your fingers will feel. It has no heart
and cannot suffer the anxiety and grief which you must suffer.
Do you see these stinging-nettles which I have in my hand?
There are many round the cave where you are sleeping and only
those that grow there, or on the graves in the churchyard, are of
use. Remember that! You must pluck them although they sting
your hands; you must trample on them with your feet and get
yarn from them, and with this yarn you must weave eleven
shirts with long sleeves. When they are all made, throw them
over the eleven wild swans and the spell will be broken. But
take heed. From the moment you begin the work you must not
speak a word, even if it occupy you for years. The first syllable

that escapes your lips will fall like a dagger into the hearts of your brothers. Their lives depend on your tongue. Remember this!'

At the same moment the fairy touched Elise's hands with a nettle which made them burn like fire, and Elise awoke. It was broad daylight, and close to her lay a nettle like the one she had seen in her dream. She fell on her knees, thanked God and went out of the cave to begin her work. She plucked the harmful nettles with her delicate hands; they burned large blisters on her arms but she bore the pain willingly in the hope of releasing her brothers. She trampled on them with her naked feet and spun the green yarn.

Her brothers came back at sunset. Elise's silence frightened them; they thought it must be the effect of some fresh spell by their wicked step-mother, but when they saw her blistered hands they found out what she was doing for their sake. The youngest brother wept and, when his tears fell upon her hands, Elise felt no more pain and the blisters disappeared.

The whole night she spent at her work, for she could not rest till she had released her brothers. All the following day she sat alone for the swans had flown away but never had time passed so quickly. One shirt was ready; she now began the second.

Suddenly a hunting-horn sounded among the mountains. She was frightened and as the noise came nearer, she heard the hounds barking. In great terror she fled into the cave, bound up the nettles which she had gathered and combed into a bundle, and sat down.

She had just done so when a large dog sprang out from the bushes. Two others followed, which barked loudly, ran away, and then returned again. It was not long before the hunters stood in front of the cave. The handsomest among them was the King of that country; he stepped up to Elise and never had he seen a lovelier maiden.

'How did you come here, you beautiful child?' said he. Elise shook her head. She dared not speak, for a word would cost her

brothers their lives. She hid her hands under her apron lest the
King should see how she was suffering.

'Come with me,' he said, 'you must not stay here! If you are
as good as you are beautiful, I will dress you in velvet and silk,
I will put a gold crown upon your head, and you shall dwell in
my palace.' So he lifted her upon his horse, while she wept and
wrung her hands. But the King said, 'I only want your happiness.
You will thank me for this some day,' and away he rode over the
mountains and valleys. When the sun set they reached the King's
capital with its churches and domes and the King led Elise into
the palace where, in a high marble hall, fountains were playing,
and the walls and ceiling were covered with the most beautiful
paintings. But Elise didn't care about all this splendour. She wept
and mourned in silence while the ladies-in-waiting dressed her
in royal robes, wove costly pearls into her hair, and drew soft
gloves over her blistered hands.

When she was fully dressed her beauty was so dazzling that the courtiers all bowed low before her and the King chose her for his bride, although the Archbishop shook his head and whispered that the 'beautiful lady of the wood who had blinded their eyes and infatuated the King's heart must certainly be a witch.'

But the King did not listen. He ordered that music should be played and a sumptuous banquet prepared. The loveliest maidens danced round the bride and she was led through fragrant gardens into magnificent halls, but not a smile was to be seen playing upon her lips or shining from her eyes. Then the King opened a small room next to her bedroom. It was adorned with costly green tapestry and exactly resembled the cave in which she had been found. On the ground lay the bundle of yarn which she had spun from the nettles, and the shirt she had completed hung on the wall. One of the hunters had brought all this with him, thinking there must be something wonderful in it.

'Here you can dream of your former home,' said the King; 'here is the work which employed you. Amid all your present splendour it may sometimes give you pleasure to imagine yourself there again.'

When Elise saw what was so dear to her heart, she smiled and the blood returned to her cheeks. She thought her brothers might still be released, and she kissed the King's hand. He pressed her to his heart and ordered the bells of all the churches in the city to be rung to announce the celebration of their wedding. The beautiful dumb maiden of the wood was to become Queen of the land.

The Archbishop whispered evil words in the King's ear but they made no impression upon him. He and Elise were married and the Archbishop himself was obliged to put the crown upon her head. In his rage he pressed the narrow rim so firmly on her forehead that it hurt her, but a heavier weight of sorrow lay upon her heart and she did not feel bodily pain. She was still silent; her eyes, however, beamed with heartfelt love to the King, who had done so much to make her happy. She became more fond of him every day. Oh! how much she wished she might confide in him but she was forced to remain silent, she could not speak until her work was finished! So she stole away every night, and went into the little room that was fitted up in imitation of the cave. There she worked at her shirts but by the time she had begun the seventh, all her yarn was spent.

She knew that the nettles she needed grew in the churchyard and that she must gather them herself. How was she to get them?

'Oh, what is the pain in my fingers compared with the anguish my hearts suffers!' she thought. 'I must go to the churchyard; the good God will not take away his protection from me!'

As fearfully as though she were about to do something wrong, she crept down to the garden one moonlight night and passed through the long avenues into the lonely road leading to the churchyard. She saw a number of ugly old witches sitting on one of the broadest tombstones. They took off their ragged clothes as if they were going to bathe and, digging with their long lean fingers into the fresh grass, drew up the dead bodies and devoured the flesh. Elise had to pass close by them and the witches glared at her with their wicked eyes; but she repeated her prayer, gathered the stinging-nettles, and took them back with her into the palace. One person only had seen her. It was the Archbishop who was awake when the others slept. Now he was convinced that there was something evil about the Queen—she must be a witch, who had won the hearts of the King and all the people by her magic.

In the Confessional he told the King what he had seen and what he feared and when the slanderous words came from his lips, the sculptured images of the saints shook their heads as though to say, 'It is untrue. Elise is innocent!' But the Archbishop explained the omen quite otherwise. He thought it was a testimony against her and that the holy images shook their heads at hearing of her sin.

Two large tears rolled down the King's cheeks; he returned home in doubt. From then on he only pretended to sleep at night and each night he saw Elise rise from her bed; every time he followed her secretly and saw her go into her little room.

His countenance became darker every day. Elise noticed it although she did not know the cause. It made her doubly unhappy; for she already suffered in her heart for her brothers and her bitter tears ran down on her royal velvet and purple like bright diamonds.

She had now nearly finished her work; only one shirt was left to do. Unfortunately the yarn had run out again and she had not a single nettle left. She must go once more to the churchyard and gather a few handfuls. She shuddered when she thought of the solitary walk and of the horrid witches, but her resolution was as firm as her trust in God. She went, and the King and the Archbishop followed her. They saw her disappear at the churchyard door, and when they came nearer they saw the witches sitting on the tombstones as Elise had seen them. Then the King turned away for he believed the woman, whose head had rested on his bosom that very evening, was amongst them. 'Let the people judge her,' said he. And the people condemned her to be burnt.

She was dragged from the King's splendid palace into a dark, damp prison, where the wind whistled through the grated window. Instead of velvet and silk they gave her the bundle of nettles she had gathered; the shirts she had woven were her mattress and counterpane. But they could not have given her anything she valued so much and she continued her work, at the same time praying earnestly to God. The boys from the town sang shameful songs about her in front of her prison and not a soul comforted her with one word of love.

Towards evening she heard the rustling of swans' wings at the grating. It was the youngest of her brothers who had at last found her, and she sobbed aloud for joy although she knew that she had only one night to live. But then her work was almost finished and her brother was near.

The Archibishop came in to spend the last evening with her as he had promised the King he would, but she shook her head at him and entreated him with her eyes and gestures to go. She **must** finish her work that night or all she had suffered, her pain, her anxiety, her sleepless nights, would be in vain. The Archbishop went away with many angry words but the unfortunate Elise **knew** herself to be perfectly innocent and went on with her work.

Little mice ran busily about and dragged the nettles to her feet, wishing to help her, and a thrush perched on the iron bars of the window and sang all night as merrily as he could so that she would not lose courage. An hour before sunrise the eleven brothers stood before the palace gates and demanded an audience with the King. They were refused admission for it was still night, the King was asleep, the people dared not wake him. They entreated, they threatened. The guard came up and the King himself at last stepped out to ask what was the matter, but at that moment the sun rose, the brothers could be seen no longer and eleven white swans flew away over the palace.

The people poured forth from the gates of the city to see the witch burnt. One wretched horse drew the cart in which Elise was placed, a coarse frock of sackcloth covered her, her beautiful long hair hung loosely over her shoulders and her cheeks were deathly pale. But her lips moved gently and her fingers wove the green yarn. Even on the way to her cruel death she did not give up her work; the ten shirts lay at her feet and the eleventh was in her hand. The crowd insulted her.

'Look at the witch, how she mutters to herself. Her accursed sorcery is in her hands. Tear it from her, tear it into a thousand pieces!'

And they all crowded round her and were on the point of snatching away the shirts when eleven white swans came flying towards the cart and settled round her, beating furiously with their wings. The crowd gave way in terror.

'It is a sign from Heaven, she is certainly innocent!' whispered some, but they dared not say so aloud.

The Executioner seized her by the hand—in a moment she threw the eleven shirts over the swans and eleven handsome Princes appeared in their place. The youngest, however, had only one arm for one sleeve in his shirt had not been quite finished.

'Now I may speak,' said she. 'I am innocent!'

And the people who had seen what had happened bowed before her as before a saint, yet she sank in her brothers' arms, exhausted with suspense, fear and grief.

'Yes, she is innocent,' cried her eldest brother and he related their wonderful history. While he spoke fragrance like millions of roses spread round about, for every piece of wood in the funeral pile had taken root and sent forth branches. A hedge of blooming red roses surrounded Elise and above all the others blossomed a flower of dazzling white colour, bright as a star. The king plucked it and laid it on her bosom, whereupon she revived and found there was peace and joy in her heart. All the church bells began to ring of their own accord, great flocks of birds appeared and the procession back to the palace was more joyful and glorious than any King had ever seen before.

The Nightingale

In China, as you know, the Emperor is a Chinaman and everyone round him is a Chinaman too. Now, the story I am going to tell you happened many years ago, so it is very important that you should hear it now before it is forgotten.

The Emperor of China's palace was the most magnificent building in the world; it was made entirely of fine porcelain, which was so brittle that it was even dangerous to touch it. The choicest flowers were to be seen in the garden and little silver bells were fastened to the most splendid of all so that nobody passed by without noticing them.

Yes, everything in the Emperor's garden was wonderfully well arranged and the garden was so big even the gardener did not know where it ended. Whoever walked right through it, however, came to a beautiful wood with very high trees, and beyond that to the sea. The wood went right down to the water which was very deep and blue. Big ships could sail close under the branches and among these branches dwelt a nightingale, who sang so sweetly that even the poor fisherman, who had so much else to do, would stand still and listen to her at night-time.

Travellers came from all parts of the world to the Emperor's city and they admired the city, the palace, and the garden, but if they heard the nightingale they all said, 'This is best of all.'

And they talked about her after they went home, and learned men who wrote books about the city, the palace, and the garden, praised the nightingale above everything else. Poets also wrote the most beautiful verses about this nightingale in the wood near the sea.

These books went round the world, and one of them at last reached the Emperor. He read and read and nodded his head at each sentence, for these splendid descriptions of the city, the palace, and the garden, pleased him greatly. But at last he read something that surprised him. The words, 'But the nightingale is the best of all,' were clearly written in the book.

'What's this?' said the Emperor. 'A nightingale! I know nothing about it. Can there be such a bird in my empire, in my own garden, without my having heard of it? It's surprising what one can learn from a book!'

So he called his Prime Minister, who was so grand a personage that no one of inferior rank might speak to him.

If one did venture to ask him a question, his only answer was 'Pish!'

'There is said to be a very remarkable bird here, called a nightingale,' said the Emperor. 'Her song, they say, is worth more than anything else in all my dominions. Why has no one ever told me about her?'

'I have never heard her mentioned before,' said the Prime Minister; 'she has never been presented at court.'

'I wish her to come and sing to me this evening,' said the Emperor. 'The whole world knows what I have, and I do not know it myself!'

'I have never heard her mentioned before,' said the Prime Minister, 'but I will seek her; I will find her.'

But where was she to be found? The Prime Minister ran up one flight of steps, down another, through halls, and through the passages, but nobody he met had ever heard of the nightingale. So he went back to the Emperor, and said, 'I cannot find it. It must have been invented by the man who wrote the book. Your

Imperial Majesty must not believe all that is written in books.'

'But the book where I read it,' said the Emperor, 'was sent to me by the high and mighty Emperor of Japan, so it must be true. I want to hear the nightingale. She must be here this evening, and if she doesn't come, the whole court shall be flogged after supper.'

In great alarm the Prime Minister set off again up stairs and down stairs, through the halls and through the passages. And half the court ran with him, for no one would have relished the flogging. Many were the questions asked about the wonderful nightingale which the whole world was talking about—except at court where no one knew anything about it.

At last they met a poor little girl in the kitchen who said, 'Oh yes. The nightingale! How she can sing! Every evening I carry scraps to my poor sick mother. She lives by the seashore and when I am coming back, I rest a little in the wood and hear the nightingale sing; it makes the tears come into my eyes.'

'Little kitchen-maiden,' said the Prime Minister, 'I will give you a good place in the kitchen and permission to see the Emperor dine, if you will take us to the nightingale, for she is expected at court this evening.'

So they went together to the wood where the nightingale used to sing, and half the court went with them. As they were on the way, a cow began to low.

'Oh!' said the court pages, 'now we have her! It is certainly an extraordinary voice for so small an animal; surely I have heard it somewhere before.'

'No, those are cows you hear lowing,' said the little kitchen-maid; 'we are still a long way away.'

The frogs were now croaking in the pond.

'There she is now!' said the Master of Ceremonies.

'No, those are frogs,' said the little kitchen-maid, 'but we shall soon hear her.'

Then the nightingale began to sing.

'There she is!' said the little girl, 'listen, listen! There she sits, she added, pointing to a little grey bird up in the branches.

'Is it possible?' said the Prime Minister. 'I should never have thought it. How simple she looks! She must certainly have changed colour at the sight of so many distinguished personages.'

'Little nightingale,' called out the kitchen-maid, 'our gracious Emperor wishes you to sing something to him.'

'With the greatest pleasure,' said the nightingale, and she sang so beautifully that everyone was enchanted.

'It sounds like glass bells,' said the Prime Minister. 'And look at her little throat, how it moves! It is extraordinary that we should never have heard her before and she will have great success at court.'

'Shall I sing again to the Emperor?' asked the nightingale, for she thought the Emperor was among them.

'Most excellent nightingale,' said the Prime Minister, 'I have the honour to invite you to a court festival, which is to take place this evening, when His Imperial Majesty will be delighted to hear you sing.'

'My song would sound far better among the green trees,' said the nightingale; but she followed willingly when she heard that the Emperor wished it.

A golden perch was erected in the middle of the grand hall where the Emperor sat. The whole court was present and the little kitchen-maid got permission to stand behind the door, for now she had the rank and title of 'Maid of the Kitchen'. Everybody was dressed in his finest clothes, and all eyes were fixed upon the little grey bird.

The Emperor nodded as a signal for her to begin. The nightingale sang so sweetly that tears came into his eyes and tears rolled down his cheeks. Then the nightingale sang more sweetly still, and touched the hearts of all who heard her, and the Emperor was so pleased that he said, 'The nightingale shall have my golden slippers to wear round her neck.' But the nightingale thanked him, and said she was already sufficiently rewarded.

'I have seen tears in the Emperor's eyes; that is the greatest

reward I can have. The tears of an Emperor have a special value.'
And then she sang again with her lovely clear voice.

'That is the most amiable coquetry we ever saw!' said the
ladies of the court and they thought they would be nightingales
too and put water into their mouths and tried to move their
throats like the nightingale when they spoke.

Even the footmen and chambermaids declared that they were
quite contented; which was a great thing to say, for of all people
they are the most difficult to satisfy. Yes, the nightingale's
success was complete. She was now to remain at court, to have
her own cage, with permission to fly out twice in the day and
once at night. Twelve attendants were appointed to hold a
silken band fastened round her foot; and they held on very
firmly.

All the city was talking of the wonderful bird and when two
people met, one would say 'night' and the other 'gale', and then

they sighed, and understood each other perfectly. Indeed eleven of the children of the citizens were named after the nightingale.

One day a large parcel arrived for the Emperor, on which was written 'Nightingale'.

'Here we have another new book about our famous bird,' said the Emperor. But it was not a book; it was a little piece of machinery lying in a box—an artificial nightingale, which was covered with diamonds, rubies and sapphires. When this artificial bird was wound up, it could sing one of the tunes that the real nightingale sang, and its tail, all glittering with silver and gold, went up and down at the same time.

'That is splendid!' said everyone, and the messenger who had brought the bird was given the title of 'Chief Imperial Nightingale Bringer'.

Then the Emperor ordered that the real and the toy nightingales should sing together. But it was not successful for the real nightingale sang in her own way, and the artificial bird produced the song mechanically.

'It is not his fault,' said the Master of Music; 'he keeps exact time, and is quite correct and methodical.'

So the artificial bird sang alone. He was just as successful as the real nightingale, and of course he was so much prettier to look at—his plumage sparkled like jewels.

Three and thirty times he sang the same tune, and yet he was not weary. Every one would willingly have heard him again. The Emperor, however, wanted the real nightingale to sing something—but where was she? No one had noticed when she flew out of the open window—flew away to her own green wood.

'What is the meaning of this?' said the Emperor and all the courtiers abused the nightingale, and called her a most ungrateful creature. 'Anyhow, we have the best bird,' they said, and for the four and thirtieth time they heard the same tune, but still they did not quite know it by heart because it was so difficult. The Master of Music praised the bird very highly; indeed, he declared it was better than the real nightingale in every way.

'Just think!' he said, 'One could never tell what was coming with the real nightingale, but everything is settled with the artificial bird. He will sing in this one way, and no other. This can be proved by taking him to pieces, and showing how the wheels move and how they all interlock.'

'That is just what *I* think,' said everybody, and the Master of Music was given permission to show the bird to the people on the following Sunday. 'They shall hear him sing too,' the Emperor said. So they heard him, and were as well pleased as if they had all been drinking tea (for it is tea that makes Chinese merry). One of the fishermen who had heard the new nightingale said, 'It sounds very pretty, almost like the real bird, but yet there is something missing, I don't know what.'

The real nightingale however, was banished from the empire.

The artificial bird had his place on a silken cushion close to the Emperor's bed. All the presents he received, gold and precious stones, lay around him. He had been given the rank and title of 'High Imperial Dessert Singer'.

And the Master of Music wrote five and twenty volumes about the artificial bird, with the longest and most difficult words that are to be found in the Chinese language. So, of course, everybody said they had read and understood them, lest they should have been thought stupid or perhaps even flogged.

Thus it went on for a year. The Emperor, the court, and all the Chinese knew every note of the artificial bird's song by heart and that was the very reason they enjoyed it so much— they could now sing with him. The little boys in the street sang 'zizzi, cluck, cluck, cluck!' and the Emperor himself sang it too.

But one evening, as the bird was singing loudly and the Emperor lay in bed and listened, there was suddenly a great bang inside the bird. Then something went 'Whrr'. All the wheels whirred round and then the music stopped.

The Emperor jumped quickly out of bed and had his chief physician summoned, but what use was he? Then a clockmaker was fetched and at last, after a great deal of discussion and consultation, the bird was put to rights again; but the clockmaker said he mustn't be made to sing too much for the pegs were almost worn out and it would be almost impossible to make new ones which would give the right notes.

There was great lamentation, for the artificial bird was allowed to sing only once a year, and that was with difficulty. However, the Master of Music made a short speech full of his favourite long words, and said the bird was as good as ever; so then, of course, it *was* as good as ever.

When five years had gone by a great distress came to the whole empire, for the Emperor was ill, and it was reported that he would not live. A new Emperor had already been chosen, and the people stood in the street outside the palace and asked the Prime Minister how the old Emperor was.

'Pish!' said he, and shook his head.

Cold and pale, the Emperor lay in his magnificent bed. All the court believed him to be already dead, and everyone hastened away to greet the new Emperor.

But the Emperor wasn't dead though he could scarcely breathe and it seemed to him that something was sitting on his chest. He opened his eyes, and saw that it was Death. He had put on the Emperor's crown, and with one hand he held the golden sword and with the other the banner. From under the folds of the thick velvet hangings the strangest-looking heads peered forth, some with very ugly faces, and others that looked extremely gentle and lovely. They were the bad and good deeds of the Emperor, which now all fixed their eyes on him while Death sat on his heart.

'Do you know this?' they whispered one after another. 'Do you remember that?' And they began reproaching him so that the sweat broke out upon his forehead.

'I have never known anything like it,' said the Emperor. 'Music, music, the great Chinese drum,' cried he, 'let me not hear what they are saying.'

They went on speaking, however, and Death went on nodding his head to every word, like a Chinese mandarin.

'Music, music!' cried the Emperor. 'You dear little artificial bird, sing, I pray you, sing!—I have given you gold and precious stones, I have even hung my golden slippers round your neck— sing, I pray you, sing!'

But the bird was silent; there was no one there to wind him up and he could not sing. Death continued to stare at the Emperor with his great hollow eyes and everywhere it was quiet, dreadfully quiet.

All at once the sweetest song was heard from the window; it was the little nightingale who was sitting on a branch outside. She had heard of her Emperor's illness and was come to sing to him of comfort and hope. As she sang, the spectral forms became paler and paler, and blood flowed more and more quickly through the Emperor's feeble limbs and even Death listened and said, 'Go on, little nightingale, go on.'

'Will you give me the golden sword? Will you give me the gay banner, and the Emperor's crown?'

Death gave up all these treasures for a song, and the nightingale sang on. She sang of the quiet churchyard where white roses blossom, where the lilac sends forth its fragrance, and the fresh grass is bedewed with the tears of sorrowing for the dead. Then Death was seized with a longing for his own garden and, like a cold white shadow, flew out at the window.

'Thank you, thank you, little bird,' said the Emperor. 'I know you well. I banished you from my realm, and you have sung away those evil faces from my bed, and death from my heart; how shall I reward you?'

'You have already rewarded me,' said the nightingale; 'I have seen tears in your eyes, as I did when I sang to you for the first time. I shall never forget them: they are the jewels which do good to a minstrel's heart. But go to sleep now, and you will wake up fresh and well; I will sing you to sleep.'

She sang and the Emperor fell into a sweet sleep. Oh, how soft and refreshing that sleep was!

The sun was shining in at the window when he woke, strong and healthy. None of his servants came in for they all thought he was dead, but the nightingale still sat and sang.

'You shall always stay with me,' said the Emperor. 'You shall only sing when it pleases you, and I will break the artificial bird into a thousand pieces.'

'Don't do that,' said the nightingale. 'He has done what he could; take care of him. I cannot stay in the palace, but let me come when I like. In the evening I will sit on the branches close to the window and sing to you so you become happy and thoughtful. I will sing about those that are happy and those that are sad. I will tell you all the good or bad deeds among your people which are hidden from you, for the singing-bird flies afar—to the fisherman's hut, to the peasant's cottage, and to all who are far distant from you and your court. I love your heart more than your crown, and yet the crown has an air of sanctity about it. I will come; I will sing. But you must promise me one thing.'

'Anything,' said the Emperor, as he stood in his imperial splendour, which he had put on by himself, and as he pressed the golden sword to his heart.

'One thing I beg of you: let no one know that you have a little bird who tells you everything, and then all will go well.' And the nightingale flew away.

The attendants came in to look at their dead Emperor—and the Emperor said, 'Good morning!'

The Emperor's New Clothes

Many years ago there was an Emperor who was so very fond of new clothes that he spent all his money on dress. He didn't worry about his army, nor did he bother to go to the theatre, or hunting, unless it gave him an opportunity to display his new clothes. He had a different suit for each hour of the day and instead of saying 'He's in the council-room' as one would with any other Emperor, people used to say 'He's in his dressing-room.'

Time passed merrily in the large town which was his capital and many strangers arrived every day at the court. One day two rogues calling themselves weavers made their appearance. They said that they knew how to weave materials of the most beautiful colours and elaborate patterns and that the clothes manufactured from them had the wonderful property of being invisible to every one who was unfit for the office he held, or who was very simple in character.

'These must indeed be splendid clothes!' thought the Emperor. 'If I had such a suit, I would find out at once which men in my realms are unfit for their office, and I could distinguish the wise from the foolish. This stuff must be woven for me immediately.' And he ordered large sums of money to be given to both the weavers so that they could begin work straight away.

So the two would-be weavers set up their looms and pretended to work very busily, though in reality they did nothing at all. They asked for the most delicate silk and the purest gold thread, put both into their own knapsacks, and then continued their work at the empty looms until late at night.

All the people throughout the city had heard of the wonderful cloth and they were all anxious to see how wise, or ignorant, their neighbours turned out to be. 'I should like to know how the weavers are getting on with my cloth,' said the Emperor to himself after some little time had elapsed. He was, however, rather embarrassed when he remembered that a simpleton, or one unfit for his office would be unable to see the material. He knew he had nothing to risk but, all the same, he thought he would rather send somebody else to report on it.

'I will send my faithful old minister to the weavers,' he said at last, after some deliberation. 'He will be best able to see how the cloth looks, for he is a sensible man, and no one can be more suitable for his office than he is.'

So the faithful old minister went into the hall where the rascals were working at their empty looms with all their might. 'What's the meaning of this?' thought the old man, opening his eyes very wide. 'I can't see the least bit of thread on the looms!' However, he did not say so aloud.

The impostors asked him politely to be so good as to come nearer their loom, and then inquired whether the design pleased him and whether the colours were not very beautiful, at the same time pointing to the empty frames. The poor old minister stared and stared; he still couldn't see anything on the looms, for the very good reason that there was nothing there. 'What!' thought he again, 'am I a simpleton? I never thought so myself and, if I am, nobody must find out. Am I unfit for office? No, I couldn't admit to that either. I will never confess that I could not see the stuff.'

'Well, Sir Minister,' said one of the knaves, still pretending to work, 'you don't say whether the material pleases you.'

'Oh, it is excellent,' replied the old minister, looking at the loom through his spectacles. 'This pattern, and the colours—yes, I will tell the Emperor at once how very beautiful I think them.'

'We are much obliged to you,' said the impostors. As they described the stuff in still greater detail the old minister listened attentively to them, in order that he might repeat the description to the Emperor; and then the knaves asked for more silk and gold, saying that it was necessary to complete what they had begun. But, of course, they put all that was given them into their

knapsacks, and continued to work with as much diligence as before at their empty looms.

The Emperor soon sent another court official to see how the men were getting on and to ask whether the cloth would soon be ready. The same happened with this gentleman as with the minister; he surveyed the looms from all sides, but could see nothing at all but the empty frames.

'Doesn't the stuff seem as beautiful to you as it did to my lord the minister?' asked the impostors, at the same time making the same gestures as before and talking of the design and colours which weren't there at all.

'I'm certainly not *stupid*,' thought the messenger. 'I must be unfit for my nice, profitable office. That's very odd! However, no one shall know anything about it.' And accordingly he praised the stuff he could not see and declared that he was delighted with both colours and patterns. 'Indeed, your Imperial Majesty,' said he to his sovereign when he returned, 'the cloth the weavers are preparing is magnificent.'

The whole city was talking of the splendid cloth which the Emperor had ordered to be woven at his own expense. And now the Emperor himself wished to see the costly stuff while it was still on the loom. Accompanied by a select number of officers of the court, among whom were the two honest men who had already admired the cloth, he went to the weavers. As soon as they noticed him approaching they went on working more diligently than ever, although they did not pass a single thread through the looms.

'Isn't the work absolutely magnificent?' said the two officers already mentioned. 'If your Majesty will only be pleased to look at it. What a splendid design! What glorious colours!' And at the same time they pointed to the empty frames, because they thought that everyone else could see this exquisite piece of workmanship.

'What's happened?' said the Emperor to himself; 'I can't see anything! This is terrible! Am I a simpleton, or am I unfit to be an Emperor? This is the worst thing that could happen—Oh! the cloth is charming,' said he aloud. 'It has my entire approval.' And he smiled most graciously and looked closely at the empty looms, for on no account would he say that he couldn't see what two of the officers of his court had praised so much. All his retinue now strained their eyes, hoping to discover something on the looms, but they could see no more than the others. Nevertheless, they all exclaimed, 'Oh, how beautiful!' and advised his Majesty to have some new clothes made from this splendid material for the procession the following day. 'Magnificent! charming! excellent!' resounded on all sides; and everyone was uncommonly gay. The Emperor shared in the general satisfaction, and presented the impostors with the riband of an order of knighthood to be worn in their button-holes and the title of 'Gentlemen Weavers'.

The rogues sat up the whole of the night and had sixteen lights burning, so that everyone might see how anxious they were to finish the Emperor's new suit. They pretended to roll the cloth off the looms, cut the air with their scissors and sewed with needles without any thread in them. 'Look! they cried at last; 'the Emperor's new clothes are ready!'

Then the Emperor, with all the gentlemen of the court, came to the weavers. The rogues pretended to hold up the clothes, saying, 'Here are your Majesty's trousers, here is the scarf, here is the mantle. The whole suit is as light as a cobweb; one might almost think one had nothing on at all, the cloth is so delicate.'

'Yes, indeed,' said all the courtiers.

'If your Imperial Majesty will be graciously pleased to take off your clothes, we will fit on the new suit.'

The Emperor was undressed, and the rogues pretended to help him into his new suit. He turned from side to side in front of the mirror and admired himself.

'How splendid his Majesty looks in his new clothes! and how well they fit!' everyone cried out. 'What a design! What colours! These are royal robes!'

'The canopy which is to be borne over your Majesty in the procession is waiting,' announced the Master of the ceremonies.

'I am quite ready,' answered the Emperor. 'Do my new clothes fit well?' he asked looking at the mirror again as if he were examining his handsome suit.

The lords in waiting, who were to carry his train, felt about on the ground as if they were lifting up the ends of the mantle, and solemnly pretended to carry it, for they would not betray anything like simplicity or unfitness for office.

So the Emperor walked under his high canopy in the middle of the procession, through the streets of his capital. And all the people standing by, and those at the windows, cried out, 'Oh! how beautiful our Emperor's new clothes are! What a magnificent train! And how neatly it fits!' Certainly, none of the Emperor's various suits had ever made so great an impression as this invisible one.

'But the Emperor has on nothing at all!' said a little child.

'Just listen to what that innocent says!' exclaimed her father, and what the child had said was whispered from one to another.

'He has nothing on at all,' cried out all the people together, and the Emperor was angry and ashamed for he knew suddenly that they were right. 'But I will have to go through with the procession,' he said to himself, so he drew himself up and the lords in waiting tightened their hold on his imaginary mantle and stalked on.

The Ugly Duckling

It was beautiful in the country; it was summer-time, the wheat was yellow, the oats were green, the hay was stacked up in the green meadows, and the stork paraded about on his long red legs, talking in Egyptian, which language he had learned from his mother. The fields and meadows were skirted by thick woods, and a deep lake lay in the midst of the woods. Yes, it really was beautiful in the country! The sunshine fell warmly on an old mansion, surrounded by deep canals, and the large burdock-leaves that grew from the walls down to the water's edge were so high that children could stand upright among them without being seen. This place was as wild and unfrequented as the thickest part of the wood, and because of this a duck had chosen to make her nest there. She was sitting on her eggs, but the pleasure she had felt at first was now almost gone because she had been there so long. She had very few visitors, for the other ducks preferred swimming on the canals to sitting gossiping with her.

At last the eggs cracked, and one little head after another appeared. 'Quack, quack!' said the duck, and all got up as well as they could, and peeped about from under the green leaves.

'How large the world is!' said the little ones.

'Do you think this is the whole of the world?' said the mother. 'It stretches far beyond the other side of the garden up to the vicar's field; but I have never been there. Are you all here?' And then she got up. 'No, I have not hatched you all yet, the largest egg is still here. How long will it take? I am so tired of it!' And she sat down again.

'Well, and how are you getting on?' asked an old duck who had come to pay her a visit.

'This one egg keeps me so long,' said the mother, 'it won't break. Still, you should see the others! They are the prettiest little ducklings I have seen in all my days.'

'Depend upon it,' said the old duck, 'it is a turkey's egg. I was cheated in the same way once myself, and I had great trouble with the young ones. They were afraid of the water, and I couldn't get them to go near it. I called and scolded, but it was all no use. But let me see the egg—ah yes! to be sure, that is a turkey's egg. Leave it, and teach the other little ones to swim.'

'I will sit on it a little longer,' said the duck. 'I have been sitting so long, that I may as well spend the harvest here.'

'Oh, well, it's none of my business,' said the old duck, and away she waddled.

The great egg cracked open at last. 'Piep, piep,' said the little one, and out it tumbled. But oh! how large and ugly it was!

The duck looked at it. 'That is a great strong creature,' said she, 'none of the others are at all like it. Can it be a young turkey-cock? Well, we shall soon find out; it must go into the water, though I push it in myself.'

The next day was wonderfully fine, and the sun shone warmly on all the green leaves when mother duck with all her family went down to the canal. Plump! she went into the water. 'Quack, quack!' she cried and one duckling after another jumped in. The water closed over their heads, but they all came up again and swam quite easily. They were all there, even the ugly grey one.

'No, it's not a turkey,' said the mother duck; 'see how prettily it moves its legs, how upright it holds itself. It's my own child, and it really is very pretty when one looks more closely at it. Quack, quack! now come with me, I will take you into the world; but keep close to me, or someone may tread on you; and beware of the cat.'

When they came into the duck-yard, two families were quarrelling about the remains of an eel which the cat got in the end.

'See, my children, such is the way of the world,' said the mother duck, wiping her beak, for she too was fond of roasted eels. 'Keep together, and bow to the old duck you see yonder. She is the most distinguished of all the birds and is of Spanish blood, which accounts for her distinguished appearance and manners. And look, she has a red rag on her leg: that is considered extremely handsome, and is the greatest honour a duck can have. Come along now and don't turn in your toes. A well-brought up duck turns its toes right out like mother and father.'

The other ducks who were in the yard looked at them and said aloud, 'Here's another brood! You'd think there weren't enough of us already. And how ugly that one is! We won't stand for it,' and immediately one of the ducks flew at him, and bit him on the neck.

'Leave him alone,' said the mother, 'he isn't doing any harm.'

'Yes, but he is so large and so strange-looking.'

'Those are fine children that our friend has there,' said the old duck with the red rag on her leg. 'They are all pretty except one, which has not turned out so well. I almost wish it could be hatched over again.'

'Certainly, he isn't handsome,' said the mother, 'but he's a very good child, and swims as well as the others—indeed rather better. I think he will grow like the others in all good time, and perhaps will look smaller.' And she scratched the duckling's neck, and stroked his whole body. 'Besides,' added she, 'he's a drake so it doesn't matter so much. I think he will be very strong, so he will make his way in the end.'

'The other ducks are very pretty,' said the old duck. 'Pray

make yourselves at home, and if you find an eel's head you can bring it to me.'

Accordingly they made themselves at home but the poor duckling who had come last out of his egg-shell and who was so ugly was bitten, pecked, and teased by both ducks and hens. And the turkey-cock (who had come into the world with spurs on and therefore fancied he was an emperor) puffed himself up like a ship in full sail, and marched up to the duckling quite red with passion. The poor thing scarcely knew what to do; he was most unhappy because he was so ugly.

So the first day passed and, afterwards, matters grew worse and

worse. Even his brothers and sisters behaved unkindly, and were constantly saying, 'I hope the cat gets you, you ugly thing!' The mother said, 'Ah, if only I hadn't hatched you!' The ducks bit him, the hens pecked him, and the girl who fed the poultry kicked him. He ran through the hedge and the little birds in the bushes were terrified. 'That's because I am so ugly,' thought the duckling, and ran on. At last he came to a wide moor, where some wild ducks lived and here he lay the whole night, tired and comfortless. In the morning the wild ducks flew up, and looked at their new companion. 'Pray, who are you?' they asked, and our duckling greeted them as politely as possible.

'You are really very ugly,' said the wild ducks; 'but that doesn't matter to us, if you don't marry into our families.'

Poor thing, he had never thought of marrying: he only wanted to lie among the reeds and drink the water of the moor. He stayed there for two whole days and on the third day there came two wild geese, or rather ganders, who had not been long out of their egg-shells—which accounts for their impertinence.

'Listen,' they said, 'you're so ugly that we like you very much. Will you come with us? On another moor, not far from this, are some pretty, wild geese, as lovely creatures as have ever said "hiss, hiss". You're on the point of making your fortune, ugly as you are.'

Bang! suddenly a gun went off and both wild geese were stretched dead among the reeds. Bang! a gun went off again, whole flocks of wild geese flew up, and another report followed.

There was a grand hunting party. The hunters lay in ambush all around and some were even sitting in the trees, whose huge branches stretched far over the moor. The hounds splashed about in the mud, bending the reeds and rushes in all directions. How frightened the poor little duck was! He turned his head, thinking to hide it under his wing, and in a moment a fierce-looking dog stood close to him, his tongue hanging out of his mouth, his eyes sparkling fearfully. He opened his jaws at the sight of our duckling, and showed his sharp white teeth, then splash,

splash! he was gone—without touching a single feather.

'Well! I must be thankful,' sighed the duckling. 'I'm so ugly that even the dog won't eat me.'

He lay still, though the shooting continued among the reeds. The noise did not cease till late in the day, and even then the poor little thing dared not stir. He waited several hours before he looked around him, and then hastened away from the moor as fast as he could. He ran over fields and meadows, though the wind was so high that he could hardly make any headway against it.

Towards evening he reached a wretched little hut, so wretched that it only stayed upright because it couldn't decide which way to fall. He noticed that the door had lost one of its hinges, and hung so crookedly that there was enough space between it and the wall to let him through. As the storm was becoming worse and worse, he crept into the room.

An old woman lived in this room with her tom-cat and her hen. The cat, whom she called her little son, could make his fur stand on end and purr. The hen was very small and was therefore called 'Shortlegs'; she laid very good eggs, and the old woman loved her as her own child.

The next morning the cat began to mew and the hen to cackle when they saw the new guest.

'What's the matter?' asked the old woman, looking round. Her eyes were not good, so she took the duckling to be a fat duck who had lost her way. 'This is a capital catch,' said she. 'I shall now have duck's eggs, if it isn't a drake. We must try.' So the duckling was tried out for three weeks, but no eggs made their appearance.

Now the cat was the master of the house, and the hen was the mistress, and they used always to say, 'We and the world,' for they imagined themselves to be not only the half of the world, but also by far the better half. The duckling thought some people might have a different opinion but the hen wouldn't agree.

'Can you lay eggs?' asked she.

'No.'

'Well, then, hold your tongue.'

And the cat said, 'Can you make your fur stand on end? Can you purr?'

'No.'

'Well, then, you shouldn't produce your own opinions when wise persons are speaking.'

So the duckling sat alone in a corner in a very bad humour. He happened, however, to think of the fresh air and bright sunshine and these thoughts gave him such a strong desire to swim again that he could not help saying so to the hen.

'What is the matter with you?' said the hen. 'You have nothing to do and therefore you brood over these fancies. Either lay some eggs, or purr, and then you will forget about them.'

'But it's so wonderful to swim,' said the duckling; 'so wonderful when the waters close over your head, and you plunge to the bottom.'

'Well, that is a queer sort of pleasure,' said the hen; 'I think you must be crazy. Ask the cat—he's the most sensible animal I know, apart from myself—whether he would like to swim, or to plunge to the bottom of the water. Ask your mistress; no one is wiser than she. Do you think she would enjoy swimming and having the waters close over her head?'

'You don't understand me,' said the duckling.

'What, we don't understand you! So you think yourself wiser than the cat and the old woman and me! Don't imagine any such thing, child, but be thankful for all the kindness that has been shown you. Aren't you living in a warm room, and haven't you the advantage of society from which you can learn something? —But you're a simpleton, and it's tedious to have anything to do with you; though, believe me, I wish you well. I may tell you unpleasant truths, but it's thus that real friendship is shown. Now, do make an effort for once and learn to purr, or to lay eggs.'

'I think I will go out into the wide world again,' said the duckling.

'Well, go,' answered the hen crossly. 'Go at once.'

So the duckling went. He swam on the surface of the water and he plunged beneath, but all animals passed him by on account of his ugliness. The autumn came, the leaves turned yellow and brown and the wind caught them and danced about with them; the air was very cold, the clouds were heavy with hail or snow, and the raven sat on the hedge and croaked. The poor duckling certainly had a bad time of it.

One evening, just as the sun was setting, a flock of large birds rose from the bushes. The duckling had never seen anything so beautiful before; their plumage was dazzling white and they had long, slender necks. They were swans. They uttered their singular cry, spread out their long, splendid wings, and flew away from these cold regions to warmer countries across the open sea. They flew so high, so very high! The ugly duckling's feelings were quite strange; he turned round and round in the water like a mill-wheel, strained his neck to look after them, and sent forth such a loud and strange cry, that he almost frightened himself. Ah! he could not forget them, those noble birds! He did not know what they were or where they were flying, yet he loved them as he had never loved anything before. Still, it was not as though he envied them. It would never have occured to him to wish such beauty for himself; he would have been quite contented if only the ducks in the duck-yard had tolerated his company.

The winter grew cold, so cold! The duckling had to swim round and round in the water to keep it from freezing. But every night the opening became smaller and smaller and he had to move his legs all the time to prevent the water from freezing entirely. At last, wearied out, he lay stiff and cold in the ice.

Early in the morning a peasant passed by and when he saw him he broke the ice in pieces with his wooden shoe, and brought him home to his wife.

The duckling soon revived. The children would have played with him, but he thought they wanted to tease him and in his terror he jumped into the milk-pail so that the milk spilled all over the room. The good woman shouted and clapped her hands. He flew into the pan where the butter was kept, and then into the meal-barrel, and out again.

The woman screamed and struck at him with the tongs; the children ran races with each other trying to catch him and laughed and screamed too. It was just as well for him that the door stood open; he fled among the bushes into the new-fallen snow, and lay there as in a dream.

It would be too sad to relate all the trouble and misery he had to suffer during the winter. He was lying on a moor among the reeds when the sun began to shine warmly again, the larks sang, and beautiful spring returned. Once more he shook his wings. They were stronger than before and carried him along swiftly, and before he realized what had happened he found himself in a large garden where the apple-trees stood in full bloom and where the syringa smelt sweetly and hung its long green branches down into the winding canal. Oh! everything was so lovely, so full of the freshness of spring!

Out of the thicket came three beautiful white swans. They rustled their wings and swam lightly down the river. The duckling recognized them and was seized with a strange sadness.

'I will go up to them, those royal birds,' said he. 'They will kill me, because I, ugly as I am, have dared to approach them, but it doesn't matter. Better be killed by them than be bitten by the ducks, pecked by the hens, kicked by the girl who feeds the poultry, and have so much to suffer during the winter!' He flew into the water, and swam towards them. They saw him and swam forward to meet him. 'Only kill me,' said the poor duckling, and he bowed his head low, expecting death. But what was this he saw in the clear water? He saw his own reflection—no longer that of a plump, ugly, grey bird, but that of a swan.

It doesn't matter if you are born in a duck-yard when you've been hatched from a swan's egg.

The larger swans swam round him, and stroked him with their beaks, and he was very happy.

Some little children were running about in the garden. They threw grain and bread into the water, and the youngest exclaimed, 'There's a new one!' The others also cried out, 'Yes, a new swan has come!' and they clapped their hands, and ran and told their father and mother. They threw more bread and cake into the water and everyone said, 'The new one is the best, so young, and so beautiful!' and the old swans bowed before him.

The young swan felt quite ashamed, and hid his head under his wing for he did not know what to do. He was all too happy, but still not proud, for a good heart is never proud.

He remembered how he had been laughed at and cruelly treated; and now he heard everyone say he was the most beautiful of all beautiful birds. The syringa bent down its branches towards him, and the sun shone warmly and brightly. He ruffled his wings, stretched his slender neck, and with joy in his heart said, 'I never dreamed of so much happiness when I was still the Ugly duckling!'

The Constant Tin Soldier

There were once five and twenty tin soldiers and they were all brothers for they had all been made out of one old tin spoon. They carried muskets in their arms and held themselves very upright; their uniforms were red and blue and they looked very gay indeed. When the lid was taken off the box they lay in, the first words they heard were, 'Tin soldiers!' It was a little boy who said this, clapping his hands at the same time. They had been given to him because it was his birthday and he now set them out on the table. The soldiers were alike in every detail. Only one was rather different from the rest; he had only one leg, for he had been made last when there was not quite enough tin left. However, he stood as firmly on his one leg as the others did on both of theirs and it is this very tin soldier whose fortunes seem most worth telling.

On the table where the tin soldiers were set out there were several other toys, but the most charming of them all was a neat little cardboard castle. One could look through its tiny windows into the rooms and in front of it stood some tiny trees which clustered round a little mirror representing a lake and some waxen swans swam on the lake and were reflected on its surface. All this was very pretty, but the prettiest thing of all was a little girl standing in the open doorway of the castle. She, too, was cut out of cardboard but she wore a frock of the finest muslin and a little sky-blue ribbon was flung across her shoulders like a scarf, and in the middle of this scarf was a bright gold wing. The little lady was a dancer and she stretched out both her arms and raised one of her legs so high in the air that the tin soldier could not see it and thought she had only one leg like him.

'She would be just the wife for me,' thought he, 'but then she is of rather too high a rank. She lives in a castle; I have only a box. Besides, the box isn't mine. There are all our five and twenty men living in it; it's no place for her! However, perhaps there wouldn't be any harm in making her acquaintance.' So saying, he stationed himself behind a snuff-box that stood on the table. From this place he had a full view of the delicate little lady who still remained standing on one leg without losing her balance.

When evening came, all the other tin soldiers were put away into the box and the people of the house went to bed. The toys now began to play in their turn. They pretended to visit, to fight battles and give balls. The tin soldiers rattled about in their box, for they wanted to play too, but the lid wouldn't open. The nut-crackers cut capers and the slate-pencil played at buying and selling on the slate. There was such a noise that the canary woke up and began to talk too and he always talked in verse. The only two who did not move from their places were the little tin soldier and the beautiful dancer. She remained in her graceful position, standing on the very tip of her toe with outstretched arms and he stood just as firmly on his one leg, never for a single moment taking his eyes off her.

Twelve o'clock struck. Ping! The lid of the snuff-box sprang open but there was no snuff inside it. Out jumped a little black goblin for it was really a Jack-in-the-box. 'Tin soldier,' said the goblin, 'please keep your eyes to yourself!'

But the tin soldier pretended not to hear.

'Well, just you wait till tomorrow!' said the goblin.

Then when morning came and the children were out of bed,

the tin soldier was placed on the window-ledge and, because of the goblin's spell or the wind, the window flew open all at once and the tin soldier fell out head foremost, from the third storey to the ground. That was a dreadful fall! His one leg turned over and over in the air, and at last he came to rest, poised on his soldier's cap with his bayonet between the paving-stones.

The maid-servant and the little boy immediately came down to look for him but, although they very nearly trod on him, they didn't see him. If the tin soldier had only called out, 'Here I am!' they might easily have found him, but he thought it wouldn't be becoming for him to cry out when he was wearing uniform.

Then it began to rain; suddenly the drops came plopping down and there was a heavy shower. When it was over, two boys came by.

'Look,' said one, 'here's a tin soldier; he shall go sailing for once in his life.'

So they made a boat out of an old newspaper and put the tin soldier into it. Away he sailed down the gutter, both the boys running along by the side and clapping their hands. The paper boat rocked to and fro and every now and then veered round so quickly that the tin soldier became quite giddy. Still, he never moved a muscle and looked straight in front of him and clasped his musket tightly.

All at once the boat sailed into a drain. He found it as dark here as at home in his own box.

'Where shall I get to next?' he thought. 'This is all that goblin's doing. Ah, if only the little maiden were sailing with me in the boat I would not mind it's being twice as dark!'

Just then a great water-rat darted out from under its nest.

'Have you a passport?' asked the rat. 'Where is your passport?'

But the tin soldier was silent and held his weapon with an even firmer grip. The boat sailed on, and the rat followed. Oh! how furiously he showed his teeth and cried out to passing sticks and straws: 'Stop him, stop him! He has not paid the toll. He hasn't shown his passport!' But the stream grew stronger and stronger. The tin soldier could catch a glimpse of bright daylight before the boat came from under the tunnel, but at the same time he

heard a roaring noise at which the boldest heart might well have trembled. Where the tunnel ended the gutter water fell into a great canal. (This was as dangerous for the tin soldier as sailing down a mighty waterfall would be for us.) Soon he was so close to the fall that he couldn't stand upright any longer. The boat darted forwards, the poor tin soldier held himself as stiff and immovable as possible and no one could even accuse him of having blinked. The boat spun round and round three, nay, four times, and filled up with water to the brim and then it began to sink.

The tin soldier stood up to his neck in water. Deeper and deeper sank the boat, softer and softer grew the paper and the water went over the soldier's head. He thought of the pretty little dancer whom he would never see again, and these words rang in his ears:

Wild adventure, mortal danger
Be thy *portion, valiant stranger.*

The paper tore apart, the tin soldier fell through the hole, but at that moment he was swallowed up by a large fish. Oh, how dark it was! worse even than in the drain, and so narrow too! But the tin soldier was as constant as ever. He lay there at full length, still shouldering his arms.

The fish turned and twisted about and made the strangest movements. At last he became quite still for it was as though a flash of lightning had darted through him. The daylight shone brightly and some one exclaimed, 'Tin soldier!' The fish had been caught, taken to the market, sold, and brought home into the kitchen, where the servant-girl was cutting him up with a large knife. She picked up the tin soldier by his middle and took him into the parlour where every one was eager to see the wonderful man who had travelled in the maw of a fish. Our little warrior, however, was not in the least proud of it.

They set him on the table and there—no, how could anything so extraordinary have happened—there was the very room which he had been in before. He saw the same children, the same toys on the table and among them the beautiful castle with the pretty little dancing maiden, who was still standing on one leg, while she held the other high in the air. She, too, was constant. That touched the tin soldier and he would have wept, but such weakness would have been unbecoming in a soldier. He looked at her and she looked at him, but neither spoke a word.

Suddenly one of the little boys snatched up the soldier and threw him unceremoniously into the stove. He did not give any reason for doing so, but no doubt the goblin in the snuff-box must have had a hand in it. The tin soldier now stood in a blaze of red light. He felt extremely hot. He didn't know whether this heat were the result of the actual fire or the flames of love within him. He lost all his colour; he looked at the little damsel and she looked at him and he felt that he was melting, but, constant as ever, he still stood shouldering his arms. A door opened, the wind seized the dancer and, like a sylph, she flew straight into the stove to join him. They both flamed up into a blaze and were gone. The soldier was melted and dripped down among the ashes and when the maid cleaned out the fireplace the next day she found his remains in the shape of a little tin heart. All that was left of the dancer was the gold wing, and that was burnt black as coal.

The Fir-Tree

Far away in the deep forest grew a pretty Fir-Tree. The sun shone on him, the breeze played with him and many friends grew round him. But the little Fir-Tree was not happy: he longed to be tall. He didn't appreciate warm sun and the fresh air; he didn't care for the gay peasant children who came to the forest to look for strawberries and raspberries, especially when, after having filled their pitchers, or threaded the bright berries to a string they sat down near the little Fir-Tree and said, 'What a pretty little tree this is!' Then the Fir-Tree would be very much vexed.

'Oh, that I were as tall as the others!' sighed the little Tree, 'then I should spread out my branches, and my top would look out over the wide world! The birds would build their nests among my branches, and when the wind blew I should bend my head very grandly, just as the others do.' He took no pleasure in the sunshine, in the song of the birds, or in the red clouds that sailed over him every morning and evening.

In the winter time, when the ground was covered with the white glistening snow, there was a hare that used to scamper about and jump right over the little Tree's head—and that was most provoking! However, two winters passed away, and by the third the Tree was so tall that the hare had to run round it instead. 'Oh! to grow, to grow, to become tall and old, that is the only thing in the world worth living for.' So thought the Tree.

That autumn the wood-cutters came and felled some of the largest trees. This happened every year and our young fir, who was by this time a good height, shuddered when he saw those grand, magnificent trees fall with a tremendous crash crackling to the earth. Their boughs were all cut off—how terribly naked and lanky and long the trunk looked! They were scarcely recognizable! They were piled up on waggons and horses drew them away, far, far away from the forest.

Where could they be going? What would happen to them?

Next spring, when the swallows and the storks returned from abroad, the Fir-Tree asked them if they knew where the felled trees had been taken.

The swallows knew nothing about it, but the stork looked thoughtful for a moment, then nodded his head and said, 'Yes, I believe I have seen them. As I was flying back from Egypt I met several ships; those ships had splendid masts. I have little doubt that they were the trees that you speak of, for they smelled like fir-wood. I may congratulate you, for they sailed gloriously, quite gloriously!

'Oh, that I too were tall enough to sail upon the sea! Tell me what it is, the sea, and what it looks like.'

'It would take much too long to explain all that,' said the stork and he walked away.

'Rejoice in your youth!' said the sun; 'rejoice in your fresh growth and the life that is within you!'

And the wind kissed the Tree, and the dew wept tears over him, but the Fir-Tree didn't understand them.

When Christmas approached, many quite young trees were cut down, trees which were just the same height as our restless Fir-Tree. These young trees were chosen because they were the most beautiful. Their branches were not cut off before they were laid in a wagon and horses drew them away, far, far away from the forest.

'Where are they going?' asked the Fir-Tree. 'They are not bigger than I am, indeed one of them was much smaller. Why do they keep all their branches? Where are they going?'

'We know! We know!' twittered the sparrows. 'We peeped in through the windows of the town near by. We know where they are going. Oh, you can't think what honour and glory they receive! We looked through the window-panes and saw them planted in a warm room, and decked out with such beautiful things, gilded apples, sweetmeats, playthings, and hundreds of bright candles.'

'And then?' asked the Fir-Tree, trembling in every bough; 'and then? What happened then?'

'Oh, that was all, but it was quite beautiful.'

'Is this to be my glorious lot too?' cried the Fir-Tree with delight. 'This is far better than sailing over the sea. How I long for the time! If only it were next Christmas! I am now tall and have many branches, like the others which were carried away last year. Oh, I wish I were in the wagon or in the warm room, decorated and honoured, and then—yes, then, something still better must happen, afterwards, or why should they take the trouble to decorate me? Something still greater, still more splendid, must happen—but what? Oh, how this waiting and longing hurts!'

'Rejoice in our love!' said the air and the sunshine. 'Rejoice in your youth and your freedom!'

But he never would rejoice. He grew and grew; winter and summer he stood there clothed in dark green foliage. The people saw him and said 'That's a beautiful tree!' and next Christmas he was the first which was felled. The axe struck sharply through the wood and the Tree fell to the earth with a heavy groan. He suffered sharp pain and a faintness that he had never expected. He quite forgot to think of his good fortune for he felt so sorry at being compelled to leave the place where he had grown up. He knew that he would never see those dear old comrades again, or the little bushes and flowers that had flourished under his shadow, perhaps not even the birds. Nor did he find the journey in the least pleasant.

He came to himself for the first time in a courtyard to which he had been taken with the other trees and he heard a man say, 'This is a splendid one, the very thing we want!'

Then two smartly dressed servants came and carried the Fir-Tree into a large and handsome room. Pictures hung on the walls, and large Chinese vases with lions on the lids stood on the mantelpiece. There were rocking-chairs, silken sofas, tables covered with picture-books, and toys. The Fir-Tree was planted in a large cask filled with sand, but no one would have known it was a cask for it was hung with green cloth and placed on a carpet woven of many gay colours. Oh, how the Tree trembled! What was to happen next? A young lady helped by the servants began to decorate him. On some branches they hung little bags cut out of coloured paper and filled with sugar-plums; gilded apples and walnuts were tied on to others so that they looked just as if they had grown there, and more than a hundred little wax tapers, red, blue and white, were placed here and there among the boughs. Dolls that looked human—the Tree had never seen such things before—danced to and fro among the leaves, and a large star of gold tinsel was fastened to the very top. How splendid it all was!

'This evening,' they said, 'this evening we will light it up.'

'If only it were evening!' thought the tree. 'What will happen next? Will the trees come out of the forest to see me? Will the sparrows fly here and look through the window panes? Shall I stand here decked out like this both winter and summer?'

He went on thinking about it. He thought till anticipation gave him backache—backaches for trees are as painful as headaches are for us.

The candles were lit—oh, what a splendid sight! The Tree trembled in all his branches so that one of them caught fire. 'Oh, help!' cried the young lady, and it was extinguished in great haste. So the tree dared not tremble again; he was so frightened of spoiling his finery in the midst of all this glory and brightness.

All of a sudden, both folding-doors were flung open and a troop of children rushed in as if they were going to jump over him; the older people followed more quietly. The little ones stood quite silent, but only for a moment. Then their chatter burst out again. They shouted till the walls re-echoed, they danced round the Tree and tore down one present after another.

'What are they doing?' thought the Tree. 'What will happen now?' The candles burnt down to the branches and went out and the children were given leave to plunder the Tree. They rushed upon him in such riot that the boughs all crackled. If he hadn't been tied firmly to the ceiling by the gold star he would have been knocked over.

The children danced about with their beautiful playthings; no one thought of the Tree any more except the old nurse. She came and peeped among the boughs, but it was only to see whether anything had been left behind.

'A story, a story!' cried the children, pulling a short thick man towards the Tree. He sat down saying, 'It is good to sit under the shade of green boughs; besides, the tree may enjoy hearing my story. But I shall only tell you one. Would you like to hear about Ivedy Avedy or about Humpty Dumpty, who fell downstairs, and yet came to the throne and won the Princess?'

'Ivedy Avedy! cried some; 'Humpty Dumpty!' cried others. There was a great uproar. Only the Fir-Tree was silent, thinking to himself, 'Ought I to make a noise as they do? or ought I to do nothing at all?' For he most certainly was one of the company, and had done all that had been required of him.

And the short thick man told the story of Humpty Dumpty who fell downstairs and yet came to the throne and won the Princess. And the children clapped and clapped their hands and called out for another. They wanted to hear the story of Ivedy Avedy too, but they did not get it. Meanwhile the Fir-Tree stood quite silent and thoughtful, for the birds in the forest had never told him anything like this. 'Humpty Dumpty fell downstairs, and yet was raised to the throne and won the Princess. Yes, yes, strange things come to pass in the world,' thought the Fir-Tree, who thought it must all be true, because such a pleasant man had said so. 'Who knows, I may fall downstairs and win a Princess!' And he looked forward to being decorated again the next day with candles and playthings, gold and fruit. 'Tomorrow I will not tremble,' thought he. 'I will rejoice in all my magnificence. Tomorrow I shall hear the story of Humpty Dumpty again and perhaps the one about Ivedy Avedy too.' And the Tree thought about this all night.

In the morning the maids came in. 'Now my state begins again,' thought the Tree. But they dragged him out of the room, up the stairs, and into an attic chamber, and there thrust him into a dark corner where not a ray of light could penetrate. 'What am I to do here? What shall I listen to here?' And he leant against the wall, and thought, and thought. He had plenty of time for thinking, for day after day and night after night passed away, and still no one ever came into the room. At last somebody did come, but it was only to push some old trunks into the corner. The Tree was now entirely hidden from sight and apparently quite forgotten.

'It is winter now,' thought the Tree. 'The ground is hard and covered with snow; they cannot plant me, so I am to stay here in shelter till the spring. Men are so prudent! I only wish it were not so dark and so dreadfully lonely!'

'Squeak! squeak!' cried a little mouse who came scrambling about just then. Another followed him; they snuffed round the Fir-Tree, and then slipped in and out among the branches.

'It is horribly cold!' said the little mice. 'Otherwise it is very comfortable here. Don't you think so, you old Fir-Tree?'

'I am not old,' said the Fir-Tree, 'there are many who are much older than I.'

'How did you get here,' asked the mice, 'and what sort of things do you know about?' They were most uncommonly curious. 'Tell us about the most delightful place on earth. Have you ever been there? Have you been into the store-room, where cheeses lie on the shelves, and bacon hangs from the ceiling; where one can dance over tallow-candles; where one goes in thin and comes out fat?'

'I don't know about that,' said the Tree, 'but I know the forest, where the sun shines and where the birds sing.' And then he spoke of his youth and its pleasures. The little mice had never

heard anything like it before. They listened very attentively and said, 'Well, to be sure! What a lot you have seen! How happy you must have been!'

'Happy!' repeated the Fir-Tree in surprise, and he thought a moment over all that he had been saying—'yes, they weren't bad times on the whole.' Then he told them about Christmas Eve when he had been decked out with cakes and candles.

'Oh!' cried the little mice, 'how happy you have been, you old Fir-Tree!'

'I am not old at all!' returned the Fir. 'It was only this winter that I left the forest; I am just in the prime of life!'

'How well you talk!' said the little mice, and the next night they came again and brought four other little mice with them who wanted also to hear the Tree's history. And the more the Tree spoke of his youth in the forest, the more vividly he remembered it, and said, 'Yes, those were pleasant times. They may come again, they may come again. Humpty Dumpty fell downstairs, and yet for all that he won the Princess; perhaps I, too, may win a princess.' And then the Fir-Tree thought of a pretty little delicate birch-tree that grew in the forest, and she seemed a real princess, a very lovely princess to the Fir-Tree.

'Who is this Humpty Dumpty?' asked the little mice. So he told the story—he could remember every word of it perfectly—and the little mice were ready to jump to the top of the Tree for joy. The following night several more mice came, and on Sunday two rats came as well. However, they said that the story was not at all amusing, which worried the little mice who decided they did not like it so much either.

'Do you know only that one story?' asked the rats.

'Only that one!' answered the Tree. 'I heard it on the happiest evening of my life, though I did not know then how happy I was.'

'It's a miserable story! Don't you know any about pork and tallow? No store-room story?'

'No,' said the Tree.

'Well, then, we have had enough!' retorted the rats, and they went away.

The little mice, too, never came again. The Tree sighed, and said, 'It was pleasant when those little mice sat round me and listened to me. Now that is all over too. However, I shall enjoy remembering it when I am taken away from here.

But when would that be? One morning some people came and routed out the lumber-room. The trunks were taken away and the Tree was dragged out of the corner. They threw him carelessly on the floor, but one of the servants picked him up and carried him downstairs. Once more he saw the light of day. 'Now life begins again!' thought the Tree. He felt the fresh air, the warm sunbeams, for he was out in the courtyard. It all happened so quickly that the Tree quite forgot to look at himself —there was so much to look at all around him. There was a garden near by where everything was fresh and blooming, the roses clustered brightly round the trellis-work, the lime-trees were in full blossom, and the swallows flew backwards and forwards, twittering.

'I shall live, I shall live!' He was filled with a wonderful hope; he tried to spread out his branches—but alas! they were all dried up and yellow. He was thrown down on a heap of weeds and nettles. The star of gold tinsel that had been left fixed on his top now shone brightly in the sunshine. The same children who had danced round the Tree at Christmas time were playing merrily in the courtyard. One of the youngest suddenly saw the gold star, and ran to tear it off.

'Look at it, still fastened to the ugly old Christmas Tree!' he cried, trampling on the boughs till they broke under his boots.

And the Tree looked on all the flowers of the garden now in their prime; he looked at himself, and he wished with all his heart that he had been left to wither alone in the dark corner of the lumber-room. He remembered his happy forest life, the Christmas Eve, and the little mice who had listened so eagerly when he related the story of Humpty Dumpty.

'Past, all past!' said the poor Tree. 'Had I but been happy, as I might have been! Past, all past!'

Then the servant came and broke the Tree into small pieces, heaped them up and set fire to them, and the children came running up and danced round the bonfire. The Tree groaned deeply, and every groan sounded like the sound of a gun. With each crackle the Fir-Tree thought of a bright summer's day, or a starry winter's night in the forest, or Christmas Eve, or of Humpty Dumpty, the only story that he knew, until at last he was burned up.

The boys went on playing in the courtyard and the youngest one stuck the gold star into his jacket. There it sparkled as it had done when the Tree had worn it on the happiest evening of his life; but that was past, and the Tree was past and the story too is past! (For all stories must come to an end some time or other.)

Thumbelina

Once upon a time there lived a young woman who longed for a little child of her own, but she did not know where she could get one, so she went to an old witch-woman and said to her, 'I want a child, a little tiny child so badly. Won't you help me, old mother?'

'Oh, that can easily be managed!' replied the witch. 'Here is a barley-corn for you; it's not exactly the same as those that grow in the farmers' fields or those that are given to the fowls in the poultry yard, but sow it in a flower-pot and then we will see.'

'Thank you, thank you!' cried the woman and she gave the witch a silver sixpence. When she got home she sowed the barley-corn as she had been directed, and a large and beautiful flower immediately shot up from the flower-pot. It looked like a tulip, but the petals were tightly folded up for it was still in bud.

'What a lovely flower!' exclaimed the peasant-woman, and she kissed the pretty red and yellow petals and as she did so the flower opened with a big pop. It was indeed a tulip, but on the small green stigma in the centre of the flower there sat a tiny little girl, so pretty and delicate that her whole body was scarcely bigger than the young woman's thumb. So she called her Thumbelina.

A pretty varnished walnut-shell was given her as a cradle, and she had blue violet-leaves for a mattress, and a rose-leaf as a coverlet. She slept here at night but in the day-time she played on the table. The peasant girl filled a plate with water and laid the flowers in it, so that the blossoms bordered the edge of the plate while the stalks lay in the water. A large tulip-leaf floated on the surface, and Thumbelina could sit on it and sail from one side of the plate to the other with two white horse-hairs which had been given her for oars. And she sang too, in such low sweet tones as were never heard before.

One night a great ugly toad came hopping in through a broken window-pane and jumped down on to the table where Thumbelina lay sleeping under the red rose-petal.

'That is just the wife for my son,' said the toad and she seized hold of the walnut-shell, with Thumbelina in it, and carried her off through the window down into the garden. There was a broad stream flowing at the bottom and the old toad and her son dwelt on its swampy banks.

'Croak, croak, brekke-ke-kex!' was all he could find to say on seeing the pretty little maiden in the walnut-shell.

'Don't make such a noise, or you'll wake her!' said old mother toad. 'She may easily run away from us, for she is as light as swans' down. I'll tell you what we'll do; we'll take her out into the brook and put her down on one of the large water-lily leaves. She's so small it will be like an island to her and she won't be able to escape. Then we can go and get ready the state-rooms down under the mud, where you and she are to dwell together.'

There were many water-lilies growing out in the brook and their broad green leaves floated over the water. The leaf which was the farthest from the shore was also the largest and old mother toad swam over to it and set down the walnut-shell with Thumbelina in it.

The poor little creature awoke quite early next morning, and, when she saw where she was, she began to weep most bitterly, for there was nothing but water on every side of her and she could in no way get back to the land.

The old mother toad was down in the mud, decorating her apartments with bulrushes and yellow buttercups so as to make them quite gay and tidy to receive her new daughter-in-law. At last she and her frightful son swam together to the leaf where she had left Thumbelina, for they wanted to fetch her pretty cradle and take it to the bridal chamber for her before she was conducted there. Old mother toad bowed low in the water, and said to her, 'Here is my son. He is to be your husband and you will dwell together very comfortably down in the mud.'

'Croak, croak, brekke-ke-kex!' said her son.

Then they took the neat little bed and swam away with it while Thumbelina sat alone on the green leaf weeping, for she did not like the thought of living with the withered old toad, and having her ugly son for a husband. But it happened that some little fish, who were swimming to and fro in the water beneath, had heard what mother toad had said and they came to the surface out of curiosity to see the little maid. When they saw her, they were charmed by her beauty and it vexed them that the hideous old toad should carry her off. No, that would never do! They surrounded the lilly leaf's green stalk and gnawed it right through, and then the leaf floated away down the brook with Thumbelina far away where the old toad could not follow.

As she was carried downstream a pretty little white butterfly kept fluttering round and round her. At last he settled down on the leaf for he loved Thumbelina very much, and she was pleased.

There was nothing to trouble her now that she had no fear of the old toad pursuing her and wherever she sailed everything was most beautiful for the sun shone down on the water, making it bright as liquid gold. She took off her sash and tied one end of it round the butterfly, fastening the other end firmly into the leaf. The leaf floated faster and faster, and Thumbelina with it.

Presently a great cock-chafer came buzzing past. He caught sight of her and fastening his claw round her slender waist, flew up into a tree with her. The green leaf still floated down the brook with the butterfly, for he was tied to it and could not get free.

Oh, how frightened Thumbelina was for herself, and how sorry she was for the butterfly! She was afraid that if he could not get away, he would perish of hunger. But the cock-chafer didn't care about that. He settled down with her on the largest leaf in the tree, gave her some honey from the flowers to eat and hummed her praises, telling her she was very pretty although she was not at all like a hen-chafer. By and by all the chafers who lived in that tree came to pay her a visit; they looked at her critically and one Miss Hen-chafer drew in her feelers, saying, 'She has only two legs, how miserable it looks!' 'She has no feelers,' cried another. 'And see how thin and lean her waist is; why she is just like a human being!' observed a third. 'How very, very ugly she is!' cried all the lady-chafers in chorus. The chafer who had carried off Thumbelina still thought she was pretty, but, as all the rest kept insisting that she was ugly, he at last began to think they must be right, and decided to have nothing more to do with her. He said that, for all he cared, she could go off wherever she wanted, so the whole swarm flew down from the tree with her and set her on a daisy. Then she wept because she was so ugly that the hen-chafers would have nothing to do with her, and yet she was the prettiest little creature that could be imagined, soft and delicate and transparent as the loveliest rose petal.

All the summer and autumn poor Thumbelina lived alone in the wide wood. She wove herself a bed of grass and hung it under a large burdock-leaf which sheltered her from the rain; she dined off the honey from the flowers and drank the dew that spangled the leaves and herbs round her every morning. But then winter came, the cold, long winter. All the birds who had sung so sweetly to her flew away, trees and flowers withered and the large burdock-leaf rolled itself up and became a dry, yellow stalk. Thumbelina was dreadfully cold, for her clothes were wearing out and she was so slight and frail she was nearly frozen to death. It began to snow, and every light flake that fell upon her made her feel as we should if a whole shovelful of snow were thrown upon us, for we are giants in comparison with a little creature only an inch long. She wrapped herself up in a withered leaf, but it gave her no warmth and she still shuddered with cold.

Close outside the wood, on whose outskirts Thumbelina had been living, lay a large corn-field. The corn had been harvested long ago, leaving only the dry, naked stubble standing up from the frozen earth, but it was like another wood to Thumbelina and oh, how she shivered with cold as she made her way through it! At last she passed a field-mouse's door, for the field-mouse had made herself a little hole under the stubble and dwelt there snugly and comfortably, having a room full of corn and a neat kitchen and store-chamber besides. Poor Thumbelina stood at the door and begged for a little piece of barley-corn, for she had had nothing to eat during two whole days.

'Poor little thing!' said the field-mouse, who was indeed a thoroughly good-natured old creature, 'come into my warm room and eat with me.'

She soon took a great liking to Thumbelina and said, 'You may stay with me for the winter if you like, if you keep my rooms clean and neat and tell me stories, for I love stories dearly.'

And Thumbelina did all that the kind old field-mouse required of her, and was made very comfortable in her new home.

'We shall have a visitor soon,' said the field-mouse; 'my next-door neighbour comes to see me once every week. He is better off than I am, he has large rooms in his house and wears a coat of most beautiful black velvet. It would be a good thing for you if you could have him for your husband, but unfortunately he is blind. He will not be able to see you and you must tell him all the prettiest stories you know.'

But Thumbelina did not care about pleasing their neighbour, Mr. Mole, nor did she wish to marry him. He came in his black-velvet suit and he was very rich and learned, and the field-mouse declared his house was twenty times larger than hers. But he could not endure the sun and the pretty flowers and he was always abusing them, although he had never seen either. Thumbelina was asked to sing for him, and by the time she had sung 'Lady-bird, lady-bird, fly away home!' and 'The Friar of Orders Grey,' the mole had fallen in love with her because of her charming voice. However, he said nothing as he was a prudent, cautious animal.

He had just been digging a long passage through the earth from their house to his, and he said the field-mouse and Thumbelina should walk in it as often as they liked. Warning them not to be afraid of a dead bird that lay in the passage, he took a piece of tinder in his mouth which shone like fire in the dark and went in front to light his friends through the long dark passage. When they came to the place where the dead bird lay, he thrust his broad nose up against the ceiling and pushed up the earth to make a hole for the light to come through. On the floor lay a swallow who had evidently died of cold; his wings clung firmly to his sides and his head and legs were drawn under the feathers. Thumbelina felt very sorry, for she loved all the little birds who had sung and chirped so merrily to her the whole summer long. But the mole kicked it with his short legs, saying, 'Here's a fine end to all its chirping! What a miserable thing it must be to be born a bird. None of my children will be birds; that's a comfort! Such creatures have no assets in life but their songs and they have to starve to death in winter.'

'Yes, indeed, that's true,' replied the field-mouse. 'Where has the bird got with all his chirping and warbling? When winter comes it must starve and freeze. And it is such a lump of a thing too!'

Thumbelina said nothing but, when the others had turned round, she bent over it, smoothed down the feathers that covered its head and kissed the closed eyes. 'Perhaps it was this one that sang so beautifully to me in the summer time,' she thought. 'How much pleasure it gave me!'

The mole stopped up the hole through which the daylight had come, and then followed the ladies home. But Thumbelina could not sleep that night, so she got out of her bed and wove a carpet out of hay and then went out and wrapped it round the dead bird. She also fetched some soft cotton from the field-mouse's room, which she laid over the bird so it should be warm in the cold earth.

'Farewell, dear bird,' she said; 'farewell. Thank you for your beautiful song in the summer time when all the trees were green and the sun shone so warmly upon us.' Then she pressed her head against the bird's breast and she was terrified to feel some-thing beating within it. It was the bird's heart. He was not dead, he had lain in a swoon, and now that he was warmer, his life returned.

Thumbelina trembled with fear, for the bird was very large in comparison with her. However, she took courage, tucked the cotton more closely round the poor swallow and, fetching a leaf which had served her as a coverlet, spread it over his head.

The next night she stole out again and found that the bird's life had quite returned, though he was so feeble that he could only open his eyes for one short moment to look at Thumbelina, who stood by with a piece of tinder in her hand.

'Thank you, little child!' said the sick swallow. 'I feel wonderfully warm now. Soon I shall recover my strength and be able to fly again, out in the warm sunshine.'

'Oh, no,' she replied, 'it is too cold up here; it is snowing and freezing. You must stay in your warm bed. I will take care of you.'

She brought the swallow some water in a flower-petal and he drank, and then he told her how he had torn one of his wings in a thorn-bush, and therefore could not fly fast enough to keep up with the other swallows who were all migrating to the warm countries. At last he had fallen to the earth, and that was all he could remember; he had no idea how he had got underground.

However, underground he remained all winter and Thumbelina was kind to him and loved him dearly, but she never said a word about him to the mole or the field-mouse, for she knew they did not like him. As soon as the spring came and the sun's warmth penetrated the earth, the swallow said farewell to Thumbelina and she opened up the hole for him that the mole had thrown back before. The sun shone in on them deliciously, and the swallow asked whether she would not go with him. She could sit upon his back and they would fly together far out into the greenwood. But Thumbelina knew it would disappoint the old field-mouse if she left her.

'No, I cannot, I must not go,' said Thumbelina.

'Farewell, then, good and pretty maiden,' said the swallow, and he flew away into the sunshine. Thumbelina looked after him and the tears came into her eyes for she loved him so much.

'Tweet, tweet,' sang the bird, as he flew into the greenwood. And Thumbelina was really sad. She was not allowed to go out into the sunshine, and the wheat that had been sown in the field above the field-mouse's house grew up so high that it seemed a perfect forest to the poor little damsel.

'This summer you must work at getting your wedding clothes ready,' said the field-mouse, for the blind, dull, mole in black-velvet suit had now proposed formally to Thumbelina.

'You shall have plenty of worsted linen and be well provided with all kinds of clothes and furniture before you become the mole's wife.' So Thumbelina had to work hard at the distaff, and the field-mouse hired four spiders to spin and weave night and day. Every evening the mole arrived and he always talked about the summer coming to an end. He said that when the sun was no longer shining so warmly and scorching the earth, till it was dry as a stone, his wedding to Thumbelina was to take place. But this sort of conversation did not please her at all; she was thoroughly weary of his dull conversation. Every morning when the sun rose, and every evening when it set, she used to steal to the door; and when the wind blew the tops of the corn aside, so that she could see the blue sky through the opening, she thought how bright and beautiful it was outside and longed to see the swallow once again. But he never came and she thought he must have been flying far away in the beautiful greenwood.

Autumn came, and Thumbelina's wedding clothes were ready.

'Four weeks more and you shall be married!' said the field-mouse. But Thumbelina wept and said she would not marry the dull mole.

'Fiddlesticks!' exclaimed the field-mouse. 'Don't be obstinate, child, or I shall bite you with my sharp white teeth. Isn't he handsome? Why, even the Queen hasn't got a black-velvet dress as fine as his! And isn't he rich—rich both in kitchens and cellars? just be thankful you've got such a husband!'

The wedding-day arrived and the mole came to take away his bride to dwell with him deep under the earth, never again to come out into the warm sunshine which she loved so much and which he could not endure. The poor child was in despair at the thought that she must now say farewell to the beautiful sun, which she had at least been allowed to see every now and then while she lived with the field-mouse.

'Good-bye, glorious sun!' she cried, throwing her arms up into the air as she walked on a little way beyond the field-mouse's door. The corn had already been harvested and only the dry stubble surrounded her. 'Good-bye, good-bye,' she repeated, as she clasped her tiny arms round a little red flower that grew there. 'Give my greetings to the swallow if you should see him.'

'Tweet, tweet'—there was a fluttering of wings just over her head. She looked up, and there was the little swallow! And how pleased he was when he saw Thumbelina! She told him that she had had to accept the disagreeable mole as a husband and that she would have to dwell underground where the sun never shone. And she could not help weeping as she spoke.

'The cold winter will soon be here,' said the swallow, 'and I shall fly far away to the warm countries. Will you come with me?

You can sit on my back and tie yourself firmly to me with your sash, and we will fly away from the stupid mole and his dark room; far away over the mountains to those countries where the sun shines brightly and it is always summer, and flowers blossom all the year round. Come away with me, little Thumbelina, who saved my life when I lay frozen in the dark cellars of the earth.'

'Yes, I will come with you,' said Thumbelina. And she sat herself on the bird's back with her feet resting on the outspread wings, and tied her girdle firmly round one of the strongest feathers. Then the swallow, soaring high into the air, flew away over forests and lakes, and mountains whose crests are covered with snow all the year round. How Thumbelina shivered as she felt the keen frosty air! However, she crept under the bird's warm feathers, her head still peeping out, eager to see all the glory and beauty beneath her. At last they reached the warm countries. There the sun shone far more brightly than in her own country for the heavens seemed twice as high and twice as blue. The loveliest green and purple grapes ranged along the sloping hills. Citrons and melons grew in the groves, the fragrance of myrtles and balsams filled the air and groups of merry children, chasing large bright-winged butterflies, played by the wayside.

But the swallow did not rest here. He flew on, and still the scene seemed to grow more and more beautiful. Near a calm, blue lake, overhung by lofty trees, stood a half-ruined palace of white marble, built long ago. Vine-wreaths trailed up the long slender pillars and on the capitals, among the green leaves and waving tendrils, many a swallow had built his nest.

'This is my house,' said the swallow, 'but if you would rather choose one of the splendid flowers growing beneath us, I will take you there and you shall make your home in the loveliest of them all.'

'That would be lovely!' she exclaimed, clapping her tiny hands.

Fragments of a white marble column lay on the green turf beneath and around these fragments twined some beautiful large white flowers. The swallow flew down with Thumbelina and set her on one of the broad petals. But what was her surprise when in the very heart of the flower she saw a little mannikin, fair and transparent as though he were made of glass, wearing a gold crown on his head and the brightest, most delicate wings on his shoulders, yet scarcely bigger than she. He was the spirit of the flower. A fairy youth or maiden lived in every flower, but he was the king of them all.

'Oh, how handsome he is!' whispered Thumbelina to the swallow. The fairy prince was quite startled at their sudden arrival for the swallow was a sort of giant compared with him, but when he saw Thumbelina he was delighted, for she was the very loveliest maiden he had ever seen. So he took his gold crown off his own head and set it upon hers, asked her her name and whether she would be his bride and reign as queen over all the flower-spirits. This, you can see, was quite a different bridegroom from the son of the ugly old toad, or the blind mole with his black-velvet coat. So Thumbelina replied 'Yes' to the beautiful prince, and all the fairies came out, each from a separate flower, to pay homage to her, and every one of them brought her a present. The best of all the presents was a pair of transparent wings; they were fastened on Thumbelina's shoulders and then she found she could fly from flower to flower, which gave her the greatest pleasure. The little swallow sat in his nest above and sang to her his sweetest song, but in his heart he was very sad for he loved Thumbelina and would have wished never to part from her.

'You shall not be called Thumbelina any longer,' said the king of flowers to her, 'for it is not a pretty name, and you are so lovely. We will call you Maia.'

'Good-bye, good-bye!' sang the swallow, and he flew away from the warm countries, back to Denmark. There he had a little nest just over the window where the man who writes stories for children lives. 'Tweet, tweet!' he sang to him, and it was from him that we learnt this story.

The Leaping Match

The flea, the grasshopper, and the frog once wanted to find out which of them could jump highest, so they invited the whole world to come and see the great sight. Three famous jumpers were they, as everyone could see.

'I will give my daughter to him who jumps highest,' said the King. 'It would be too bad for you to have the trouble of jumping, and for no one to offer you a prize.'

The flea was the first to introduce himself. He had very polite manners, and bowed to the company on every side for he was of noble blood; besides, he was accustomed to human society, which had been a great advantage to him.

Next came the grasshopper. He was not quite so slightly and elegantly formed as the flea, but he, too, knew how to behave perfectly and he wore a green uniform, which belonged to him by right of birth. Moreover, he said he had sprung from a very ancient and honourable Egyptian family. In his present home, he said, he was very highly esteemed; so much so, indeed, that he had been taken out of the field where he learned to jump and put into a house of cards that was three stories high. This house was built specially for him, and was all made of court-cards, the coloured sides being turned inwards. As for the doors and windows in his house, they were cut out of the body of the Queen of Hearts.

'And I can sing so well,' added he, 'that sixteen parlour-bred crickets, who have chirped and chirped and chirped ever since they were born (and yet never succeeded in getting anybody to build them a house of cards), heard me and have fretted themselves ten times thinner than ever, out of sheer envy and vexation!'

Both the flea and grasshopper knew well how to make the most of themselves, and each considered himself a match quite good enough for a Princess.

The frog didn't say a word; however, perhaps he thought the more. The house dog, after going sniffing him very carefully, confessed that he must be of a good family. And the King's old and trusted councillor, who was ordered three times to hold his tongue in vain, declared that the frog must be gifted with the spirit of prophecy because one could read on his back whether there was to be a severe or a mild winter—which is certainly more than can be read on the back of the man who writes the weather almanac.

'Ah! I say nothing for the present,' remarked the old King, 'but I watch everything, and form my own opinion. Let them show us what they can do.'

And the match began.

The flea jumped so high that no one could see what had happened to him, and so they insisted that he had not jumped at all, 'which was disgraceful, after he had made such a fuss!'

The grasshopper only jumped half as high, but unfortunately he jumped right into the King's face, and the King declared he was quite disgusted by his rudeness.

The frog stood still as if lost in thought; at last people thought he didn't mean to jump at all.

'I'm afraid he is ill,' said the dog; and he went sniffing at him again to see if he could find out what was wrong, when, all at once, the frog made a little sidelong jump into the lap of the Princess, who was sitting on a low stool near by.

Then the King gave his judgment.

'There is nothing higher than my daughter,' he said, 'therefore it is obvious that he who jumps up to her jumps highest. Only a person of good understanding would ever have thought of that, so the frog has shown that he has understanding. He has brains in his head, so he has!'

And thus the frog won the Princess.

'I jumped highest, for all that!' exclaimed the flea. 'But it's all the same to me, let her have the stiff-legged, slimy creature, if she likes him! I jumped highest, but I am too light and airy for this stupid world; the people can neither see me nor catch me; dullness and heaviness win the day.

And so the flea went away and fought in foreign wars, where it is said he was killed.

As for the grasshopper, he sat on a green bank, meditating on the world and its strange goings on, and at length he repeated the flea's last words. 'Yes,' he said, 'dullness and heaviness win the day, dullness and heaviness win the day!' And then he began singing his own peculiar, melancholy song again and it is from him that we have learnt this strange story; and yet, my friend, though you read it here in a printed book it may not be perfectly true.

The Drop of Water

You know what a microscope is, don't you?
That wonderful glass which makes everything appear a hundred
times larger than it really is. If you look through a microscope
at a single drop of water from an ordinary stream you will see
more than a thousand strange-shaped creatures which you would
never imagine dwelt in the water. It looks rather like a plate of
shrimps, all crowded together and jumping about. They are so
ferocious that they will tear off each other's arms and legs without
mercy, yet it is their way of being happy and gay.

Now there was once an old man whom all his neighbours
called Cribbley Crabbley—a curious name certainly. He always
liked to make the best of everything and when he could not
manage it any other way he tried magic. So one day he sat with
his microscope held up to his eye, looking at a drop of ditch
water. Oh, what a strange sight it was! Thousands of little
creatures in the water were springing about, devouring each
other.

'Really, this is too horrible!' said old Cribbley Crabbley;
'there must surely be some way of making them live in peace and
quiet.' And he thought and thought but still he could not think
what to do. 'I must give them some colour,' he said at last, 'then
I shall be able to see them more clearly.' So he let a tiny drop of
something fall into the water. It looked like wine but it was

really witches' blood. The little creatures immediately went red all over like the Red Indians and the drop of water looked like a whole townful of naked wild men.

'What have you got there?' asked another old magician, who had no name at all which made him even more remarkable than Cribbley Crabbley.

'Well, if you can guess what it is,' replied Cribbley Crabbley, 'I will give it you; but I warn you, you'll not find it out very easily.'

And the anonymous magician looked through the microscope.

The scene he beheld resembled a town where all the inhabitants were running about without clothing; it was a horrible sight. But it was still more horrible to see how they kicked and hit, struggled and fought, pulled and bit each other. All those that were lowest down strove to get to the top, and all those that were highest up were thrust down. 'Look, look!' they seemed to be crying out, 'his leg is longer than mine; pah! off with it. And there is one who has a little lump behind his ear, quite an innocent little lump but it hurts him, and it shall hurt him even more!' And they seized hold of him and devoured him, merely because of this little lump. Of all the creatures only one was quiet and still; it sat by itself, like a little shy young girl wanting nothing but peace and rest. But the others would not have it; they pulled the little damsel forward and punched her mercilessly.

'This is uncommonly diverting,' remarked the anonymous magician.

'Do you think so? Well, but what is it?' asked Cribbley Crabbley. 'Can you guess or can't you? That's the question.'

'Of course I can guess,' said his friend,' it's easy enough. It is either Copenhagen or some other large city; I don't know which, for they are all alike. It is some large city.'

'It is a drop of ditch water!' said Cribbley Crabbley.

The Buckwheat

If you go through a field of buckwheat after a storm, you will see that it has become as black as if it had been burned. I will tell you the reason for this as I was told it from a sparrow, who in its turn heard it from the old willow tree that dwelt near a field of corn and buckwheat. This willow tree is tall and highly respectable but, at the same time, old and wrinkled. Its trunk has been riven asunder from top to bottom; grass and brambles grow out of the gap; the tree bends forward and the branches hang down to the ground like long green hairs.

There were a good many different kinds of corn growing in the fields around the buckwheat. The corn ears were richly blessed, and the fuller they were, the lower they bowed. The proud buckwheat, however, held his head high and erect.

'I have as many golden ears as the corn,' he said, 'and I am far prettier. My flowers are as beautiful as apple blossom. Have you ever seen anything more lovely than I am, old willow tree?'

The willow tree only nodded his head.

'The stupid tree!' cried the buckwheat. 'He is so old that grass is growing in his brain!'

Just then a great storm arose. All the flowers of the field folded their petals together and bent down their little heads. The buckwheat stood erect and proud.

'Bend your head as we do,' said all the flowers.

'I will not,' said the buckwheat. 'I will not bend my head.'

'Close your flowers and fold in your leaves,' said the old willow tree. 'Do not look up at the lightning, for you will see right into heaven. Even men are blinded if they look; what then will happen to us weeds if we dare to raise our heads?'

'Weeds, indeed!' cried the buckwheat with scorn; 'I'm not afraid of seeing heaven.' In his pride he looked upward and for a moment the whole world seemed to be in flames.

Soon the storm had passed over and how sweet everything was after the rain! The flowers breathed again, and the corn waved in the wind. But the buckwheat lay on the ground, withered and charred. The old willow tree shook his head in the wind and a big drop of rain-water fell from his leaves. It was as if he wept. The sparrows chirped: 'Why do you weep? Can't you feel the fragrance of the flowers and leaves? Why are you crying, old willow tree?' The willow told them what had happened to the proud buckwheat and I heard it all from the sparrows one evening when I asked them for a story.

The Shepherdess and the Chimney Sweep

Have you ever seen an old-fashioned wood cabinet, quite black with age and varnish and covered with carvings? Just such a piece of furniture, which had once belonged to its present mistress's great-grandmother, stood in a parlour. It was carved from top to bottom with roses, tulips, and little stags' heads with long branching antlers peering from the curious scrolls and foliage surrounding them. Moreover in the central panel of the cabinet was the full-length figure of a man. He always seemed to be smiling at himself; he was really a most ridiculous figure. He had crooked legs, small horns on his forehead and a long beard. The children of the house used to call him 'the crooked-legged Field-Marshal-Major-General-Corporal-Sergeant,' for this was a long, hard name, and not many figures, whether they were wood or stone, could boast of such a title. There he stood with his eyes fixed on the table under the mirror, for on this table was a pretty little porcelain shepherdess, whose mantle was gathered gracefully round her and fastened with a red rose. Her shoes and hat were gilt, her hand held a crook; oh, she was charming! Close by her stood a little chimney sweep, likewise of porcelain. He was as clean and neat as any of the other figures. Indeed, the manufacturer might just as well have made him into a prince for, although most of him was as black as a coal, his face was as fresh and rosy as a girl's, which was certainly a mistake—it ought to have been black. He kept his station close by the little shepherdess with his ladder in his hand. They had been placed side by side at the very beginning and had always remained on the same spot, and it was not unnatural they had plighted their troth to each other. They suited each other well for they were both young people made of the same kind of porcelain, fragile and delicate.

Not far off stood a figure three times as large as the others. He was an old Chinese mandarin, who could nod his head and because he was porcelain too, he declared that he was grandfather to the little shepherdess. He could not prove this but he insisted that he had authority over her, and so, when 'the crooked-legged Field-Marshal-Major-General-Corporal-Sergeant' proposed to the little shepherdess, he nodded his head in token of consent.

'Now you will have a husband,' the old mandarin said to her: 'a husband who I believe is made of mahogany. You will be the wife of a Field-Marshal-Major-General-Corporal-Sergeant, of a man who has a whole cabinet full of silver plate and a store of no one knows what in the secret drawers.'

'I will not go into that dismal cabinet,' declared the little shepherdess. 'I have heard that eleven porcelain ladies are already imprisoned there.'

'Then you will be the twelfth, and you will be in good company,' retorted the mandarin. Your wedding shall be celebrated this very night, as sure as I am a Chinese mandarin!'

Whereupon he nodded his head and fell asleep.

But the little shepherdess wept and turned to her sweetheart, the porcelain chimney sweep.

'I'm afraid I will have to ask you to take me away into the wide world,' she said, 'for we cannot stay here.'

'I will do anything you want,' replied the little chimney sweep; 'let's go at once. I think I can earn enough to support you.'

'If you could only get off the table!' she sighed. 'I shall never be happy till we are out in the wide world.'

And he comforted her, and showed her how to climb down the

carved edges and gilded foliage twining round the leg of the table, till at last they reached the floor. But turning to look at the old cabinet they saw everything in great commotion; all the carved stags were poking out their little heads, waving their antlers and twisting their necks round, while 'the crooked-legged Field-Marshal-Major-General-Corporal-Sergeant' sprang up and shouted out to the old Chinese mandarin, 'Look, they're eloping! They're eloping!'

Then they were frightened, and jumped quickly into an open drawer for protection. In this drawer there were three or four incomplete packs of cards and a little puppet-theatre. A play was in progress and all the queens, whether of diamonds, hearts, clubs or spades, sat in the front row fanning themselves with the flowers they held in their hands, while the knaves stood behind them, showing that they had each two heads, one at the top and one at the bottom, as most cards have. The play was about two people who were crossed in love, and the shepherdess wept at it, for it was just like her own story.

'I cannot bear this!' she said. 'Let's leave the drawer at once.' But when they reached the floor again they looked up and saw that the old Chinese mandarin had woken up and was rocking his whole body to and fro with rage.

'Oh, the old mandarin is coming,' cried the little shepherdess, and down she fell on her porcelain knees in the greatest distress.

'I have an idea,' said the chimney sweep. 'Suppose we creep into the big pot-pourri vase that stands in the corner? We can rest there on roses and lavender, and throw salt in his eyes if he comes near us.'

'That won't do at all,' she said; 'for I know that the old mandarin was once betrothed to the pot-pourri vase, and no doubt they're still friendly. No, there's nothing for it but to go out into the wide world.'

'Have you the courage to come with me?' asked the chimney sweep. 'Have you thought how large it is, and how we may never come home again?'

'I have,' she said.

The chimney sweep looked at her keenly, and then he said, 'My road leads up the chimney. Have you really got the courage to creep through the stove with me, through the flues and the tunnel? Well, I know the way. We will climb so high that they won't be able to catch us, and at the top there's a hole that leads into the wide world.'

And he led her to the door of the stove.

'Oh, how black it looks!' she sighed, but she went on with him through the flues and through the tunnel where it was dark, pitch dark.

'Now we're in the chimney,' he said, 'and look, what a lovely star is shining above us!'

And there actually was a star in the sky, shining as if to show them the way. They crawled and climbed and crawled and climbed, higher and higher. What a dangerous performance it was! But the chimney sweep guided and supported the shepherdess and showed her the best places to put her tiny porcelain feet, till at last they reached the top of the chimney. There they sat down to rest, for they were very tired.

The sky with all its stars was above them, the town with all its roofs lay beneath them and the wide, wide world surrounded them. The poor shepherdess hadn't been prepared for any of this; she leant her little head on the chimney sweep's arm and wept so bitterly that the gold ran down off her girdle.

'It's too big!' she said. 'The world is much too big! Oh, would I were on the little table under the mirror again. I shall never be happy till I am back there. I have followed you out into the wide world; surely you can follow me home again, if you love me.'

The chimney sweep talked very sensibly to her, reminding her of the old chinese mandarin and 'the crooked-legged Field-Marshal-Major-General-Corporal-Sergeant.' But she cried so hard and kissed her chimney sweep so fondly that at last he yielded to her request, unreasonable though it was.

So with great difficulty they crawled down the chimney, crept through the flues and the tunnel, and at last found themselves in the dark stove once more. But they waited behind the door and listened, before they dared return to the room. Everything was quite still. They peeped out. Alas! the old Chinese mandarin lay on the ground. In trying to follow the runaways, he had fallen down off the table and had broken into three pieces. His head lay nodding in a corner. 'The crooked-legged Field-Marshal-

Major-General-Corporal-Sergeant' stood where he had always stood, thinking over what had happened.

'Oh, how shocking!' exclaimed the little shepherdess. 'Old grandfather is broken in pieces, and we are the cause of it. I shall never survive it!' and she wrung her delicate hands.

'He can be put together again,' replied the chimney sweep. 'In fact, he can very easily be put together again. Don't be so impatient! If they glue his back together and put a strong rivet in his neck, he'll be as good as new again, and will be just as rude and overbearing as before.'

'Do you really think so?' she asked. And then they climbed up on to the table to the place where they had always stood.

'Look how far we've been!' said the chimney sweep; 'we might have saved ourselves all the trouble.'

'If we could only have old grandfather put together!' said the shepherdess. 'Will it cost very much?'

He was put together; the family had his back glued and his neck riveted. He was as good as new, except he couldn't nod his head any more.

'You've got very proud since you broke into pieces!' remarked the crooked-legged Field-Marshal-Major-General-Corporal-Sergeant, 'but I must say I don't see there is anything to be proud of. Am I to have her, or am I not? Just answer me that!'

And the chimney sweep and the little shepherdess looked imploringly at the old mandarin; they were so afraid he might nod his head. But nod he could not, and it would have been unpleasant for him to confess to a stranger that he had a rivet in his neck. So the young porcelain couple remained together, and they blessed the grandfather's rivet, and went on loving each other till they were eventually broken.

The Shadow

In hot countries the sun's rays burn fiercely. People have their complexions dyed a mahogany-brown colour, and in the very hottest regions of all they are scorched into negroes. Our story, however, concerns not equatorial regions but one of the moderately hot countries, which was visited once upon a time by a learned man from the cold, cold north. This learned man thought at first that he could run about as easily as he had been used to do at home, but he was soon to learn better and, like all other reasonable people, he remained in his house all day long, keeping the doors and window-shutters closed just as though everybody were asleep or away from home. The narrow street of tall houses where he lived was so situated that the sun fell full on it from dawn of day till dusk, and the learned man from the cold country felt as though he were sitting in an oven. He was a young as well as a wise man, and the sun injured his health; he became quite thin. His shadow, too, was considerably smaller during the day-time than it had used to be, for the sun affected both of them. However, at night, after the sun had set, both man and shadow revived a little.

It was really a pleasure to see the change. As soon as lights were brought into the room the shadow reached up the wall, sometimes even as far as the ceiling. It seemed stretching itself to the utmost in order to recover its original size. The learned man used to go out on the balcony—that was *his* place for stretching—and when the stars shone forth in the clear, balmy atmosphere, he felt a new life breathing through his limbs. Figures of men and women appeared on all the balconies in the street (and in hot countries every single window has a balcony, for people must have air even though they are mahogany-coloured). Above and below, everything became full of life; butchers and bakers, cobblers and tailors, moved about the streets; chairs and tables were brought out and thousands of lamps were lit. One shouted, another sang, some walked, some drove, some rode on donkeys —klingelingeling, the little bells on their harness tinkled merrily as they passed—little boys let off squibs and crackers, the church-bells pealed, psalms were sung, and many a solemn funeral procession moved along. Yes, the street really was alive then.

Only in the house which stood exactly opposite the northern man's was there silence. And yet it could not be uninhabited, for flowers filled the balcony—they flourished in spite of the sun's burning heat, which they could never have done unless they had been constantly watered. Besides every evening the balcony window used to open and, although it was quite dark in the first room, notes of music were heard from some deeper recess. It was incomparably delicious music—at least so our stranger thought, but this might have been only imagination as, according to him, everything in this hot country was incomparably delicious—except for the sun. The stranger's landlord said that he did not know who occupied the house opposite, for no one had ever been seen there. As for the music, it seemed dreadfully dull. 'It is,' said he 'just like a person sitting and practising a piece which he cannot play—always the same piece. "I shall be able to play it eventually," he keeps on saying, but it is plain that he never will, with all his practising.'

One night the stranger was asleep close by the open window when the curtains were waved aside by the wind so that the opposite balcony was clearly visible. It was decorated with great splendour: all the flowers shone like flames of the loveliest and most varied hues, and amongst them stood a tall, graceful maiden, surrounded by a dazzling light. He woke up with a start and with one spring he was on the floor. He crept softly behind the curtain, but suddenly the lady was gone, the glory which had dazzled his eyes was gone, the flowers shone no longer, the soft and plaintive music sounded again from within the half-open door. Surely this was some sort of magic!

One evening the stranger was sitting on his balcony. Lights were burning in the room behind him and consequently his shadow fell on the opposite wall. There it sat among the flowers of the balcony and whenever its master moved, the shadow moved also, as a matter of course.

'I really think my shadow is the only thing stirring over there,' said the learned man. 'See how comfortably it is sitting among the flowers! The door is half open—I do wish it would have the sense to walk in, look about, and then come back to me and tell me what it had seen there. Well, will you go?' he continued, jestingly; and he nodded to the shadow, and the shadow nodded back in return. 'Go on, then, but remember not to stay too long!' He got up and his shadow on the opposite balcony rose also. Then he turned round, and the shadow turned round too, and a close observer might have seen that the shadow went through the half-opened door into the room in the opposite house just as the stranger retired to his own room, closing the long curtains behind him.

Next morning he went out to drink coffee and read the newspapers. 'What's this?' he exclaimed, as he came out into the sunshine. 'Why, I haven't got a shadow! Then it really did go into that house yesterday evening, and it hasn't come back. Upon my word, this is the most provoking thing ever heard of!'

He was angry, not so much because his shadow had gone, as because he knew that there was already a story about a man without a shadow which was well known to most people in his own country, so that if he were to tell his own story, everybody would call him a plagiarist. That didn't appeal to him at all, so he determined to say nothing about it, and this was certainly a wise decision.

In the evening he went back on to the balcony, having first placed the candles behind him, for he knew that a shadow always requires its master to act as its screen. Yet he could not entice it forth. He stretched himself, he contracted himself, but no shadow made its appearance. He said, 'Hem, hem!' but that was of no avail either.

All this was irritating. However, in hot countries everything grows very fast. After eight days had gone by, he noticed, to his great delight, that a new shadow was beginning to spring out from under his feet—the root must have remained there—and in three weeks' time he had once more a very tolerable shadow. Soon he was travelling homewards and the shadow increased rapidly in size during the journey, until at last it became so long and so broad that half of it would have been sufficient for him.

So this same learned man returned to his cold homeland and he wrote books about all that was true and good and beautiful in the world. Days passed on—and weeks passed on—and years passed on—many years.

One evening when he was sitting alone in his room, he heard a low tapping at the door.

'Come in,' he said but no one came in, so he got up and opened the door. Before him stood a man so unaccountably thin and meagre that the sight startled him. This stranger was, however, exceedingly well dressed and appeared to be a person of rank. 'With whom have I the honour of speaking?' inquired the scholar.

'Ah! I thought as much!' replied the thin gentleman. 'I thought you would not recognize me. I have gained so much body lately—I have gained both flesh and clothes—I dare say you never thought to see me in such excellent condition. Do you not remember your old shadow? Ah! you must have imagined I never meant to return at all. Things have gone so well with me since I was last with you, I've become quite wealthy. I can easily ransom myself if necessary.' And with these words he passed his hand over the heavy gold watch-chain which he wore round his neck and rattled the large bunch of costly seals which hung from it—and how his fingers glittered with diamond rings! And all this was real!

'I must pull myself together,' exclaimed the scholar. 'What can this mean?'

'It is certainly rather extraordinary,' said the shadow. 'But then you yourself are by no means an ordinary man, and as you know, I have trod in your steps from childhood. As soon as you thought I was capable of going alone, I made my own way in the world. My luck was good, yet nevertheless a sort of yearning came over me to see you once more before you die. Besides, I wanted to see this country again, for one cannot help loving one's own fatherland. I know that you have another shadow now. Have I to pay you anything for it? Be good enough to tell me how much you want for it.'

'Is it really and truly yourself?' cried the scholar. 'This is indeed incredible! I could never have believed that my old shadow would return to me as a man!'

'Tell me what I am to pay you,' repeated the shadow; 'for on no account would I remain in anyone's debt.'

'How can you speak like that?' said the scholar. 'Why talk about debts? You are perfectly free and I am exceedingly glad to hear of your good fortune. Come, old friend, sit down and tell me how it has all happened and what you saw in that mysterious house just opposite mine in the hot country.'

'Well, I will tell you,' said the shadow as he sat down, 'but you must first promise that you will never let anyone in this town know that I was once your shadow, for you may meet me again here. I am thinking of getting married as I have the means to support more than one family.'

'Have no fear,' replied the scholar, 'I won't tell anyone what you really are. Here is my hand—I promise on my honour as a gentleman.'

'Then I will tell you the truth, on my honour as a shadow,' said the mysterious visitor, and indeed he could hardly have expressed himself otherwise.

It was quite wonderful to see how much of a man he had become. He was dressed all in black, the finest black cloth, with shining boots and a hat which could be squeezed up so that it was only crown and brim, not to speak of things we have already mentioned—gold chain, seals, and diamond rings. Yes, the shadow was uncommonly well dressed and, in fact, it was his dress which made him appear so completely like a man.

'Well then, I will tell you all about it,' said the shadow, and he planted his legs, with their shining boots, as firmly as he could upon the arm of the scholar's new shadow, which lay like a poodle at its master's feet. This was done, perhaps out of pride but more probably with the idea that he might entice it into staying with him. And the recumbent shadow lay still, anxious not to miss a single word, for it was eager to learn how it too might free itself and become its own master.

'Can you guess who turned out to be living in the opposite house?' asked the shadow triumphantly. 'It was Poetry—most beautiful, most charming Poetry! I was there three weeks and that is as good as if I had lived there three thousand years and had read all that was imagined and written during that time. I tell you this and it is true; I have seen all, and I know all!'

'Poetry!' cried the scholar. 'Ah yes! she often lives as a hermitess in the very heart of a bustling city. Poetry—yes. I have seen her too, but it was only for one moment, when sleep had charmed my eyes. She stood at the balcony, radiant as the Northern Lights. Oh, tell me, please tell me! You were on the balcony, you went through the door, and then—'

'Why, then I was in the hall,' said the shadow. 'You remember you used to sit looking across into it. It was not lit, but was in a kind of twilight. But door after door, all open, led through a long suite of rooms and in the distance there were plenty of lights, quite an illumination in fact. The glare would have killed me had I gone on into the lady's apartment.'

'And what did you see?' inquired the scholar.

'I saw everything.'

'What were the inner rooms like?' asked the scholar again. 'Were they like fresh woods? Or like a holy church? Or like the starry sky?'

'Everything that is beautiful was there,' said the shadow. 'I didn't go in; I stayed in the twilight of the outer room—but that was an excellent position. I saw everything, and I know everything! I have been at Poetry's Court—I have stood in the hall.'

'But what did you see? Did all the ancient gods pass through spacious halls? Didn't bold heroes and chivalrous knights do battle there as in olden times? Were there pretty children playing together and telling each other their dreams?'

'I repeat that I was there, and I beg you to understand that I saw everything which was to be seen and I became a man

Had you gone over possibly you might have become something more; but this is what happened to me. I gained knowledge of my inmost nature, my talents, and the relationship I bore to Poetry. During the time I spent with you I thought little about these matters. Whenever the sun rose or set, as you know, I became wonderfully tall, perhaps by moonlight I was even more distinguished than you—but I did not understand my own nature. In that antechamber all was made plain—I became a man. I left the place completely altered. You were no longer in the hot country, and I was ashamed to go about as the man I was then. I wanted boots and clothes; in short, all that human paraphernalia which distinguishes a man, or rather makes him known as such. I made my way under the kitchen-maid's cloak. I hid myself in it and she little thought whom she was sheltering. It was evening when I first went out—I ran along the street in the moonlight, I stretched myself up along the wall (it is so pleasant and cooling to one's back) I ran up and I ran down; I peeped into every room in the street, even the attics. I saw what no one else could see.

This is only a poor, miserable sort of a world after all! I wouldn't be a man if it weren't for the honour of the thing. I saw the most incredible, unheard of things among all ranks and classes. I saw,' continued the shadow emphatically, 'what no one knows but what everybody would like to know—*their neighbour's secret evil deeds*. Had I published a new magazine, wouldn't people have read it! But, instead of this, I wrote to the individuals themselves whose private doings I had spied out, and thus I raised wonder and fear in every town I visited. They were so afraid of me and they loved me so much! Professors made me a professor; tailors gave me new clothes—you will observe how prosperous I am. Coiners minted money for me, and women declared I was very handsome! And thus I became the man you see. And now, I must bid you farewell. Here is my card. I live on the sunny side of the road, and am always at home when it rains.'

And the shadow took his leave.

'Strange, certainly, very strange!' said the scholar.

Days and years passed away—the shadow came again.

'How are you?' he asked.

'Alas!' sighed the scholar, 'I still write what is true and good and beautiful, but no one wants to hear about it. I'm in despair. I suppose I take it to heart too much.'

'I never do that,' returned the shadow. 'I am growing fat, as everyone should try to be. Ah, you don't understand the world, and so you let yourself be disgusted with it. You should travel. I'm going to make a tour this summer; suppose you come with me? I should like to have a companion—will you travel with me as my shadow? It would be a great pleasure to me to have you with me. I will pay your expenses.'

'An odd proposal, certainly,' and the scholar smiled at the idea.

'What does it matter, when it suits both of us? Travelling will do wonders for you. Be my shadow, and you shall have everything you want.'

'This is too absurd; you are mad!'

'If I am, all the rest of the world is mad too, and mad it will be to the end.' And with this the shadow went away.

Meantime the scholar's affairs grew worse and worse. He was pursued by sorrow and care and his writing about the true, and the good, and the beautiful did as much good to the multitude as casting pearls before swine. At last he became downright ill.

'Actually, you look like a shadow,' said his friends, and a shiver went through the scholar's frame on hearing the words.

'You must go to the baths,' said the shadow at his next visit; 'there is nothing else for it. I'll take you with me for old acquaintance' sake. I'll pay the expenses of the journey, and you shall write descriptions and entertain me on the way. I want to go to the baths myself; my beard doesn't grow quite as it should do and that's as bad as a disease, for one cannot do without a beard. Now, be reasonable and accept my offer. We shall travel as friends.'

And so they travelled. The shadow was now the master, and the master was the shadow. They drove, they rode, they always walked together, sometimes side by side, sometimes before or behind one another, according to the position of the sun. The shadow always took care to take the place of honour for himself. But the scholar cared little about this for he was really a kind-hearted man and of an exceedingly mild and placid temper.

They arrived at one of the spas. There were many strangers and amongst them a King's daughter who was very beautiful. Her disease was that she was too sharp-sighted—so much so that she was quite uncomfortable.

Of course she saw at once that the new-comer was quite a different sort of person from all the other visitors. 'They say,' she said, 'that he comes here because his beard won't grow, but I see the real cause well enough. He hasn't got a shadow.'

Her curiosity was excited. Accordingly, meeting him on her walk one day, she took the opportunity of accosting him. Being a King's daughter, she didn't have to stand on ceremony; so she said at once, 'Your disease is that you can't cast a shadow.'

'I am delighted to find that your Royal Highness is so much better,' came the shadow's reply. 'I know that it has been your misfortune to be too keen-sighted; but that disease must be cured, for the fact is that I have a very unusual shadow. Don't you see the person who always walks close to me? Other men have mere

common shades for their shadows, but I do not like anything that is common. You may have noticed that people often give their servants finer clothes for their liveries than they wear themselves. In the same way I have allowed my shadow to dress himself up like a man and, in fact, as you see, I have even given him a shadow of his own. This has been rather expensive, certainly but I love to be out of the ordinary.'

'Ah!' thought the Princess, 'am I really recovered? There is nothing like these baths! The waters have had almost miraculous powers lately. But I shall not leave the place at present; it is only just beginning to grow amusing. This stranger pleases me very much.'

That evening, in the grand assembly room, the Princess danced with the shadow. She was very light, but he was still lighter: she had never had such a partner before. She told him what country she came from, and he knew the country. He had been there, though at a time when she was not at home. He had peeped in at both upper and lower windows of the palace so he had seen many curious things, and he could answer the questions of the Princess and make startling revelations to her. Surely he must be the wisest man living! She was struck with wonder and awe, and by the time they had danced the second dance she was fairly in love with him. The shadow soon became aware of this as her eyes were continually piercing him through and through. They danced a third time and she was very near telling him what she thought but, prudently, she restrained herself, remembering her land and heritage, and the multitude of beings over whom she would reign at some future period.

'He is a wise man,' thought she, 'and he dances charmingly, but has he solid accomplishments? These are most important, too. I must test him.' So she began to ask him various questions, so difficult that she could not have answered them herself; and the shadow made a very strange face.

'Then you cannot answer me?' said the King's daughter.

'Oh, I learned all that in the days of my childhood,' replied her new acquaintance. 'I believe that my shadow, who is standing at the door over there, could answer you.'

'Your shadow! That would be rather remarkable.'

'Mind, I'm not positive that he can, but I should think so; he has followed me and listened to all I have said for so many years—yes, really, I should think he could answer you. But your Royal Highness must first let me warn you that he prides himself upon passing for a man so, to keep him in good-humour (and without that you will get nothing out of him), he must be treated as if he really were one.'

'Oh, of course!' said the Princess. So she went up to the learned man standing at the door, and began asking him many things. And he answered her in a manner which proved his wisdom and learning.

'What a wonderful man he must be who has so wise a shadow!' thought the Princess. 'It would be a real blessing to my kingdom and people if I were to choose him for my husband. And I will.'

And they soon agreed, the King's daughter and the shadow, but no one was to know of their engagement before the Princess returned to her own country. 'No one shall know, not even my shadow!' declared the future bridegroom, and for this arrangement, no doubt, he had his own reasons.

So they went off to the Princess' country.

'Listen to me, my good friend,' said the shadow to the scholar. 'I have now arrived at the height of happiness and power—I must think of doing something for you. You shall always live with me at the palace, drive out with me in the royal carriage and receive an annuity of a hundred thousand dollars. But, in return, you must let everyone call you a shadow—you must never tell anyone that you have been a man, and once every year when I sit publicly in the balcony in the sunshine, you must lie meekly at my feet as every shadow should lie. For, listen to this, I'm going to marry the King's daughter and the wedding will be celebrated this very evening.'

'No, this is too much!' exclaimed the scholar; 'it would be deceiving the whole country, not to speak of the King's daughter. I will make everything public; how that I am the man and you the shadow—that you are only dressed like a man.'

'No one would believe you,' retorted the shadow. 'Be reasonable, please, or I shall call the guard.'

'I am going straight to the King's daughter!' cried the scholar.

'But I am going first,' said the shadow, 'and you are going to prison.' And to prison he went, for of course the guard obeyed whoever their Princess had chosen as her husband.

'You're trembling,' said the Princess when the shadow entered her room; 'has anything happened? You must not be ill this evening—our wedding evening!'

'I have lived to see a most fearful thing,' said the shadow. 'You would never believe it—but alas! a poor shadow-brain cannot bear much—just imagine it! My shadow has gone mad; he actually believes that he is a man and that I—only think—that I am his shadow!'

'This is certainly shocking!' said the Princess; 'I hope he is locked up?'

'Of course; I'm much afraid he will never recover himself.'

'Poor shadow! he is very unlucky; it would be a kindness to free him from the little life he possesses. And, indeed, when I think how ready people are these days to take the part with the lower classes against the great, it seems to me that the best thing we can do is to have him quietly done away with.'

'It is hard, very hard, for he has been a faithful servant.' And the shadow pretended to sigh deeply.

'You have a most noble nature,' exclaimed the King's daughter.

That evening the whole city was illuminated; cannons were fired—boom!—and the soldiers presented arms. All this was done in honour of the royal wedding, and the King's daughter and the shadow went out on the balcony to show themselves and hear 'Hurrah!' shouted again and again.

But the scholar heard none of these grand doings, for he had already been executed.

The Little Match Girl

It was dreadfully cold, the snow fell thick and fast and it was almost dark. The last evening of the old year was drawing in. But, cold and dark as it was, a poor little girl with bare head and feet was still wandering about the streets. When she left home she had slippers on but they were much too large for her, for they really belonged to her mother, and they had dropped off her feet when she was running very quickly across the road to get out of the way of two carriages. One of the slippers couldn't be found and the other had been snatched up by a little boy, who ran off with it.

So now the little girl walked on, her bare feet quite blue with cold. She carried a small bundle of matches in her hand and a good many more in her tattered apron. No one had bought any of them the whole day—no one had given her a single penny. Trembling with cold and hunger, she crept on, looking the picture of sorrow.

The snowflakes fell on her long, fair hair, which curled in pretty ringlets over her shoulders, but she wasn't thinking about her own beauty or of the cold. Lights were glimmering through every window, and the smell of roast goose reached her from several houses; it was New Year's eve, and it was this that she was thinking about.

She sat down in the corner of two houses, drawing her little feet close under her, but in vain, for she couldn't warm them up. She dared not go home as she hadn't sold any matches and perhaps her father would beat her. Besides, her home was

almost as cold as the street: it was an attic, and although the largest of the many chinks in the roof were stopped up with straw and rags, the wind and snow often came through. Her hands were nearly dead with cold; perhaps one little match from her bundle would warm them, if she dared light it. She drew one out, and struck it against the wall. It was a bright, warm flame, and she held her hands over it. For a moment there was something magic about it and it seemed to her as though she were sitting before a large iron stove with brass ornaments. The fire burnt so brightly that the child stretched out her feet to warm them too. Alas! in a moment the flame had died away, the stove vanished and the little girl sat cold and comfortless again with the burnt match in her hand.

She struck a second match against the wall; it kindled and blazed, and wherever its light fell the wall became transparent like glass. The little girl could see into the room within. She saw a table spread with a snow-like damask cloth and covered with shining china dishes. The roast goose stuffed with apples and dried plums stood at one end, smoking hot, and—which was best of all to see—the goose, jumped down from the dish, and waddled along the floor as though he were coming right up to the poor child. The match was burnt out, and only the thick hard wall was beside her.

She kindled a third match. Again the flame shot up—and now she was sitting under a most beautiful Christmas-tree, far larger and far more prettily decked out than the one she had seen last Christmas-eve through the door of a rich merchant's house. Hundreds of wax tapers lit up the green branches and tiny painted figures, such as she had seen in the shop windows, looked down from the tree. The child stretched out her hands in delight, and in that moment the light of the match was quenched. Still, however, the Christmas candles burned higher and higher— she saw them shining like stars in heaven. One of them fell, the light streaming behind it like a long, fiery tail.

'Some one is dying,' said the little girl softly, for her old grandmother—the only person who had ever been kind to her and who had died long ago—had told her that whenever a star falls, an immortal spirit returns to the God who gave it.

She struck yet another match against the wall; it flamed up and there appeared before her that same dear grandmother, surrounded by its light. She looked gentle and loving as she always had done, but now she was bright and happy too.

'Grandmother!' cried the child, 'oh, take me with you! I know you will leave me as soon as the match goes out—you will vanish like the warm fire in the stove, like the splendid New Year's feast, like the beautiful large Christmas-tree,' and she hastily lit all the remaining matches in the bundle, lest her grandmother should disappear. They burned with such a blaze of splendour that noon-day could scarcely have been brighter. Never had the good old grandmother looked so tall and stately, so beautiful and kind. She took the little girl in her arms, and they flew together— joyfully and gloriously they flew—higher and higher, till they were at last in Paradise, where neither cold, nor hunger, nor pain, is ever known.

But in the cold morning hour, crouching in the corner of the wall, the poor little girl was found—her cheeks glowing, her lips smiling—frozen to death on the last night of the Old Year. The New Year's sun shone on the lifeless child; motionless she sat there with the matches in her lap, one bundle of which was quite burnt out.

'She has been trying to warm herself, poor thing!' the people said; but no one knew the sweet visions she had seen, or how gloriously she and her grandmother were celebrating their New Year's festival.

The Bell

Every evening when the sun was setting and the clouds shone like gold among the high chimneys of the town, one or two people heard a strange deep sound like the pealing of a church bell. Sometimes it was one person, sometimes another, and then it was only for a moment for there was such an incessant rumbling of carts and carriages, such a bustle and coming and going, such a noise of singing and shouting, that one was well-nigh bewildered and it quite drowned the distant chime. 'Listen! there is the evening bell,' people used to say; 'the sun is just setting.' If you went beyond the town into the suburbs where the houses stood farther apart with gardens and meadows lying between them, you would see the evening sky arrayed in still more bright and beautiful colours and hear the tones of the unknown bell ringing far more loudly and sweetly. It seemed as though the sound came from some church deep within the distant forest and you could not help casting a glance towards it, and feeling slightly awed.

Time went on; the bell still pealed as regularly as ever. At last people said, 'Can there be a church in the forest? The tone of the bell is strange and exceedingly beautiful; why shouldn't we go and clear up this mystery?' And accordingly the rich drove there in their carriage, and the poor walked on foot; but they found the distance longer than they had expected and when they reached the willow grove that skirted the forest, they had to sit down and rest in the shade. They looked up into the branches overhead and thought themselves already in the forest. And soon the chief confectioner in the town came out and spread his stall there, and this provoked a rival confectioner to do the same except that he hung up a bell right over his tent. The bell was covered with tar to keep the rain out, but it had no clapper. So when the people returned home, they said that they had enjoyed themselves very much, and that it was a romantic excursion—quite apart from tea.

There were three people who boasted of having penetrated right through to the other side of the forest, and they said that there, too, they had heard the distinctive tones of the supposed bell; but that the sound then seemed to come from the town. And one man wrote a long poem about the bell, comparing it to the voice of a mother speaking to a beloved child, and declaring that no other melody could ever be so mellow or so sweet.

The poem came to the attention of the Emperor of that country, and he promised that whoever discovered the cause of this mysterious sound should bear the title of 'Universal Bell-ringer', even though it turned out that there was no bell at all.

So, in hopes of obtaining this distinction, several people went rambling all over the forest, but only one returned with any pretence at an explanation. Not that he penetrated much deeper than the others. He said that the bell-like tones came from a very large owl in a hollow tree. It was the Owl of Wisdom, he said, and she was constantly striking her head against the tree; but he admitted he could not decide whether the sound proceeded from her head or from the hollow trunk. Nevertheless, he was appointed 'Universal Bell-ringer', and published every year a short treatise 'On the Owl of Wisdom'. In spite of this people were just about as wise as they were before.

It was a Confirmation-day; the Bishop addressed the children kindly and earnestly, bidding them remember that this day was a most important day for them and that the blessing of God had

been called upon their heads. The glorious sun shone brightly as
the newly confirmed boys and girls walked all together out of
the town, and suddenly the marvellous, incomprehensible bell
was heard pealing loudly from the distant forest. Immediately

the young children were seized with a longing to go and search
for the cause of the sound. All but three agreed to set out at once.
One of these wanted to go home and try on her ball-dress—and,
indeed, had it not been for the ball, she would not have cared
about being confirmed that year. Another was a poor boy who
had borrowed his confirmation coat and boots from the innkeeper's son, and had promised to return them within a fixed

time. And as for the third, he declared that he never went to any strange place without his parents; he had always been a good child, and intended to be so still, although he was confirmed, and they ought not to laugh at him for it. However, they did laugh at him very loudly.

So three went back to the town, whilst the rest sped merrily on their way. The sun shone, the birds sang, and the children sang with them. They had none of them yet entered upon the business of life; they were like brothers and sisters, all equal, all children of the good God above them.

But very soon two of the youngest became weary and turned back, and two little girls sat down by the wayside to weave garlands; they stayed so long that it seemed no use trying to overtake the rest. And when the party reached the willow grove where the confection's stall stood, they said to each other, 'See, here we are at last! After all, there is really no such thing as the bell, it is only a fancy of ours!' However, that moment the bell pealed again out of the depths of the forest with such sweet and solemn tones that four or five of them decided to go on.

The trees grew close together, many-branched and thickly leaved, and it was no easy task to make a path through. Anemones and the sweet-scented woodruff grew almost too high, honey-suckle and wild convolvulus hung in long wreaths from tree to tree; the nightingales sang, and the sunbeams peeped in here and there through the boughs. Oh! the forest was most beautiful, though certainly it was no place for girls; they would have torn their frocks to ribbons among the brambles. Several large blocks of stone, covered with lichens of every colour formed a basin from which sprung a fountain of fresh spring-water. It gushed merrily with a strange, gurgling noise, like 'cluck, cluck!' 'And what if this should be the bell?' suggested one of the young adventurers, and he crouched down on the ground to listen. 'I must examine this thoroughly.' So there he stayed examining it and let the others go on without him.

They came to a cottage built with bark and boughs which had

a large tree bearing wild crab-apples leaning over it. A rose-bush was trained up the front wall, its green leaves and bright-red flowers clustering thickly round the gable end, and just under this gable end hung a little bell. Could this be the bell they sought? Yes, they all agreed that it was, excepting for one boy who said it was far too small and low to have been heard at such a distance, and that the chimes which had stirred the hearts of all men so powerfully were not at all the same. It happened that this boy was a King's son; so the others said, 'This is always the way; these grand folks think they are wiser than all the rest of the world put together.'

So they let him go his way alone, and as he wandered on he felt his spirit more and more impressed with the silent beauty of the forest. He could still hear the little bell ringing, whose sight had so delighted his comrades and at times, too, the wind carried the sound of the confectioner's bell as it summoned the holiday-makers to tea. But the deep, solemn strokes that had brought them all out of the town sounded above them all, growing louder and louder and more and more like the music of an organ. And he thought this singular music proceeded from some place to his left, from the side where the heart beats.

Suddenly there was a rustling among the bushes. The King's son turned round and saw beside him a little boy wearing wooden shoes and a jacket with sleeves so short that his wrists were quite bare. The King's son recognized him immediately; it was the boy who could not come with the rest in search of the bell, because he had to give back his borrowed confirmation clothes. This he had done, and had then followed the others, for the bell rang with so insistent a melody that he felt he must come and look for it.

'Well, then, we can go on together,' said the King's son. But the poor boy in the wooden shoes was very shy. He tugged at his short jacket sleeves, and said he was afraid he could not walk so quickly; besides he thought that the bell would be somewhere towards the right, because the right-hand side was always the place of honour.

'Well, we're not going to agree about anything!' replied the King's son, and he nodded a friendly farewell to the poor boy, who went on into the deepest, thickest recesses of the wood where the thorns tore his clothes to pieces and made his face, hands and feet bleed terribly. The King's son, too, did not escape without a few sharp scratches, but his path was much sunnier. We shall follow him, for he had a truly noble heart.

'I must, and will, find the bell,' he said, 'even if I have to go to the end of the world for it.'

Hideous grinning monkeys sat chattering and grinding their teeth among the branches. 'Shall we cudgel him?' they cried. 'Shall we thrash him? He is a King's son.'

But nothing daunted, on he went, deeper and deeper into the forest shades, where the loveliest and strangest flowers grew. Large white lilies with blood-red stamens, and sky-blue tulips, waving to and fro in the wind sprang up at his feet, and apple-trees reached out with their tempting fruit, shining like great soap-bubbles in the shafts of sunlight. Here and there were seen clear spots of the freshest green where hart and hind played together under the shade of magnificent oaks and beeches and, wherever the tree trunks had split open with age, grass and long creepers covered the cleft. He saw calm, glassy lakes, too, with white swans swimming upon them. He often paused to look and listen; often he thought that the bell-like tones must come from the depths of one of these unruffled lakes. However, he was soon convinced of his mistake: he still heard the bell pealing; it still came from some distant region of the forest. At last the sun set, the firmament glowed as if on fire, the forest seemed more silent, more sacred than ever. He knelt down, sang his evening hymn, and when it was ended said to himself, 'I'll never find it! The sun is setting; night, dark night is coming on. I would like to see the round, red sun once more before it sinks beneath the earth. I will climb up that group of rocks; the centre one is as high as the tallest tree in the forest.' And, seizing hold of roots and shrubs, he clambered up the moist stones, where water-snakes lay writhing their long, smooth coils and toads sat croaking at him. On and on he climbed and reached the top just before the sun had quite disappeared. Oh, what a magnificent scene appeared before him! The sea—the great, glorious sea—was spread before him, dashing its foaming billows on the coast and the sun shone like a rich golden altar where sea and sky met, melting into each other with the same glowing colours. The forest sang, the sea sang, and his heart sang with them. All nature seemed one vast and holy church where the trees and the light, hovering clouds formed the arched pillars together, flowers and grass were woven into a soft velvet carpet at his feet while heaven itself hung like a spacious dome overhead. And, as he gazed, the bright-red hues faded rapidly away. The sun had quite vanished but, one by one, millions of stars burst out, just as though millions of diamond lamps had been suddenly kindled. The King's son raised his arms gratefully towards heaven, sea, and forest, and just at that moment the poor youth in wooden shoes and the short jacket came forward from the right-hand side. Each following his own path, they had ended up in the same spot. They ran to meet each other, and stood together, hand in hand, in that vast natural church; while the invisible bell pealed above them and angels hovered round, praising God in heavenly chorus.

The Snow Queen

Which tells of The Mirror and Its Fragments.

There was once a wicked troll who was more wicked than anybody else. One day he was in a very happy frame of mind for he had just constructed a mirror which made everything good and beautiful shrink up to nothing when it was reflected in it, but all those things that were ugly and useless were magnified and made to appear ten times worse than before. In this mirror, the loveliest landscapes looked like boiled spinach and the handsomest persons appeared odious and their features were so distorted that their friends could never have recognized them. Moreover, if one of them had a freckle it seemed to spread right over his nose and mouth; and if a good or pious thought glanced across his mind, a wrinkle was seen in the mirror. The troll thought all this was highly entertaining, and he chuckled with delight at his clever invention.

Those who studied at the school of magic where he taught spread abroad the fame of this wonderful mirror, and said that for the first time the world and its inhabitants could be seen as they really were. They carried the mirror from place to place, until at last there was no country or person that had not been misrepresented in it. Then they flew up to the sky with it, to see if they could carry on their sport there. But the higher they flew the more wrinkled the mirror became; they could scarcely hold it together. They flew on and on, higher and higher, till at last the mirror trembled so fearfully that it escaped from their hands and fell to the earth, breaking into a million billion little pieces. And then it caused far greater unhappiness than before for fragments of it scarcely as large as a grain of sand flew about in the air, and got into people's eyes, making them see everything the wrong way and have eyes only for what was peverted and corrupt, for each little fragment retained the peculiar properties of the whole mirror. Some people were unfortunate enough to get a little splinter into their hearts and that was disastrous for their heart became cold and hard, like a lump of ice. Some pieces were large enough to be used as window-panes, but it was no use looking at one's friends through panes like these. Other fragments were made into spectacles, and did much harm to everybody who put them on. The wicked troll was greatly amused with all this, and he laughed till his sides ached.

Some little splinters of this mischievous mirror are still flying about in the air and we shall hear more about them very soon.

The First Story

A LITTLE BOY AND A LITTLE GIRL

In a large town, where there were so many houses and inhabitants that there was not enough room for everybody to have a little garden of their own and many people had to be content with keeping a few plants in pots, there dwelt two poor children whose garden was somewhat larger than a flower-pot. They were not brother and sister, but they loved each other just as much as if they had been, and their parents lived in two attics which were exactly opposite each other. The roof of one house nearly joined the other, the gutter ran along between them, and there was a little window in each roof, so that you could stride across the gutter from one window to the other. The parents of each child had a large wooden box in which they grew herbs for the kitchen, and they put these boxes on the gutter, so that they almost touched each other. A beautiful little rose-tree grew in each box, scarlet-runners entwined their long shoots over the windows, and, uniting with the branches of the rose-trees, formed a flowery arch across the street. The boxes were very high and the children knew that they weren't allowed to climb over them, but they often used to sit on their little stools under the rose trees, and thus they passed many a delightful hour.

When winter came this wasn't possible any more. The windows were often frozen over, and then they heated a half-penny on the stove, held the warm copper against the frozen pane and thus made a little round peep-hole through which they could see each other.

The little boy was called Kay and the little girl's name was Gerda. In summer they could get out of the window and jump over to each other, but in winter there were stairs to run down and stairs to run up, and sometimes outside the wind roared and the snow fell.

'Those are the white bees swarming there,' said the old grandmother.

'Have they a Queen bee?' asked the little boy, for he knew that real bees have one.

'They have,' said the grandmother. 'She flies about over there where they swarm so thickly. She is the largest of them all and she never stays on the earth, but flies up again into the black cloud. Sometimes on a winters' night she goes through the streets of the town and breathes with her frosty breath on the windows, covering them with strange and beautiful forms like trees and flowers.'

'Yes, I have seen them!' said both the children, so they knew that this was true.

'Can the Snow Queen come in here?' asked the little girl.

'If she comes in,' said the boy, 'I'll put her on the hot stove, and then she'll melt.'

And the grandmother stroked his hair and told him stories.

That same evening, after little Kay had gone home and was half undressed, he crept on to the chair by the window and peeped through the little round hole. Just then a few snowflakes fell outside, and one, the largest of them, remained lying on the edge of one of the flower-pots. The snowflake grew larger and larger and at last took the form of a lady dressed in the finest white silk, her robes made up of millions of star-like particles. She was exquisitely fair and delicate, but entirely made of ice— glittering, dazzling ice. Her eyes gleamed like two bright stars, but there was no rest or repose in them. She nodded at the window and beckoned with her hand. The little boy was frightened and jumped down from the chair to hide but afterwards he thought he saw something like a large bird fly past the window.

There was a clear frost next day, and soon afterwards spring came. The trees and flowers budded, the swallows built their nests, the windows were opened and the little children sat once more in their little garden upon the gutter that ran along the roofs of the houses.

That summer the roses blossomed so beautifully that the little girl learned a hymn in which there was something about roses; it reminded her of her own. So she sang it to the little boy, and he sang it with her.

> *Our roses bloom and fade away,*
> *Our Infant Lord abides alway;*
> *May we be blessed His face to see,*
> *And ever little children be!*

And the children held each other by the hand, kissed the roses, and looked up into the blue sky, talking away all the time. What glorious summer days were those! How wonderful it was to sit under those rose-trees, which looked as though they never intended to stop flowering!

One day Kay and Gerda were sitting looking at their picture-books full of birds and animals, when suddenly Kay exclaimed, 'Oh, dear! what was that shooting pain in my heart, and oh, something has gone into my eye!'

The little girl turned and looked at him. He blinked his eyes; no, there was nothing to be seen.

'I think it has gone,' said he, but it had not. It was one of those glass splinters from the Magic Mirror, the wicked glass which made everything great and good appear little and hateful, and which magnified everything ugly and mean. Poor Kay had a splinter too in his heart and it became hard and cold like a lump of ice. He no longer felt the pain, but the splinter was there.

'Why are you crying?' he asked. 'You look so ugly when you cry! There is nothing the matter with me. Oh!' he exclaimed again, 'this rose has an insect in it. And just look at this! They are ugly roses after all, and it is an ugly box they grow in!' Then he kicked the box, and tore off the roses.

'Oh, Kay, what are you doing?' cried the little girl. But when he saw how it distressed her, he tore off another rose and jumped down through his own window, away from his once dear little Gerda.

Ever afterwards, when she brought out the picture-book he called it a baby's book, and when her grandmother told stories, he interrupted her with a 'but', and sometimes, whenever he could manage it, he would get behind her, put on her spectacles and speak just as she did. He did this in a very droll manner and so people laughed at him. Very soon he could mimic everybody in the street. All that was singular and awkward about them Kay could imitate, and his neighbours said, 'What a remarkable brain that boy has!' But no, it was the glass splinter which had fallen into his eye, the glass splinter which had pierced his heart—it was these which made him regardless whose feelings he hurt and even made him tease little Gerda.

He played quite different games now from the ones he had before. One winters' day when it snowed he came out with a big magnifying glass and held it against the blue tail of his coat where the snow flakes fell on it.

'Now look at the glass, Gerda,' he said.

Every flake of snow was magnified and looked like a splendid flower, or ten-pointed star. 'See how clever it is!' Kay said, 'that's much more interesting than real flowers, and the design is absolutely flawless.'

Soon after he came in with thick gloves on his hands and his sledge slung across his back. He called out to Gerda, 'I've got permission to drive on the great square where the other boys are playing,' and away he went.

The boldest boys in the square used to fasten their sledges to the wagons of the country people and get pulled behind them, which was particularly good fun. While they were in the middle of the game, a large sledge painted white passed by; in it sat a person wrapped in a rough white fur, and wearing a rough white cap. When the sledge had driven twice round the square,

Kay bound his little sledge to it and was carried on with it. On they went, faster and faster, into the next street. The person driving the sledge turned round and nodded kindly to Kay, just as if they were old friends, and every time Kay was going to loose his little sledge, the person turned and nodded again, as if to signify that he must stay. So Kay sat still and they passed through the gates of the town. Then the snow began to fall so thickly that the little boy could not see his own hand, but he was still carried on. He tried hastily to undo the cords and free himself from the large sledge, but it was no use; it wouldn't come undone and he was carried on, swift as the wind. Then he cried out as loudly as he could, but no one heard him. The snow fell and the sledge dashed on; every now and then it sprang up as if it were bouncing over the top of the hedges and ditches. He was very frightened; he would have repeated 'Our Father', but he could remember nothing but the multiplication tables.

The snow-flakes seemed to be getting larger and larger, till at last they looked like great white birds. All at once they parted, the large sledge stopped, and the person who drove it rose from the seat. Kay saw that the cap and coat were entirely of snow, that that driver was a lady, tall and slender, and dazzlingly white—it was the Snow Queen!

'We have driven fast,' she said, 'but no one likes to be frozen. Creep under my bear-skin.' And she seated him in the sledge by her side, and spread her cloak around him—he felt as if he were sinking into a drift of snow.

'Are you still cold?' asked she, and then she kissed his brow. Oh! her kiss was colder than ice. It went to his heart, although that was half frozen already and he thought he should die. This feeling however, only lasted for a moment; directly afterwards he was quite well and no longer felt the intense cold around.

'My sledge! Do not forget my sledge!' He thought about that straight away. So they fastened it to one of the white birds which flew behind with it on his back. The Snow Queen kissed Kay again, and he entirely forgot little Gerda, her grandmother, and everyone at home.

'Now you must have no more kisses,' said she, 'or I shall kiss you to death.'

Kay looked at her. She was very beautiful; a more intelligent, more lovely countenance, he could not imagine. She no longer appeared to him as cold as ice, as she had when she sat outside the window and beckoned to him. In his eyes she was perfect and he now felt no fear. He told her how good he was at mental arithmetic, even with fractions, and how he knew the number of square miles of every country, and the number of the inhabitants in different towns. She smiled, and then it occurred to him that perhaps he did not yet know so very much after all. He looked up into the wide, wide space, and she flew with him high into the black cloud where the storm was raging which seemed to Kay to be singing songs of olden times. They flew over woods and over lakes, over sea and over land. Beneath them the cold wind whistled, the wolves howled, the snow glittered, and the black crow flew cawing over the plain, but above them the moon shone cold and clear.

Thus did Kay spend the long, long winter night and all day he slept at the feet of the Snow Queen.

The Second Story

THE ENCHANTED FLOWER GARDEN

But how did little Gerda get on when Kay never returned? Where could he be? No one knew. The boys said they had seen him fasten his sledge to another larger and very handsome one which had driven into the street, and then swept through the gates of the town. No one knew where he was and many tears were shed over him. Little Gerda wept and wept, for the boys said he must have been drowned in the river that flowed not far from the town. Oh, how long and dismal the winter days were now! At last the spring came, with its warm sunshine.

'Alas, Kay is dead and gone,' said little Gerda.

'I do not believe it,' said the sunshine.

'He is dead and gone,' said she to the swallows.

'We do not believe it,' they replied and at last little Gerda herself did not believe it.

'I will put on my new red shoes,' said she one morning, 'the ones which Kay has never seen, and then I will go down to the river and ask after him.'

It was quite early. She kissed her old grandmother, who was still sleeping, put on her red shoes and went alone through the gates of the town towards the river.

'Is it true,' said she, 'that you have taken my little playfellow away? I will give you my red shoes if you will give him back to me!'

And the waves of the river flowed towards her in a strange way; so she thought that they were going to accept her offer. She took off her red shoes—though she prized them more than anything else she possessed—and threw them into the stream; but the little waves bore them back to her, as though they would not take them from her because they had not got little Kay. However, she thought she had not thrown the shoes far enough, so she stepped into a little boat which lay among the reeds by the shore, and, standing at the farthest end of it, threw them far into the water. The boat was not fastened, and the movement inside it made it glide away from the shore. Seeing this she hurried to the other end, but by the time she reached it, it was more than a yard from the land; she could not escape and the boat moved on.

Little Gerda was much frightened and began to cry, but no one besides the sparrows heard her. They could not carry her back to the land, but they flew along the banks and sang, as if to comfort her, 'Here we are, here we are!' The boat followed the stream.

'Perhaps the river will take me to Kay,' she thought and then she became more cheerful, and amused herself for hours by looking at the lovely countryside around her. At last she glided past a large cherry orchard, in which was a little cottage with thatched roof and curious red and blue windows. Two wooden soldiers stood at the door and they presented arms when they saw the little vessel approach.

Gerda called to them, thinking they were alive, but naturally enough they made no answer. She came close up to them, for the stream carried the boat towards the land.

She called still louder and an old lady came out of the house, supporting herself on a crutch. She wore a large hat with the most beautiful flowers painted on it.

'Poor little child!' said the old woman. 'The mighty river has indeed brought you a long way.' And she walked right into the water, seized the boat with her crutch, drew it to land and took the little girl out. Gerda was glad to be on dry land again, although she was a little afraid of the strange old lady.

'Come and tell me who you are, and how you came here,' said she.

So Gerda told her everything and the old lady shook her head, and said, 'Hum! hum!' And when Gerda asked if she had seen little Kay, the lady said that he had not arrived there yet, but that he would be sure to come soon and in the meantime Gerda must not be too sad. She could stay with her and eat her cherries and look at her flowers, which were prettier than any picture-book and would each tell her a story.

Then she took her by the hand and they went together into the cottage, and the old lady shut the door. The windows were very high and had panes of different-coloured glass, so that when the bright daylight streamed through them various and beautiful colours filtered into the room. A plate of very fine cherries was placed on a table in the centre and Gerda was allowed to eat as many as she liked. While she was eating them, the old dame combed her hair with a golden comb and the bright flaxen ringlets fell on each side of her pretty, gentle face, which looked as round and as fresh as a rose.

'I have long wished for a dear little girl like you,' said the old lady. 'We will see if we can live very happily together.' And, as she combed little Gerda's hair, the child thought less and less of Kay, for the old lady was an enchantress. She did not, however, practise magic for the sake of mischief, but merely for her own amusement.

Now she wanted very much to keep little Gerda to live with her and, fearing that if Gerda saw her roses she would be re-minded of her own flowers and of little Kay, she went out into the garden, waved her crutch over all her rose-bushes and although they were covered with leaves and blossoms, they immediately sank into the black earth.

Then she led Gerda into this garden. Flowers of all seasons and all climates grew there in profusion—certainly no picture-book could be compared with it. Gerda danced with delight and played among the flowers till the sun set behind the cherry-trees. Then a little bed, with crimson silk cushions and a mattress stuffed with blue violet-leaves, was made ready, and she slept sweetly there and had dreams such as a queen might have on her bridal eve.

The next day she played again among the flowers in the warm sunshine, and she spent many more days in the same manner. She knew every flower in the garden but, numerous as they were, it seemed to her that one was missing, though she could not tell which. Then one day she was sitting looking at her hostess's hat, which was the one with the flowers painted on it, and, behold, the loveliest among them was a rose. The old lady had entirely forgotten about it.

'Why,' cried Gerda, 'there are no roses in the garden!' She ran from one bed to another looking everywhere, but no rose was to be found. She sat down and wept, and it so happened that her tears fell on a spot where a rose-tree had formerly stood. As soon as her warm tears had moistened the earth, the bush sprang up again, as fresh as it was before it had sunk into the ground. Gerda threw her arms round it, kissed the flowers and immediately remembered Kay. 'Oh, how could I stay here so long!' she exclaimed. 'I left home to look for Kay. Do you know where he is?' she asked of the roses. 'Is he dead?'

'He is not dead,' said the roses. 'We have been down in the earth; the dead are there, but not Kay.'

'Thank you,' said little Gerda, and she went to the other flowers, and asked, 'Do you know where little Kay is?'

But every flower stood in the sunshine dreaming its own little dream. They told their stories to Gerda, but none of them knew anything about Kay.

So away she ran to the end of the garden.

The gate was closed, but she pressed down upon the rusty lock till it broke. The gate sprang open, and little Gerda ran barefooted out into the wide world. She looked back three times; there was no one following her. She ran till she could run no longer, and then sat down to rest upon a large stone. Looking round she saw that summer was over and it was now late in the autumn. She had not noticed this in the enchanted garden where there were sunshine and flowers all the year round.

'How long I must have stayed there!' said little Gerda, 'so it's autumn now. Well, then, there is no time to lose!' and she rose to go on her way.

Oh, how sore and weary her little feet were! And everything round about looked so cold and barren. The long willow-leaves had already turned yellow and the dew trickled down from them like water. The leaves fell off the trees one by one; the sloe alone bore fruit and its berries were sharp and bitter. Cold and grey and sad the world seemed that day.

The Third Story

THE PRINCE AND THE PRINCESS

Gerda soon had to stop and rest again. Suddenly a large raven hopped upon the snow in front of her, saying, 'Caw!—Caw!—Good day!—Good day!' He sat for some time on the withered branch of a tree just opposite, eyeing the little maiden and wagging his head; then he came forward to talk to her and ask her where she was going all alone. Gerda told the raven the story of her life and fortunes, and asked if he had seen Kay.

And the raven nodded his head, half doubtfully, and said, 'That is possible—possible.'

'Do you think so?' exclaimed the little girl, and she hugged the raven so enthusiastically that it is a wonder she did not squeeze him to death.

'Gently, gently!' said the raven. 'I think I know. I think it may be little Kay, but he has certainly forsaken you for the princess.'

'Does he live with a princess?' asked Gerda.

'Listen to me,' said the raven; 'but it is so difficult to speak your language. Do you understand Ravenish? If so, I can tell you much better.'

'No, I have never learned Ravenish,' said Gerda; 'but my grandmother knew it. Oh, how I wish I had learnt it from her!'

'Never mind,' said the raven, 'I will tell you as best I can.'

'In the kingdom where we are now there dwells an uncommonly clever princess. Immediately after she came to the throne, she began to sing a new song, the burden of which was this, "Why should I not marry me?" "There is some sense in this song!" said she, and she determined she would marry, but declared that the man whom she would choose must be able to answer sensibly whenever people spoke to him, and must be good for something else beside merely looking grand and stately. Believe me,' continued the raven, 'every word I say is true, for I have a sweetheart who hops about the palace as she pleases and she has told me all this.

'Proclamations, adorned with borders of hearts, were immediately issued, proclaiming that every well-favoured youth was free to go to the palace, and that whoever should talk and show himself intelligent and at ease with the princess would be the one she would choose for her husband.

'The people all crowded to the palace, but it was all no use. The young men could speak well enough while they were outside the palace gates, but when they went in and saw the royal guard in silver uniform and the lackeys on the staircase in gold and the spacious rooms all lighted up, they were quite confounded. They stood before the throne where the princess sat, and when she spoke to them they could only repeat the last word she had uttered. It was just as though they had been struck dumb the moment they entered the palace, for as soon as they got out they could talk fast enough. There was a regular procession constantly moving from the gates of the town to the gates of the palace.'

'But Kay, little Kay, when did he come?' asked Gerda. 'Was he among the crowd?'

'Presently, presently; we have just come to him. On the third day arrived a youth with neither horse nor carriage. Gaily he marched up the the palace. His eyes sparkled like yours; he had long beautiful hair, but was very meanly clad.'

'That was Kay!' exclaimed Gerda. 'Oh, then I have found him!' and she clapped her hands with delight.

'He carried a knapsack on his back,' said the raven.

'No, not a knapsack,' said Gerda, 'a sledge, for he had a sledge with him when he left home.'

'It is possible,' rejoined the raven, 'I did not look very closely, but I heard from my beloved that when he entered the palace gates and saw the royal guard in silver, and the lackeys in gold upon the staircase, he did not seem in the least confused. He nodded pleasantly and said to them, "It must be very tedious standing out here, I prefer going in." The halls glistened with light, cabinet councillors and Lords in Waiting were walking about bare-footed and carrying golden keys—it was just the place to make a man solemn and silent and the youth's boots creaked horribly—yet he was not at all afraid.'

'That certainly was Kay!' said Gerda; 'I know he had new boots: I have heard them creak in my grandmother's room.'

'They really did make a noise,' said the raven, 'but he went merrily up to the princess who was sitting on a pearl as large as a spinning-wheel. All the ladies of the court, the maids of honour and their handmaidens, stood ranged in order on one side, and all the gentlemen in waiting, with their gentlemen, and their gentlemen's gentlemen who also kept pages, stood ranged in order on the other side, and the nearer they were to the door the prouder they looked.

'The young man spoke as well as I speak when I converse in Ravenish. He was handsome and lively. He did not come to woo her, he said, he had only come to hear the wisdom of the princess. And he liked her much, and she liked him in return.'

'Yes, to be sure, that was Kay,' said Gerda. 'He was so clever, he could do arithmetic in his head, even fractions! Oh, will you take me to the palace?'

'Ah! that is easily said,' replied the raven, 'but how is it to be done? I will talk it over with my sweetheart. She will advise us what to do, for I must tell you that such a little girl as you will never get permission to enter publicly.'

'Yes, I shall!' cried Gerda. 'When Kay knows that I am here, he will immediately come out and fetch me.'

'Wait for me at the trellis over there,' said the raven. He wagged his head and away he flew.

He did not return till late in the evening. 'Caw, caw,' he said. 'My sweetheart greets you kindly and sends you a piece of bread which she took from the kitchen. There is plenty of bread there, and you must certainly be hungry. As you have bare feet, the royal guard in silver uniform and the lackeys in gold would never permit you to enter the palace; but do not weep, you shall go there. My sweetheart knows a little back staircase leading to the bedrooms, and she also knows where to find the key.'

So they went into the garden and down the grand avenue, and, when the lights in the palace had been extinguished one by one, the raven took Gerda to a back door which stood half-open. Oh, how Gerda's heart beat with fear and expectation! It was just as though she was about to do something wrong, although she only wanted to know whether Kay was really there. She would see if his smile was the same as it used to be when they sat together under the rose-trees. He would be so glad to see her, to hear how far she had come for his sake, and how everyone at home mourned his absence. Her heart trembled with fear and joy as she went on.

They climbed the staircase. A small lamp placed on a cabinet gave a glimmer of light and on the floor stood the tame raven, who first turned her head on all sides and then looked at Gerda, who made her curtsy as her grandmother had taught her.

'My betrothed has told me much about you, my good young maiden,' said the tame raven; 'your adventures, too, are extremely interesting. If you will take the lamp, I will show you the way. We are going straight on: we won't meet anyone now.'

They entered the first room. Its walls were covered with rose-coloured satin and embroidered with gold flowers. Some dreams rustled past them, but with such rapidity that Gerda could not see them. Each room that they went through vied with the next in splendour, until at last they reached the sleeping-hall. In the centre of this room stood a pillar of gold like the stem of a large palm-tree whose leaves of costly glass fashioned the ceiling. Hanging down from the tree on thick golden stalks were two beds in the form of lilies. One was white, and in it rested the princess. The other was red, and in it Gerda hoped to find her playfellow Kay. She bent aside one of the red leaves and saw a brown neck. Oh, it must be Kay! She called him by his name aloud, and held the lamp close to him. The dreams rushed by—he awoke, turned his head, but behold! it was not Kay.

The princess looked out from under the white lily petals, and asked what was the matter. Then little Gerda wept and told her the whole story and what the ravens had done for her. 'You poor child!' said the prince and princess, and then they praised the ravens, and said they were not angry with them, but that they weren't to do it again. This once, however, they should be rewarded.

'Would you like to fly away freely to the woods?' asked the princess, addressing the ravens, 'or would you rather have appointments as Court-Ravens with the perquisites belonging to the kitchen, such as crumbs and leavings?'

And both the ravens bowed low and chose the appointment at court, for they thought of old age, and said it would be so comfortable to be well provided for in their declining years. Then the prince rose and made Gerda sleep in his bed.

The next day she was dressed from head to foot in silk and velvet. She was invited to stay at the palace and enjoy all sorts of diversions, but she begged only for a carriage and a horse, and a pair of little boots. All she wanted was to go back into the wide world to look for Kay.

They gave her the boots and a muff besides, and as soon as she was ready there drove up to the door a carriage of pure gold with the arms of the prince and princess glittering like a star and whose coachman, footman and outriders all wore gold crowns. The princess and prince themselves helped her into the carriage and wished her success and the wood raven, who was now married, accompanied her the first three miles. The carriage was well provided with sugar-plums, fruit, and gingerbread nuts.

'Farewell, farewell!' cried the prince and princess. Little Gerda wept, and the raven wept out of sympathy. Then he flew up to the branch of a tree and flapped his black wings at the coach till it was out of sight.

The Fourth Story

THE LITTLE ROBBER-MAIDEN

They drove through the dark, dark forest. The carriage shone like a torch and unfortunately its brightness attracted the eyes of the robbers who dwelt in the shadows of the forest.

'That is gold!' they cried. They rushed forward, seized the horses, stabbed the outriders, coachman, and footman to death and dragged little Gerda out of the carriage.

'She is plump, she is pretty, she has been fed on nut-kernels,' said the old robber-wife, who had a long, bristly beard and eyebrows hanging like bushes over her eyes. 'She is like a little fat lamb, and how smartly she is dressed!' And she drew out her bright dagger, glittering most terribly.

'Oh, oh!' cried the woman for, the very moment she had lifted her dagger to stab Gerda, her own wild and wilful daughter jumped on her back and bit her ear violently. 'You naughty child!' said the mother.

'She shall play with me,' said the little robber-maiden. 'She shall give me her muff and her pretty frock, and sleep with me in my bed.' Then she bit her mother again, till the robber-wife sprang up and shrieked with pain, while the robbers all laughed, saying, 'Look at her playing with her young one!'

So spoiled and wayward was the little robber-maiden that she always had her own way, and she and Gerda sat together in the carriage and drove farther and farther into the wood. The little robber-maiden was about as tall as Gerda, but much stronger; she had broad shoulders and a very dark skin; her eyes were quite black, and had an almost melancholy expression. She put her arm round Gerda's waist and said, 'She shan't kill you so long as I love you. Aren't you a princess?'

'No,' said Gerda; and then she told her all that had happened to her, and how much she loved little Kay.

The robber-maiden looked earnestly in her face, shook her head and said, 'She shall not kill you even if I do quarrel with you; then, indeed, I would rather do it myself!' And she dried Gerda's tears, and put both her hands into the pretty muff that was so soft and warm.

The carriage stopped at last in the middle of the courtyard of the robbers' castle. This castle was half ruined, crows and ravens flew out of the openings and some fearfully large bulldogs, looking as if they could devour a man in a moment, jumped round the carriage. They did not bark, for that was forbidden them.

The maidens entered a large, smoky hall, where a tremendous fire was blazing on the stone floor. A huge cauldron full of soup was boiling on the fire, while hares and rabbits were roasting on the spit.

'You shall sleep with me and my little pets tonight,' said the robber-maiden. Then they had some food, and afterwards went to the corner where there was some straw and a piece of carpet. Nearly a hundred pigeons were perched on staves and laths around them. They were asleep, but started up when the little maidens approached.

'These all belong to me,' said Gerda's companion and seizing hold of one of the nearest, she held the poor bird by the feet and swung it round. 'Kiss it,' she said, flapping it into Gerda's face. 'The rabble from the wood sit up there,' continued she, pointing to a number of laths fastened across a hole in the wall; 'those are wood-pigeons, they would fly away if I didn't keep them shut up. And here is my old favourite!' She pulled forward a reindeer who wore a bright copper ring round his neck, by which he was fastened to a large stone. 'We have to chain him up, or he would run away from us. Every evening I tickle his neck with my sharp dagger; it makes him so frightened of me!' And the robber-maiden drew out a long dagger from a gap in the wall and ran it down the reindeer's throat. The poor animal struggled and kicked, but the girl laughed, and then she pulled Gerda into bed with her.

'Are you going to keep the dagger in your hand while you sleep?' asked Gerda, looking timidly at the dangerous plaything.

'I always sleep with my dagger by my side,' replied the little robber-maiden. 'One never knows what may happen. But now tell me all over again what you told me before about Kay, and the reason for your coming into the wide world all by yourself.'

So Gerda told her story again and the imprisoned wood-pigeons listened but the others were fast asleep. The little robber-maiden threw one arm round Gerda's neck and, holding the dagger with the other, was also soon asleep. But Gerda could not close her eyes throughout the night—she didn't know what would become of her or whether she would even be allowed to live. The robbers sat round the fire drinking and singing. Oh, it was a dreadful night for the poor little girl!

Then the wood-pigeons spoke, 'Coo, coo, coo! we have seen little Kay. A white bird carried his sledge; he was in the Snow Queen's chariot which passed through the wood whilst we sat in our nest. She breathed on us young ones as she passed, and all died of her breath excepting us two—coo, coo, coo!'

'What are you saying?' cried Gerda. 'Where was the Snow Queen going? Do you know anything about it?'

'She travelled most likely to Lapland, where ice and snow abide all the year round. Ask the reindeer tied up there.'

'Yes, ice and snow are there all through the year; it is a glorious land,' said the reindeer. 'There, free and happy, one can roam through the wide sparkling valleys. There the Snow Queen has her summer tent; her strong castle is a long way off, near the North Pole on an island called Spitzbergen.'

'Oh, Kay, dear Kay!' sighed Gerda.

When morning came Gerda told the little robber-maiden what the wood pigeons had said and the little robber-maiden looked grave for a moment, then she nodded her head. 'Do you know where Lapland is?' asked she of the reindeer.

'Who should know better than me!' returned the animal, his eyes kindling. 'There was I born and bred; how often have I bounded over the wild icy plains there!'

'Listen to me!' said the robber-maiden to Gerda. 'You see all our men are going out but my mother is still here and will stay behind. Towards noon she will drink a little out of the great flask, and after that she will sleep—then I will do something for you.

When her mother was fast asleep, the robber-maiden went up to the reindeer and said, 'I should have great pleasure in stroking you a few more times with my sharp dagger, for you look so comic; but never mind, I will undo your chain and help you to escape, on condition that you run as fast as you can to Lapland and take this little girl to the castle of the Snow Queen, where her playfellow is. You must have heard her story, for she speaks loud enough and you're good at eavesdropping!'

The reindeer bounded with joy, and the robber-maiden lifted Gerda on his back, taking care to bind her on firmly as well as to give her a little cushion to sit on. 'And here,' she said, 'are your fur boots. You will need them in that cold country. The muff I will keep for myself; it is too pretty to part with. But you won't be frozen. Here are my mother's huge gloves; they reach up to the elbow. Put them on—now your hands look as clumsy as my old mother's!'

Gerda shed tears of joy.

'I cannot bear to see you crying!' said the little robber-maiden. 'You ought to look glad. See, here are two loaves and a piece of bacon for you, so you're not hungry on the way.' She fastened this food on to the reindeer's back too, opened the door, called away the great dogs and then, cutting the reindeer's rope with her dagger, shouted to him, 'Now then, run! but take good care of the little girl.'

Gerda stretched out her hands to the robber-maiden and bade her farewell, and the reindeer bounded through the forest, over stock and stone, over desert and heath, over meadow and moor. The wolves howled and the ravens shrieked. There was a noise in the sky, 'Tcho, tcho,' a red light flashed—one might almost have thought the sky was sneezing.

'Those are my dear old Northern Lights,' said the reindeer. 'Look at them, aren't they beautiful!' And he ran faster than

ever, night and day. The loaves were eaten, so was the bacon—
and then, at last, they were in Lapland.

The Fifth Story

THE LAPLAND WOMAN AND THE FINLAND WOMAN

They stopped at a little hut. It was a miserable building; the
roof very nearly touched the ground and the door was so low
that whoever wished to go either in or out had to crawl on
hands and knees. No one was at home except an old Lapland
woman who was busy boiling fish over an oil lamp. The reindeer
told her Gerda's whole story—but not, however, till after he had
made her acquainted with his own, which seemed to him to be
much more important. Poor Gerda, meanwhile, was so over-
powered by the cold that she could not speak.

'Ah, poor thing!' said the Lapland woman, 'you have still a
long way before you. You have a hundred miles to run before
you can arrive in Finland. The Snow Queen dwells there, and
burns blue lights every evening. I will write a few words on a
piece of dried stock-fish—for paper I have none—and you may
take it with you to the wise Finland woman who lives there. She
will advise you better than I can.

So when Gerda had warmed herself well and eaten some food,
the Lapland woman wrote a few words on the stock-fish, told
Gerda to take care of it and bound her once more firmly on the
reindeer's back.

They sped onwards. The wonderful Northern Lights, which
were now the loveliest, brightest blue colour, shone all through
the night and with these splendid lights they arrived in Finland,
and knocked on the wise woman's chimney, for she had no door
to her house.

It was very hot inside—so much so that the wise woman wore
scarcely any clothing. She was low in stature and very dirty.
She loosened little Gerda's dress, took off her fur boots and thick
gloves, laid a piece of ice on the reindeer's head and then read

what was written on the stock-fish. She read it three times. After the third reading she knew it by heart so she threw the fish into the porridge-pot, for it would make a very excellent supper, and she never wasted anything.

The reindeer then repeated his own story, and when that was finished he told her about little Gerda's adventures, and the wise woman twinkled her wise eyes but never said a word.

'Won't you mix this little maiden that wonderful draught which will give her the strength of twelve men, so she can over-come the Snow Queen?' said the reindeer.

'The strength of twelve men!' repeated the wise woman, 'that would be a lot of good!' And she walked away, drew out a large parchment roll from a shelf and began to read. She read so intently that perspiration ran down her forehead.

At last her eyes began to twinkle again and she drew the reindeer into a corner, and putting a fresh piece of ice upon his head, whispered: 'Little Kay is still with the Snow Queen, where he finds everything so much to his liking that he believes it to be the best place in the world. But that is because he has a glass splinter in his heart and a glass splinter in his eye. Until he has got rid of them he will never feel like a human being, and the Snow Queen will always have power over him.'

'But can't you give something to Gerda that will overcome all these evil influences?'

'I can give her no power as great as that which she already possesses. Her power is greater than ours because it comes from her heart, from her being a loving and innocent child. If it cannot give her access to the Snow Queen's palace and help her to free Kay's eye and heart from the glass fragment, then we can do nothing for her. The Snow Queen's garden is two miles hence. Carry the little maiden there and put her down by the bush bearing red berries and half covered with snow: don't waste any time about it, and hasten back!'

Then the wise woman lifted Gerda on to the reindeer's back, and away they went.

'Oh, I've left my boots behind! I have left my gloves behind!' cried little Gerda, but it was too late. The cold was piercing but the reindeer dared not stop. He ran on until he reached the bush with the red berries. Here he set Gerda down, kissed her, the tears rolling down his cheeks the while, and ran quickly back again—which was the best thing he could do. And there stood poor Gerda, without shoes, without gloves, alone in that barren region, that terribly icy-cold Finland.

She ran on as fast as she could. A whole regiment of snow-flakes came to meet her. They did not fall from the sky, which was cloudless and bright with the Northern Lights, they ran straight along the ground and the farther Gerda advanced the larger they grew. Then she remembered how large and curious the snowflakes had appeared to her the day she had looked at them through a magnifying-glass. These, however, were very much larger; they were living forms. They were, in fact, the Snow Queen's guards and their shapes were the strangest that could be imagined. Some looked like great ugly porcupines, others like snakes rolled into knots with their heads peering out, and others like little fat bears with bristling hair. Little Gerda began to repeat the Lord's prayer, and it was so cold that she could see her own breath, which, as it escaped from her mouth, ascended into the air like vapour. The cold grew intense, the vapour more dense, and at length it took the form of little bright angels which, as they touched the earth, became larger and more distinct. They wore helmets on their heads, and carried shields and spears in their hands; their numbers increased so rapidly that, by the time Gerda had finished her prayer, a whole legion stood round her. They thrust their spears among the horrible snowflakes which fell into thousands of pieces, and little Gerda walked on unhurt and undaunted. The angels touched her hands and feet and then she scarcely felt the cold, and approached the Snow Queen's palace boldly.

But before we accompany her there, let us see what Kay is doing. He is certainly not thinking of his little Gerda; least of all does he think that she is now standing at the palace gate.

The Sixth Story

THE SNOW QUEEN'S PALACE

The walls of the palace were made of the driven snow, its doors and windows of the cutting winds. There were a hundred halls, the largest of them many miles long, all illuminated by the Northern Lights; all alike were vast, empty, icily cold, and dazzlingly white. In the middle of the empty, interminable snow lay a frozen lake. It was broken into exactly a thousand pieces, and these pieces were so exactly alike that it might well be thought a work of more than human skill. The Snow Queen always sat in the centre of this lake when at home.

Little Kay was quite blue, nay, almost black with cold, but he did not notice it for the Snow Queen had kissed away the shrinking feeling he used to experience, and his heart was like a lump of ice. He was playing among the icy fragments, joining them together in every possible way just as people do with Chinese puzzles. Kay could make the most curious and complete figures—and in his eyes these figures were of the utmost importance. He often spelt out whole words, but there was one word he could never succeed in forming—it was *Eternity*. The Snow Queen had said to him 'When you can put that word together, you shall become your own master, and I will give you the whole world and a new pair of skates besides.'

But he could never do it.

'Now I am going to the warm countries,' said the Snow Queen. 'I shall sail through the air, and look into the black cauldrons'— she meant volcanoes Etna and Vesuvius. 'I shall whiten them a little; that will be good for the citrons and vineyards.' So she flew away, leaving Kay sitting all alone in the large empty hall of ice. He looked at the fragments and thought and thought, till his head ached. He sat so still and stiff that one would have thought he was frozen too.

The winds blew keenly when little Gerda passed through the palace gates, but she repeated her evening prayer and they immediately sank to rest. She entered the huge empty hall; she saw Kay, she recognized him, she flew to him and fell upon his neck, she held him fast, and cried, 'Kay! dear, dear Kay! I have found you at last!'

But he sat as still as before—cold, silent, motionless. His unkindness wounded poor Gerda deeply. She shed hot, bitter tears; they fell on his breast, they reached his heart, they thawed the ice and dissolved the tiny fragment of glass within it. He looked at her while she sang her hymn:

> Our roses bloom and fade away.
> Our Infant Lord abides alway.
> May we be blessed His face to see,
> And ever little children be.

Then Kay burst into tears. He wept till the glass splinter floated in his eye and fell with his tears. He knew his old companion immediately, and exclaimed with joy, 'Gerda, my dear little Gerda, where have you been all this time?—and where have I been?'

He looked round him. 'How cold it is here! how wide and empty!' Then he hugged Gerda, while she laughed and wept. Even the pieces of ice took part in their joy; they danced about merrily and when they were weary they lay down forming of their own accord the mystical letters which made Kay his own master.

Gerda kissed his cheeks, whereupon they became fresh and glowing as ever. She kissed his eyes, and they sparkled like her own. She kissed his hands and feet, and he was once more healthy and merry. The Snow Queen might come home as soon as she liked—it didn't matter; Kay's charter of freedom stood written on the lake in bright icy characters.

They took each other by the hand and wandered out of the palace and, as they walked on, the winds were hushed into a

calm, and the sun burst out in splendour from among the dark
storm-clouds. When they arrived at the bush with the red berries,
they found the reindeer waiting for them. He had brought
another and younger reindeer with him, whose udders were full
and who gladly gave her warm milk to refresh them.

Then the old reindeer and the young hind carried Kay and
Gerda back to the little hot room of the wise woman of Finland
where they warmed themselves, and received advice as to how
to proceed on their long journey home. Afterwards they went
to the Lapland woman, who made them some new clothes and
provided them with a sledge.

The whole party now ran on together till they came to the
boundary of the country, but, just where the green leaves began
to sprout, the Lapland woman and the two reindeers took their

leave. 'Farewell, farewell!' they all said. The first little birds they had seen for many a long day began to warble their pretty songs, and the trees of the forest were bowed down with richly tinted leaves. Suddenly the green boughs parted and a spirited horse galloped up. Gerda knew it well, for it was one which had been harnessed to her golden coach; and on it sat a young girl wearing a bright scarlet cap, and with pistols on the holster before her. It was no other than the robber-maiden! Weary of her home in the forest she had taken to travelling, first to the North and afterwards to other parts of the world. She at once recognized Gerda, and Gerda had not forgotten her. Their greeting was particularly joyful.

'A fine gentleman you are, to be sure, you graceless young truant!' said she to Kay. 'I should like to know whether you deserved anyone running to the end of the world on your account.'

But Gerda stroked her cheeks, and asked after the prince and princess.

'They are gone travelling into foreign countries,' replied the robber-maiden.

'And the raven?' asked Gerda.

'Ah! the raven is dead,' returned she. 'Now his sweetheart is a widow, she hops about with a piece of flannel wound round her leg; she moans most piteously, and chatters more than ever! But tell me now all that has happened to you, and how you managed to pick up your old playfellow.'

And Gerda and Kay told their story.

'Snip-snap-snurre-basselurre!' said the robber-maiden. She pressed the hands of both, promised that if ever she passed through their town she would pay them a visit, and then bade them farewell and rode on through the wide world.

Kay and Gerda walked on hand in hand, and wherever they went it was spring, beautiful spring, with its bright flowers and green leaves. They arrived at a large town, the church bells were ringing merrily, and they immediately recognized the high towers rising into the sky—it was the town where they had lived. Joyfully they passed through the streets, and stopped at the door of Gerda's grandmother. They walked up the stairs and entered the well-known room. The clock said 'Tick, tick!' and the hands moved as before. They could only find one difference, and that was in themselves, for they saw that they were now fully grown people. The rose-trees on the roof blossomed in front of the open window, and there beneath them stood the children's stools. Kay and Gerda went and sat down on them, still holding each other by the hand; they forgot the cold, hollow splendour of the Snow Queen's palace, it seemed like an unpleasant dream. The old grandmother sat in the bright sunshine and read these words from the Bible, 'Unless ye become as little children, ye shall not enter into the kingdom of heaven.'

And Kay and Gerda gazed on each other and all at once they understood the words of their hymn:

> Our roses bloom and fade away,
> Our Infant Lord abides alway;
> May we be blessed His face to see,
> And ever little children be!

There they both sat, grown up and yet children—children at heart—and it was summer, beautiful, warm summer.

The Flying Trunk

There was once a merchant who was so rich that he might have paved the whole street where he lived with silver and had enough left over for the little lane. But he didn't do this: he had better ways of using his money and whenever he spent a shilling he gained a crown in return.

When he died all his money went to his son. But the son lived merrily and spent all his time on pleasure, went to masquerades every evening, made bank-notes into paper kites, and played at ducks and drakes in the pond with gold pieces instead of stones. In this manner his money soon vanished until at last he had only a few pennies left and his wardrobe was reduced to a pair of slippers and an old dressing-gown. His friends no longer cared about him as they could no longer go merry-making with him. However, one of them who was more good-natured than the rest sent him an old trunk, with this advice, 'Pack up, and be off!' That was all very fine but he had nothing that he *could* pack up, so he put himself into the trunk.

It was a wonderful trunk. When the lock was closed down it could fly. The merchant's son pressed the lock, and lo! the trunk flew up with him through the chimney, high into the clouds, on and on, higher and higher. The lower part cracked, which rather frightened him, for if it had broken in two he would have had a terrible fall.

The trunk, however, descended safely and he found himself in Turkey. He hid it under a heap of dry leaves in a wood and walked into the next town. There he found that everybody was clad as he was in dressing-gown and slippers. He met a nurse carrying a little child in her arms and he asked her what palace it was he saw close by the town.

'The King's daughter dwells there,' replied the nurse; 'it has been prophesied that she shall be made very unhappy by a lover and therefore no one may visit her except when the King and Queen are with her.'

'Thank you,' said the merchant's son and he immediately went back into the wood, sat down on his trunk, flew up to the roof of the palace, and crept through the window into the Princess's apartment.

She was lying asleep on the sofa. She was so beautiful that the merchant's son couldn't help kissing her. At this she awoke, and was not a little frightened at the sight of this unexpected visitor; but he told her that he was the Turkish prophet, and had come down from the sky on purpose to woo her, and she was well pleased. So they sat down side by side, and he talked to her about her eyes, how they were beautiful dark-blue seas, and her thoughts and feelings floated like mermaidens in them; and he spoke of her brow, how it was a fairy snowy mountain. And many other such things he told her.

Thus he wooed the Princess, and she immediately said 'Yes'.

'But you must come here on Saturday,' said she; 'the King and Queen have promised to come to tea with me. They will be very proud and pleased when they hear that I am to marry the Turkish prophet! And mind you tell them a very pretty story for they are exceedingly fond of stories; my mother likes them to be very good and aristocratic, and my father likes them to be merry, to make him laugh.'

'Yes, I shall bring no other bridal present than a tale,' replied the merchant's son.

Then they parted, but not before the Princess had given her

lover a sabre all covered with gold. He had a very good idea what he would do with this present.

So he flew away, bought a new dressing-gown, and then sat down in the wood to compose the tale which was to be ready by Saturday.

At last he was ready, and at last Saturday came.

The King, the Queen, and the whole court were waiting for him at the Princess's palace. The suitor was received with much ceremony.

'Will you not tell us a story?' asked the Queen; 'a story that is instructive and full of deep meaning.'

'But let it make us laugh,' said the King.

'With pleasure,' replied the merchant's son. And this is what he told them:

'There was once a bundle of matches who were all extremely proud of their high descent, for their genealogical tree (that is to say, the tall fir-tree from which they had all been splintered) had been a very ancient tree, taller than all the other trees of the forest. The matches were lying on the mantelpiece between a tinder-box and an old iron saucepan and they often talked to them about their youth. 'Ah, when we were on the green branches,' they said, 'when we really lived upon green branches— that was a happy time! Every morning and evening we had diamond tea—that's dew: the whole day we had sunshine—at least whenever the sun shone—and all the little birds used to tell stories to us. You can easily see how rich we were, for the other trees were clothed with leaves only during the summer, whereas our family could afford to wear green clothes both summer and winter. But at last the wood-cutters came: there was the great revolution and our family was dispersed. The paternal trunk got a job as mainmast to a magnificent ship which could sail round the world if it chose; the boughs were carried off to various places and our vocation is henceforth to kindle lights for common people. Now you will understand how it comes to pass that persons of such high descent as we are should be living in a kitchen.'

'Mine is indeed a very different history,' remarked the iron saucepan, which the matches were lying near. 'Ever since I came into the world, I have been rubbed and scrubbed and boiled over and over again—oh, how many times! I love to have dealings with good solid food, and I'm really most important in this house. My only recreation is to stand clean and bright upon this mantelpiece after dinner and hold some rational conversation with my companions. However, except for the water-pail who goes out into the courtyard now and then, we all of us lead a very quiet domestic life here. Our only news bringer is the shopping basket, but he talks in such a democratic way about "government" and the "people"—why, I assure you, not long ago, there was an old jar standing here who was so much shocked by what he said that he fell down from the mantelpiece and broke into a thousand pieces! That shopping basket is a Liberal, that's the fact.'

'Now, you talk too much,' interrupted the tinder-box and the steel struck the flint, so that the sparks flew out. 'Why shouldn't we spend a pleasant evening?'

'Yes, let's decide who is of highest rank among us,' proposed the matches.

'Oh no. For my part, I would rather not speak of myself,' objected the earthenware pitcher. 'Suppose we have an intellectual entertainment. I will begin. I will relate something of everyday life such as we have all experienced, one can easily identify oneself with it and that is so interesting. Near the Baltic, among the Danish beech-groves—'

'That is a capital beginning!' cried all the plates at once; 'it will certainly be just the sort of story for me!'

'Yes, there I spent my youth in a very quiet family. The furniture was rubbed, the floors were washed, clean curtains were hung up every fortnight.'

'How very interesting! What a charming way you have of describing things!' said the broom. 'Everyone would know immediately that it is a lady who is speaking, the tale breathes such a spirit of cleanliness!'

'Very true; so it does!' exclaimed the water-pail and in the excess of his delight he gave a little jump, so that some of the water splashed on the floor.

So the pitcher went on with her tale and the end proved as good as the beginning.

All the plates clattered applause and the hair-broom swept some green parsley out of a dusty hole and crowned the pitcher. He knew that this would vex the others but he thought, 'If I crown her today, she will crown me tomorrow.'

'Now I will dance,' said the fire-tongs, and accordingly she danced and oh! it was wonderful to see how high she threw one of her legs up into the air—the old chair-cover in the corner tore with surprise at seeing her. 'Am I not to be crowned too?' asked the tongs, and she was crowned forthwith.

'They're only common people after all,' thought the matches.

The tea-urn was now called to sing. But she had a cold. She said she could only sing when she was boiling which, of course, was all pride and affectation. The fact was she never bothered to sing except when she was standing on the parlour table before company.

On the window-ledge lay an old quill-pen which the maids used for writing. There was nothing remarkable about her except that she had been dipped too low in the ink but she was proud of that. 'If the tea-urn does not choose to sing,' she said, 'she needn't bother; there is a nightingale in the cage hung just outside—he can sing. He has never learnt the notes—but never mind, we will not speak evil of anyone this evening.'

'I think it very improper,' observed the tea kettle, who was the best singer in the kitchen and a half-brother of the tea urn's, 'that we should listen to a foreign bird. Is it patriotic? I appeal to the shopping basket.'

'I am worried,' said the shopping basket. 'I am deeply worried that such things are thought of at all. Is it a becoming way of spending the evening? Would it not be much more rational to reform the whole house and establish a totally new order of things rather more according to nature? Then everyone would get his right place. I would undertake to direct the revolution. What say you to it? That would be something worth doing!'

'Oh yes, we will make a grand commotion!' they all cried. Just then the door opened—it was the servant-maid. No one dared stir, yet there was not a single kitchen utensil among them who wasn't thinking about the great things he could have done if he had been so minded and how superior he was to the others.

'Ah, if only I had chosen it,' each of them thought, 'what a merry evening we might have had!'

The maid took the matches and struck a light—oh, how they sputtered and blazed up!

'Now everyone may see that we are of highest rank;' thought the matches. 'What a splendid light we give, how dazzling!' And in another moment they were burnt out.'

'That's a good story,' said the Queen.' I felt as though I was really in the kitchen. Yes, you shall have our daughter.'

'Willingly,' said the King; 'on Monday you shall marry our daughter.'

On the evening before the wedding the whole city was illuminated; cakes, buns, sugar-plums were thrown about among the crowd; all the little boys in the streets stood upon tiptoe and shouted and whistled through their fingers.

'Well, I suppose I ought to do something about it too!' thought the merchant's son. So he went and bought sky-rockets, squibs, Catherine-wheels, Roman-candles and every conceivable kind of fireworks, put them all into his trunk and flew up into the air, letting them off as he flew.

All the Turks jumped up to look, so hastily that their slippers flew about their ears. They had never seen such a meteor before. Now they were quite sure that it was the prophet who was to marry their Princess.

As soon as the merchant's son had returned to the wood, he said to himself, 'I will now go into the city and hear what people say about me, and what sort of figure I made in the air.'

Oh, what strange accounts were given! Everyone he accosted had seen the bright vision in a different way, but all agreed that it was marvellously beautiful.

'I saw the great prophet with my own eyes,' declared one. 'He had eyes like sparkling stars, and a beard like foaming water.'

'He flew wrapped in a mantle of fire,' said another, 'and the prettiest little cherubs were peeping out from its folds.'

Then he went back to the wood, intending to get into his trunk again, but, alas! the trunk was burnt. One spark from the fireworks had been left in it, and set it on fire. The trunk lay in ashes and the poor merchant's son could never fly again—could never visit his bride again.

She sat the whole day on the roof of her palace waiting for him. She is waiting still. Meanwhile he goes about the world telling stories, but none of his stories now is so pleasant as the one which he told in the Princess's palace about the Brimstone Matches.

Great Claus and Little Claus

Once upon a time two men bearing the very same name lived in the same village. One of them had four horses and the other had only one horse, so to distinguish them the proprietor of four horses was called 'Great Claus,' and he who owned only one horse was known as 'Little Claus'.

All week long Little Claus ploughed for Great Claus with his one horse, and in return Great Claus lent him his four horses on Sunday. Little Claus was a proud man that day and he brandished his whip over his five horses for he thought all five were his for this one day at least. The people were dressed in their best and walking to church, and as they passed they looked at Little Claus driving his five horses and he was so pleased that he kept cracking his whip and crying out, 'Hip, hip, hurrah! five fine horses, and all of them mine!'

'You mustn't say that,' said Great Claus. 'Only one of the horses is yours; you know that well enough.'

But when another party of church-goers passed close by him, Little Claus quite forgot what he had been told and cried out again, 'Hip, hip, hurrah! five fine horses, all mine!'

'Didn't I tell you to hold your tongue?' exclaimed Great Claus, very angrily. 'If you say that again, I'll give your one horse such a blow on the forehead, it will strike him dead on the spot and then that'll be an end to your boasting about your five fine horses.'

'Oh, but I'll never say it again, indeed I won't!' said Little Claus, and he really did mean to keep his word. But presently some more people came by and, when they nodded a friendly 'Good morning' to him he was so delighted and it seemed to him such a grand thing to have five horses to plough his bit of a field that he could not contain himself. He flourished his whip aloft, and shouted out, 'Hip, hip, hurrah! five fine horses; every one of them mine!'

'I'll soon cure you of that!' cried Great Claus in a fury and taking up a large stone, he flung it at Little Claus's horse. The stone was so heavy that the poor creature fell down dead.

'Alas, now I have no horses at all!' cried Little Claus and he began to cry. As soon as he had recovered himself a little, he set to work to flay the skin off his dead horse, dried the skin thoroughly in the air and then putting it into a sack, he slung the sack across his shoulders, and set out for the nearest town to sell the skin. He had a long way to go and the road led him through a large and thickly grown wood. Here a violent storm came on and the clouds, the rain and the dark trees, whipped to and fro by the wind, so bewildered poor Claus that he lost his path and before he could find it again evening had darkened into night. Not far off stood a large farm-house. The window-shutters were closed, but Little Claus could see lights shining out through the cracks. So he went up to the house and knocked at the door. The farmer's wife came and opened it to him but, when she heard what he wanted, she told him very politely he must go and ask elsewhere. He couldn't come into her house as her husband was away from home and she didn't like receiving strangers in his absence.

'Well, then, I must sleep outside, under this stormy sky,' replied Little Claus, and the farmer's wife shut the door in his face.

Close by stood a hay-stack, and between it and the house there was a little penthouse with a flat straw roof.

'I'll get up there,' said Little Claus to himself when he saw it.

'It will make me a capital bed—only I hope the stork over there doesn't take it into his head to fly down and bite my legs.' For a stork had made his nest on the roof and had mounted guard beside the nest and was as wide-awake as could be, although it was night.

So Little Claus crept up on the penthouse and there he turned and twisted till he had made himself a really comfortable bed. The window-shutters did not close properly at the top, so that from his high and airy position he could see all that went on in the room. He saw a large table spread with bread and wine, roast meat and fried fish. The farmer's wife and the clerk sat at table; no one else was there. The farmer's wife was pouring out a glass of wine for the clerk, who, meantime, was eagerly helping himself to a large slice of fish—he happened to be particularly fond of fish. 'Too bad, really, to keep it all to themselves!' sighed Little Claus. 'If they would only give me a bit!' and he wriggled as close to the window as he could. Oh, what a magnificent cake he could see then! Why, this was quite a banquet!

Presently he heard the sound of hoof-tramps approaching from the road. It was the farmer riding home.

This farmer was a good-hearted fellow but he had one peculiar weakness, namely, that he could never endure the sight of a clerk, it made him half mad. Now, the clerk of the neighbouring town happened to be first cousin to his wife, and they were old playmates and good friends. So that evening, knowing that the farmer would be away from home, he came to pay his cousin a visit and the good woman, being very pleased to see him, had brought out all the choice things in her larder to feast him with. But now, when they heard the tramp of the farmer's horse, they both started up and the woman told the clerk to creep into a large empty chest that stood in a corner of the room. He did so, for he knew that the poor farmer would be driven wild if he came in and saw a clerk standing unexpectedly before him. The farmer's wife then bustled about and hid all the wine, and the dishes inside her baking-oven, for she feared that her husband would ask who she had been preparing for if he saw them.

'Oh dear, oh dear!' sighed Little Claus from his bed on the penthouse when he saw the feast all put away.

'Anybody up there?' said the farmer hearing the voice, and he looked up and saw Little Claus. 'Why are you lying up there? Come down into the house with me.'

And Little Claus explained that he had lost his way and asked the farmer if he would give him shelter for the night.

'To be sure, I will,' replied the good-natured man. 'Come in quickly, and let's have something to eat.'

The woman received them both with a great show of welcome, set one end of the long table and brought out a large dish of oatmeal. The farmer set to with a good appetite but Little Claus could not eat for thinking of the good roast meat, the fish, the wine, and the delicious cake which he had seen stowed away inside the oven. He put his sack containing the horse's skin under the table, and as he did not relish the oatmeal porridge, he began trampling the sack under his feet till the dry skin creaked aloud.

'Hush!' muttered Little Claus, as if he were speaking to his sack, but at the same moment he trod upon it again and made it creak louder than before.

'What have you got in your sack?' asked the farmer.

'Oh, I've got a little magician there,' replied Little Claus, 'and he says we shouldn't be eating oatmeal porridge any more, for he has conjured up a feast of beef-steak, fried fish, and cake and put it into the oven specially for us.'

'A magician, did you say?' exclaimed the farmer, and up he got in a great hurry to look into the oven and see whether the conjurer had spoken the truth. And there were fish, and steak, and cake; the conjurer had been as good as his word. The farmer's wife didn't dare utter a syllable of explanation. Almost as much bewildered as her husband, she set the food on the table and the farmer and his guest began to eat the good food before them.

Presently Little Claus trampled on his sack again, and again made the skin creak.

'Well, what does your magician say now?' asked the farmer.

'He says,' replied Little Claus, 'that he has also conjured up three bottles of wine for us. You will find them standing just in the corner of the oven.' So the woman had to bring out the wine that she had hidden, and the farmer poured himself out a glass and began to think it would be a fine thing to have such a useful magician as this.

'This is a real proper magician of yours!' he observed at last. 'I should rather like to see him. Do you think he would let me?'

'Oh, of course,' returned Little Claus; 'he will do anything I ask him. You will, won't you?' he asked, treading on his sack again. 'Didn't you hear him say "Yes"? But I warn you he will look somewhat dark and unpleasing; perhaps it is scarcely worth while seeing him after all.'

'Oh, I shall not be afraid. What will he look like?'

'Why, he will look for all the world like a clerk.'

'A clerk!' repeated the farmer. 'That's a pity! You should know that I cannot endure the sight of a clerk: but never mind. Since I shall know that this is not a real clerk but only your magician, I shan't care about it. Oh, I've plenty of courage—only don't let him come too near me!'

'Well, I'll ask about it again,' said Little Claus, and he trod on his skin till it went 'creak, creak, creak,' and bent his ear down as though he were listening.

'What does he say now?'

'He says he will transport himself into the chest over in that corner. You have only to lift up the lid and you will see him, but you must be careful to shut the lid down again.'

'Will you help me to hold up the lid? It's very heavy,' said the farmer, and he went up to the chest where his wife had hidden the real clerk who lay curled up and trembling lest he should be discovered. The farmer raised the lid of the chest gently, and

peeped under it. 'Ugh!' he cried, and immediately started back in alarm. 'Oh dear, oh dear! I saw him; he looked exactly like our clerk in the town—oh, how horrible!'

However, he sat down at table again and began to drink glass after glass of wine, by way of recovering from the shock. The wine soon revived his fallen courage. Neither he nor his guest ever thought of going to bed; they sat, talking and feasting, till late in the night.

'Did you ever see your magician before?' inquired the farmer of Claus.

'Not I,' replied Little Claus, 'I should never have thought of asking him to appear if you hadn't thought of it. He knows he's not handsome so he doesn't want to make himself noticeable in company. He talks to me, and I to him; isn't that enough?'

'Oh, indeed it is!' said the farmer quickly. Then after a minute's hesitation he went on, 'Do you know, I should like to own your magician very much. Would you mind selling him to me? Name your own price; I don't care if I give you a whole bushelful of silver on the spot.'

'Oh, how can you ask such a thing?' exclaimed Little Claus. 'Such a useful, such a faithful servant as he is, how could I think of parting with him? Why, he's worth his weight in gold ten times over.'

'I can't offer you gold,' replied the farmer, 'but I should like very much to have him; that is, provided he never shows his ugly self again.'

'Oh, there's no danger of that,' said Little Claus; 'and really, since you have been kind enough to give me shelter tonight, I don't think I can refuse your request. I will let you have my magician for a bushel of silver—only the bushel must be cram-full, you know.'

'Certainly, it shall,' answered the farmer, 'and the chest, too, you shall have that into the bargain. I don't want it to remain in the house an hour longer, it will always be reminding me of the odious clerk's face I saw inside it.'

So the bargain was struck. Little Claus gave the farmer his sack with the dry skin in it and got a whole bushelful of silver instead. The farmer also gave him a large wheel-barrow to take his money and his chest home in.

'Good-bye!' cried Little Claus, and drove the wheel-barrow away with the unfortunate clerk still lying hidden in the chest.

On the opposite side of the wood flowed a broad, deep river. The current was so strong that no one could swim against it and recently a bridge had been built over it. Little Claus made his way over the bridge but he stopped short in the middle of it, saying very loudly, so that the man in the chest could hear him, 'Now, what use is this great wrackety chest to me? It's as heavy as if it were filled with stones and I'm quite worn out. I'll tip it into the river and if it chooses to float home to me, well and good. If not, I'll do without it quite happily. It's all the same to me.'

And he lifted the chest as though he were going to throw it into the water.

'Oh, please don't do that,' cried the clerk in the chest; 'Please, please, let me out first.'

'Oh, ho!' exclaimed Little Claus; 'the chest is bewitched! The sooner I get rid of it, the better.'

'Oh, no, no, no,' cried the clerk; 'let me out, and I'll give you another whole bushelful of money.'

'Ah, that's quite another matter,' said Little Claus, and he set down the chest immediately and opened the lid. Out crept the clerk with great relief. He kicked the empty chest into the water and then took Little Claus home with him, where he gave him the bushelful of money as they had agreed on. Little Claus now had a whole wheel-barrow full of money.

'I must say I've been well paid for my horse's skin,' said he to himself, as he entered his own little room and overturned all his money in a great heap on the floor. 'It will anger Great Claus, I'm afraid, when he finds out how rich my horse's skin has made me.'

And he sent a little boy to Great Claus to borrow a measure from him.

'What can he want with a measure, I wonder?' thought Great Claus, and he cunningly smeared the bottom of the measure with clay, hoping that some part of whatever was measured might stick to it. And it was returned to him, he found three silver coins sticking at the bottom. 'Fine goings on, I must say,' exclaimed Great Claus, in amazement; and off he set to his namesake's house. 'Where did you get all that money?' he thundered.

'Oh, I got it for my horse's skin which I sold yesterday,' was the reply.

'Really?' exclaimed Great Claus. 'What, are horses' skins so dear as that? Who would have thought it?' And he ran home quickly, took an axe, and struck all his four horses on the head with it, then flayed off the skins, and drove into the town. 'Skins, skins, who will buy skins?' he cried, as he passed through the streets.

All the shoemakers and tanners in the town came running up to him and asked the price.

'A bushelful of money for each,' replied Great Claus.

'Are you mad?' they cried. 'Do you think we reckon our money by bushels?'

'Skins, fresh skins, who will buy skins?' he shouted again; and he still said he wanted a bushelful of money for each of them.

'The rude boor! he is trying to make fools of us,' declared one of his customers at last in very great wrath.

'Skins, fresh skins, fine fresh skins,' they all cried, mimicking him. 'Out of the town with him, the great ass, or he shall have no skin left on his own shoulders.' And Great Claus was ignominiously thrust out of the town.

'Little Claus shall pay for this,' he muttered. 'Sleep soundly tonight, Little Claus, for you shall not wake again.'

It so happened that Little Claus's grandmother died that same evening. She had always been very cross and ill-natured with him in her lifetime, but now, finding her dead, he felt really sorry for her. He laid the dead woman in his own warm bed in hopes that

the warmth might bring her to life
again and spent the night in a
chair in a corner of the room
as he had often done before.

About midnight the door opened and Great Claus, his axe in his hand, strode in. He knew where Little Claus's bed was, so he went straight up to it and struck the dead grandmother a violent blow on the forehead.

'There's for you!' he cried. 'Now you'll never make a fool of me again.' And with that he went out of the room and returned home.

'What a very wicked man he is,' sighed Little Claus. 'So he wanted to kill me! It was a good thing that old grandmother was dead already or that blow would have hurt her very badly.'

The next evening he met Great Claus in a lane near the village. Great Claus started back and stared at him. 'What, aren't you dead? I thought I killed you last night.'

'Yes, you wicked man,' replied Little Claus; 'I know you came into my room intending to kill me but my grandmother, not I, was lying in bed. It was she that you struck with your pick-axe, and you deserve to be hanged for it.'

'Are you going to tell everybody about it?' said Great Claus. 'You shall never do that!' He was carrying a very large sack and, seizing Little Claus by the waist, he thrust him into it, crying out, 'I will drown you at once, and that will be the end of your tale-telling.'

But he had a long way to walk before he reached the river, and Little Claus was no light burden. The road led past the church and the organ was playing, for the service had just begun. Among the congregation Great Claus saw a man he wanted to speak to. 'Little Claus cannot get out of the sack by himself,' he thought, 'and no one can help him, for everybody is in church. I shall just go in and call that man back into the porch for a minute.' So he set down the heavy sack and ran into church.

'Oh dear, oh dear!' sighed Little Claus inside the sack. He turned and twisted in vain but he couldn't get the string loose. Just then a very, very old cattle-driver passed by, his hair white as snow, and with a stout staff in his hand. He was driving a large herd of cows and bullocks before him and he had many more than he could manage. One of them charged past the sack, and turned it over and over. 'Oh, help me, please!' cried Little Claus, 'I am so young to die! Help me out of the sack.'

'What, is there a man in the sack?' The ancient cattle-driver bent down, though with some difficulty, and untied the string. 'The bullock has not hurt you, I hope?' But Little Claus sprang out briskly, showing he was not hurt, and immediately began to uproot the withered stump of a tree which stood by the roadside. This he rolled into the sack and tied the string, leaving the sack exactly as Great Claus had left it. Meantime the cattle had passed on.

'Will you drive these cattle home to the village for me?' asked the old man. 'I am so weary, and I want to go into the church so much.'

'I will help you gladly since you have helped me,' replied Little Claus, and he took the cattle-driver's goad from his hand and took his place behind the herd.

Presently Great Claus came running back. He took up the sack and flung it across his shoulders again, thinking, 'How much lighter the burden seems now; it always does one good to rest, even for a short time.' So he trudged on to the river, flung the sack out into the water, and shouted after it, 'There now, Little Claus, you shall never cheat me any more!' He then turned homewards, but when he came to the next crossroads whom should he meet but Little Claus with his cattle.

'How did this happen?' exclaimed Great Claus. 'Is it really you? Didn't I drown you then, after all?'

'I believe you meant to drown me,' said Little Claus. 'You threw me into the river just about half an hour ago, didn't you?'

'But how did you come by all these beautiful cattle?' asked Great Claus in utter amazement, his eyes wandering admiringly over the herd.

'These are sea-cattle,' said Little Claus. 'Ah, I'll tell you the whole story. I am really much obliged to you for drowning me —it has made me richer than ever, as you can see. I was very frightened when I lay in the sack, and the wind whistled very uncomfortably in my ears when you threw me down from the bridge into the cold water. I sank to the bottom at once, but I wasn't hurt for I was landed on the softest, freshest grass. Immediately the sack was opened and the most beautiful young girl you can imagine took me by the hand, saying, 'Are you Little Claus? Here are some cattle of yours, and a mile farther up the road another and larger herd is grazing; I will give you it too." And then I understood that the river was a sort of high-road for the people of the sea, and that they used it to drive their cattle from the sea far up into the land where the river rises, and thence back to the sea again. No place could be as beautiful as it is at the bottom of the river: and what gaily-dressed people I saw there and such multitudes of cattles grazing in enclosed fields!'

'Then why were you in such a hurry to come up again?' inquired Great Claus.

'Didn't I tell you?' said Little Claus. 'The sea-lady told me that a mile up the road—and by the road she could only mean the river, she can't travel on our land roads—there was another and larger herd of cattle for me? But I knew that the river makes a great many turns, and I thought I'd just spare myself half a mile by taking the short cut across the land. So here I am, you see, and I shall soon get to my sea-cattle.'

'Oh, what a lucky man you are!' exclaimed Great Claus. 'Don't you think that I might have some cattle given to me too, if I went down to the bottom of the river?'

'How can I tell?' asked Little Claus.

'You scoundrel! I believe you want to keep all the beautiful sea-cattle for yourself, I warrant!' cried Great Claus. 'Either you will carry me to the water's edge, and throw me over, or I will take out my great knife and kill you. Make your choice.'

'Oh, no, please don't be so angry!' entreated Little Claus. 'I can't carry you to the river; you're too heavy for me. But if you walk there yourself and then creep into the sack, I will throw you over with all the pleasure in the world.'

'But if I find no sea-cattle, I shall kill you all the same when I come back, remember that!' said Great Claus. And to this arrangement Little Claus made no objection.

They walked together to the river. As soon as the thirsty cattle saw the water, they ran on as fast as they could, crowding eagerly against each other and all wanting to drink at once.

'Only look at my sea-cattle!' said Little Claus. 'See how they are longing to be at the bottom of the river.'

'That's all very well,' said Great Claus, 'but you must help me first.' And he crept quickly into the great sack which had lain across the shoulders of one of the oxen. 'Put a heavy stone in with me,' said he, 'otherwise I may not sink to the bottom properly.'

'No fear of that!' replied Little Claus. However, he put a large stone into the sack, tied the strings, and pushed the sack into the water. Plump! it fell straight to the bottom.

'I'm afraid he won't find his sea-cattle,' said Little Claus, and he drove his own herd home to the village.

The Top and the Ball

A top and a ball were lying close together in a drawer among the other playthings.

The top said to the ball:

'Why shouldn't we marry since we are thrown together so much?'

But the ball, who was made of morocco leather and thought herself a very fashionable young lady, wouldn't hear of such a proposal.

The next day, the little boy to whom the playthings belonged came to the drawer. He painted the top red and yellow and drove a brass nail through his middle and after that he looked very splendid spinning.

'Look at me now!' said he to the ball; 'what do you say to me now? Why shouldn't we become man and wife? We suit each other so well. You can jump and I can spin. It wouldn't be easier to find a couple happier than we should be.'

'Do you think so?' said the ball. 'Perhaps you don't know that my father and mother were morocco slippers, and that I have a cork in my body.'

'Yes, but I'm made of mahogany,' said the top. 'The Mayor made me with his own hands, for he has a lathe of his own and took great pleasure in turning me.'

'Are you being truthful about this?' said the ball.

'Certainly. May I never be whipped again if I lie,' said the top.

'You sound all right,' said the ball; 'but I'm not free. I'm as good as engaged to a young swallow. Whenever I fly up in the air, he puts his head out of his nest and says: "Will you marry me?" I have said "Yes" to him in my heart, and that is almost the same as being engaged. But one thing I promise you: I will never forget you.'

'That's a fat lot of good!' said the top, and no more was said on the subject.

Next day the ball was taken out. The top saw her fly like a bird into the air, so high that she could be seen no longer. She came back again but every time she touched the ground she sprang higher than before. Either love or the cork she had in her body, must have been the cause of this.

The ninth time she did not return and though the boy looked and looked for her, he could not find her; she was gone.

'I know where she is,' sighed the top; 'she's in the swallow's nest celebrating her wedding.' The more the top thought of it, the more beautiful the ball seemed to him, and his love became the more vehement when he realized the ball could never be his. She had preferred someone else; he could not forget that! And the top spun and hummed, but was always thinking of the dear ball, who in his imagination grew more and more lovable. Thus several years passed. He *was* a constant lover!

But the top was no longer young. One day, however, he was gilded all over, so he had never looked so handsome before. He was now a gilt top, and spun most bravely, humming all the time. All at once he sprang too high, and disappeared! They looked everywhere, even in the cellar; but he was nowhere to be found.

Where was he?

He had jumped into a barrel full of all sorts of rubbish—cabbage-stalks, sweepings, dust and so on which had fallen in from the gutter.

'Alas! here I lie; my gilding will soon be spoiled; and what sort of trumpery have I fallen in with?' And he peeped at a long cabbage-stalk which lay fearfully near him, and at a strange, round thing somewhat like an apple. But it was not an apple. It was an old ball, which had lain several years in the gutter and was quite sodden with water.

'Thank goodness! At last I see an equal I may speak to,' said the ball, looking at the gilt top. 'I am made of real morocco, sewed together by a young lady's hands, and I have cork in my body, but I shall never again be noticed by anyone. I was going to marry a swallow when I fell into the gutter. There I lay for five years and at last I was washed down into this place. I am wet through! Only think what a weary time it is for a young lady to be in such a situation!'

But the top didn't answer. He thought of his long-lamented companion and the more he heard, the more certain he became that it was she.

Just then the servant-maid came along and was going to turn the barrel over. 'Oh good!' she exclaimed, 'there is the gilt top.'

And the top was brought back to the playroom and was used and admired as before. But nothing more was heard of the ball, nor did the top ever even speak of his former love for her, for such a feeling must have passed away. How could it be otherwise when he found that she had lain five years in the gutter, she was so much altered that he scarcely knew her again when he met her in the barrel among rubbish?

The Darning-Needle

There was once a darning-needle who was so fine that she imagined herself to be a sewing-needle.

'Now be careful; hold on to me tightly,' she said to the fingers that picked her up. 'Don't drop me, please! If I fall down you will never be able to find me again, I'm so fine!'

'That's what you think,' said the fingers.

'I'm coming with my train,' said the darning-needle, drawing a long thread without a single knot in it after her.

The fingers guided the needle to the kitchen maid's slippers; the upper leather was torn and had to be sewn together.

'This is menial work!' said the darning-needle; 'I shall never get through. 'I'll break—I'll break'—and break she did. 'Didn't I say so?' she continued; 'I am too delicate.'

The kitchen maid dropped some sealing-wax on the broken darning-needle, and then stuck it into her scarf.

'Look, I'm a brooch now!' said the darning-needle. 'I knew I should be honoured. When one *is* somebody, one always becomes somebody.'

And she laughed at this. There she sat, as proud as if she were driving in her carriage and bowing on every side.

'May I inquire if you are made of gold?' she asked the pin that was her neighbour. 'You have a pleasant appearance and a very distinguished head. It is very small, though; you must take care that it grows, for it is certainly not everyone that has sealing-wax dropped upon her, no indeed!'

And the darning-needle drew herself up so proudly that she fell into the sink where the cook was busy washing-up.

'Now I shall travel!' said the darning-needle; 'but I hope I shan't go very far.' However she did travel a long way, a very long way.

'I am too dainty for this world,' she said as at last she sat still in the gutter. 'However, I know who I am, and that is always a consolation.'

So she held herself upright and did not lose her good temper. All sorts of things sailed past her.

'Look how they sail along!' said the darning-needle. 'They don't know I'm beneath them. There goes a splinter—he thinks of nothing in the world but himself, splinter as he is! There's a straw —see how it turns round and round! No, don't be so conceited, you may easily float on to one of the stones. There's a newspaper —everybody's forgotten what was written in it, yet how it spreads itself out! *I* sit patiently and quietly. I know who I am and I shall always stay as I am!'

One day something happened to pass close by her which glittered so prettily that she felt sure it must really be a diamond although it was really only a piece of glass. The darning-needle addressed it, introducing herself as a brooch. 'Surely you're a diamond, aren't you?'

'Why, yes, something of the sort,' was the reply. So each believed the other to be a rare and costly ornament, and they both began to complain of the extraordinary snobbishness of the world.

'Yes, I lived in a box belonging to a young lady,' said the darning-needle, 'and this young lady was a kitchen-maid. She had five fingers on each hand, and anything so conceited as those five fingers I have never known; and, after all, what were they good for? For nothing, but to hold me, to take me out of the box, and put me back in the box!'

'And were they at all bright—did they glitter?' asked the piece of glass.

'Glitter!' repeated the darning-needle; 'not they! But they were proud all the same. The first (he was called the Thumb) was short and thick; he generally stood out of line in front of the others. He used to say that if he were cut off from a man, that man would no longer be fit for military service. Foreman, the second, used to push himself forward all the time and meddle with everything. Longman was so tall that he could look over the others' heads; Ringman wore a gold belt round his body; and as for Littleman, he did nothing at all—and was proud of that, I suppose. Indeed, they were so proud that I took myself off into the gutter!'

'And now we sit and glitter together instead!' said the piece of glass.

Just then some more water was poured into the gutter; it overflowed its boundaries and carried the piece of glass along with it.

'So he has gone on farther,' observed the darning-needle. 'I stay here, I am too fine; but I am proud to be so, it is honourable. I can almost believe I was born of a sunbeam, I am so delicate; and yet the sunbeams don't seem to look for me under the water. Alas! I am so fine that even my mother cannot find me. If I still had my eye, which was broken, I believe I should weep. Oh no I wouldn't, though; it is not well-bred to weep.'

One day some boys were raking about in the gutter, hunting for old nails, pennies and such like. It was a very dirty pastime, but they enjoyed it. 'Hullo!' cried one, pricking himself with the darning-needle; 'here's something else!'

'I'm not a thing, I'm a young lady,' protested the darning-needle, but nobody listened to her. The sealing-wax had worn off, and she was quite black. Black, however, makes a person look thin so she thought she was finer than ever.

'There goes an egg-shell,' said the boys; and they stuck the darning-needle into the shell.

'White walls and a lady in black,' said the darning-needle; 'that is very fetching. Now everyone can see me. But I hope I shan't be sea-sick, for then I will break.' Her fears were needless; she was not sea-sick neither did she break. 'Nothing is so good for preventing sea-sickness as remembering one has a stomach of steel and that one is just a little better than a human. The finer one is, the more one can endure.'

Crash! went the egg-shell. A wagon rolled over it. 'Ugh, what a pressure!' sighed the darning-needle; 'I shall be sea-sick after all. I shall break, I shall break!' But she didn't break, although the wheel had gone over her. She lay there for a long time, and she may die there.

The Fellow Travellers

Poor Hans was very unhappy for his father was very ill and could not get well again. There was no one but he to tend the sick man in his little low-roofed room. The lamp on the table burned with a faint, dying light, and it was already quite late in the evening.

'You have always been a good and dutiful son to me, Hans,' said the sick man; 'don't be afraid; our Lord will be with you and help you through the world.'

As he spoke, he looked fondly at the boy with his grave, loving eyes and then, with a deep sigh, he died, as calmly as though he had only fallen asleep. But Hans wept bitterly, for now he had no friend or relative in all the wide world—neither father nor mother, neither sister nor brother. Poor Hans! He knelt down beside the bed, kissed his dead father's hand and wept bitter tears till, at last, his eyes closed through utter weariness, and he fell asleep, his head resting against the hard corner of the bedstead.

He dreamed a strange dream. He saw sun and moon bowing before him, and he saw his father fresh and healthy again and heard him laugh as he used to laugh when he was well and happy. A beautiful girl, with a golden crown on her long dark hair, held out her hand to Hans with a smile and his father said, 'See what a lovely bride you have won!' She is the loveliest maiden in the world.' Then he awoke to find all the glory and beauty of his dream was gone, his father lay cold and dead in the bed and there was no one with him. Poor Hans!

The funeral took place the next week. Hans followed close behind the coffin; he watched it until only one corner was left uncovered; then one more shovelful of earth and that, too, was hidden and he felt as though his heart would burst with sorrow. The congregation round him were singing a psalm; words and music melted into each other so sweetly that they brought the tears into his eyes—he wept, and weeping eased the violence of his grief.

His first thought was to carve a large wooden cross for his father's grave. He finished it that same evening and found that the grave was already strewn with sand and flowers. Stranger hands had done this, for everybody had loved the good man who was dead.

Early next morning Hans packed up his little travelling bundle and carefully tucked his whole fortune into his belt. It consisted of fifty-six dollars and a few silver pennies, with which he intended to start on his wanderings through the wide world. First, however, he went to the churchyard and repeated the Lord's Prayer over his father's grave and then said, 'Farewell, dear father. I will be good so that you may still ask the Almighty to be my guide and shield.'

By the side of the footpath where Hans was walking there grew many wild flowers. They looked so fresh and bright in the warm sunshine and whenever the wind passed that way, they nodded to Hans, as if to say, 'Welcome to the green meadowlands! Isn't it pleasant here?' Then he began to think of the great number of beautiful things that he would see in the world and he walked faster and faster, farther and farther, by roads that he had never been along before. He didn't know the villages he passed through, nor the people he met—he was in quite a strange land and surrounded by strangers.

The first night he was forced to sleep in a haystack under the open sky for he had no other bed. He was perfectly satisfied and thought that even the King could not be better lodged than he was. The wide meadow with the blue heavens spread above formed a beautiful state bedchamber. The green turf, with its tiny red and white flowers was his carpet; the elder bushes and wild roses were better than vases of flowers, and the brook, with the reeds growing on its banks and nodding to him a friendly 'good morning' and 'good evening' provided him with water. Finally the moon was like a large night lamp, hung high amid the blue canopy of heaven yet without any danger of setting fire to the curtains, so he could sleep in perfect safety. Sleep he did, and so soundly he did not wake till the sun had risen and all the little birds around him sang loudly. 'Good morning, good morning, why aren't you up?'

He wandered on, and when he reached the next village he heard the church bells ringing. It was Sunday and all the people were going to church. And Hans went with them, sang hymns and listened reverently to the Word of God, and felt as though he were once again in his own parish church where he had been baptized and had, Sunday after Sunday, knelt by his father's side.

In the churchyard outside there were many graves, and on some of them high grass was growing. 'Perhaps my father's grave will soon look like these,' thought Hans. 'Now I'm away there is no one to pluck out the grass and plant flowers on it.' So he began to busy himself with clearing the graves here and there from weeds. He stood up the wooden crosses that had fallen down and put back the wreaths which had been blown away. 'Someone may do the same for my father's grave, since I cannot do it,' he thought. At the churchyard gate stood an old beggar-man, leaning on his crutch. Hans gave him his few silver pennies and then went on his way, cheerful and contented.

Towards evening a violent storm got up. Hans made great haste to get under shelter, but the dark night had gathered round him before he had caught sight of a building where he could take refuge. At last he found he was close to a little church, which stood alone on the summit of a hill. The door was ajar and he crept in, determined to stay till the storm was over.

'I will sit down in this corner,' he said, 'I am tired out, and it will do me good to rest a while.' And after saying his evening prayer, he leaned his head back against the wall and quickly fell into a sound sleep while the thunder and lightning continued outside.

When he awoke it was midnight, the storm had passed by, and the moonlight shone in through the high church windows on to an open coffin in the middle of the church. A dead man lay in the coffin which had been taken into the church and left there till the grave was dug for it next morning, because he was a stranger with no house of his own and no relatives to take charge of him. Hans was not frightened, for he had a clear conscience and knew that the dead can do no harm to anyone—it is only the living, the wicked, who do evil. And there were two wicked living men standing by the coffin. They were come to take the poor corpse out of the coffin and throw it out at the church door.

'Why do you want to do that?' asked Hans, when he discovered this. 'It is very wicked of you. In God's name, let the dead rest in peace.'

'Rest, indeed!' cried one of the men; 'he has made fools of us both by borrowing money from us which he could not repay. But we'll have our revenge, we will, and he shall lie like a dog

outside the church door!'

'I have only fifty dollars,' said Hans, 'it is the whole of my fortune, but I will gladly give them to you, if you will promise me, on your honour, to leave this poor dead man in peace. I'll manage without the money, no doubt; I'm strong and healthy, and our Lord will help me.'

'Of course,' replied the two wicked men, 'if you pay his debts, we shall do him no harm, you can depend on that!' And so they took the money that Hans offered them, laughed loudly and scornfully at his simplicity, and went their way. Hans then laid the corpse back in the coffin, folded the cold, stiff hands, and bade the dead man farewell.

He left the church and walked with a light heart through the wood. Here and there the moonbeams pierced through the surrounding trees and wherever their clear light fell he saw tiny elves playing merrily, and not in the least startled by his approach. They knew that he must be good and innocent, since none but those who are free from evil thoughts had power to see them. Some of them were no bigger than one of his fingers, and had their long flaxen hair fastened with golden combs. They see-sawed upon the heavy drops of dew that spangled the leaves and grass; every now and then a dewdrop trickled down, and a pair of them were flung down into the long grass, to the amazement of the rest. They sang, too, and Hans recognized all their songs which he had heard often when he was a little boy. Great brown spiders, with silver crowns on their heads, were spinning long suspension bridges and palaces from one tree to another for them, and the dew fell upon these delicate structures so they glistened like glass in the clear moonlight. Thus their play went on till sunrise when the elves crept into the flowers to sleep, and the winds took hold of their airy castles and bridges and bore them away.

Hans had just stepped out from the wood, when a deep manly voice shouted from behind him, 'Hallo, comrade, where are you going?'

'Out into the wide world,' said Hans, 'I have neither father nor mother. I am a poor friendless lad, but I trust the angels will look after me.'

'I, too, am going into the world,' rejoined the stranger. 'Suppose we join up?'

'Why not?' answered Hans, so they went on together, talking, and became good friends. Hans quickly discovered that his stranger comrade was much cleverer and more experienced than he was. He seemed to have travelled in every country on earth and to have learnt about everything.

It was almost noon and the sun was high above them when they sat down under a wide spreading tree to eat their breakfast. While they were eating, it happened that a crooked old woman came

hobbling by on her crutch. She carried a bundle of faggots over her shoulder and three bundles of ferns and willow-boughs projected from a corner of her apron. Just as she was passing them her foot slipped, she fell and gave a shrill cry of pain, for she had broken her leg, poor old woman! Hans instantly sprang up to help her and suggested that they should carry her home, but his companion calmly unpacked his knapsack, took out a little box and said that there he had a healing ointment which would heal her leg at once. But if he did this for her he wanted her to do something for him, namely, give him the three bundles of ferns and willow-boughs which she carried in her apron.

'So you insist on being well paid, do you, doctor?' said the old crone, with a strange, uncomfortable smile. She didn't like to part with her willow-twigs, she said, for she had gone to a lot of trouble to get them; still it was not very pleasant either to lie on the road with her leg broken and she gave up the contents of her apron to the stranger. In return he bent over her and anointed her leg with his precious ointment, and at once the old woman rose up and hobbled onward with considerably less difficulty than before she had fallen down. It was a marvellous ointment! But one couldn't get it at a chemists.

'What can you want with that dry wood?' Hans asked his companion.

'A whim of mine,' was the reply. 'In my eyes they are prettier and more fragrant than branches of roses. None of us can account for our whims, you know.'

'I think we shall have another storm again soon,' said Hans, after a pause, pointing to some dark, threatening forms that rose into the sky over the horizon. 'What terribly black, thick clouds.'

'What a mistake,' said his companion; 'they are not clouds at all, they are mountains! You can't imagine how fresh and keen is the air on their summit above the level of the clouds; and there's such a good view! We are getting on famously!'

But though these mountains seemed so near, the wanderers walked on the whole day without getting close to them. Black fir woods clothed the mountain-sides, and stones as large as towns lay scattered about. It would cost them a lot of hard work, the stranger said, to cross the mountains. So he and Hans agreed to turn into an inn and rest, so that they might start fresh and strong the next day.

They found the guest-room in the inn crowded with people,

for a man with a puppet-show had just arrived and made ready his little theatre, and the people had been gathering together to see it. So they sat round on chairs, but the best place of all in the front row had been taken by a stout old butcher and his mastiff—a grim-looking animal—who sat by his side, and stared with all his might, just like any other spectator.

Then the show began. A King and Queen appeared sitting on magnificent thrones, and wearing gold crowns on their heads and with long trains to their robes. The neatest little wooden dolls with glass eyes and thick moustaches were stationed at the doors and windows, which they kept opening and shutting so that their Majesties might have a current of cool air. It was a very pretty show and everything was going on smoothly and pleasantly, no tears, no bloodshed, nothing sad and tragic—it was a perfect comedy—when unfortunately, just as the Queen rose up from her throne and walked across the floor, the great mastiff—whom the stout butcher had quite forgotten to keep hold of—sprang up, and, clearing the stage with one bound, seized the pretty Queen by her slender waist so roughly that she was nearly broken in two. The poor showman was so much grieved by this misfortune that he was very nearly in tears. The Queen was his very best doll and the mastiff had bitten her head off before he could be forced to give her up. However, when the spectators had gone home, Hans' fellow-traveller went up to the poor man and comforted him, assuring him he would find a remedy. Taking out his knapsack, he produced the little jar which he had used to heal the old woman's leg and rubbed some of the ointment over the wounded doll. Not only was it perfectly healed at once but it received the power of moving by itself, without there being any need of pulling the wires. Indeed it was like a living human being except that it could not speak. The showman was delighted to see his Queen-doll dance and walk by herself, for none of his other dolls could do so.

Late that night, when all the people in the inn were in bed, there was a great groaning and sighing and it went on so long that at last everybody got up to see what was the matter. The puppet showman rushed to his little theatre in a hurry, for it sounded to him as though the noise was coming from it. And a strange sight met his eyes. The King and the soldiers were lying heaped one upon the other, groaning perpetually and trying to make their glassy eyes show their great longing, for they were all wanting some of the ointment so that they, too, might be able to move by themselves. Meantime, the Queen knelt on

one knee and lifted her pretty gold crown on high as though she were saying, 'Take my crown, if you like, only anoint my consort and my courtiers!' and the showman was so much affected by this scene that he immediately offered to give the stranger all the money he took at the play the following evening if he would anoint four or five of his best dolls with his wonder-working ointment. But the stranger said he did not want any money; he only wanted the large sabre which the showman wore by his side. When it had been given him, he readily anointed six of the dolls, which instantly danced so prettily and gracefully that all the young girls in the inn who were present felt an irresistible urge to begin dancing too. And dance they did, coachman and kitchen-maid, waiter and chamber-maid, and all the guests as well. Even the fire-tongs scrambled up and led out the shovel to perform the mazurka, but no sooner had they made the first stamp than they both fell down on top of one another. Oh, what a merry night was that!

Next morning Hans and his fellow-traveller started early to climb up the high mountains through the vast pine-wood. They climbed up so high that the church-towers far beneath them looked like little red berries scattered among the green of the landscape and they could see over many, many miles of country. Hans had never seen so much of the beauty of this fair world before, the sun shone warmly amid the blue vault of heaven and the wind bore him the faint notes of hunting horns, notes so sweet and wild that the tears stood in his eyes with transport and gratitude. His comrade, meantime, stood by with folded hands, as though in deep reverie; yet nothing above or beneath, in sky or mountain gully, in wood or town, escaped his keen glance. Presently a strain of deep, unearthly music seemed to float over their heads. Hans looked up, and behold! a large white swan hovered in the air above, singing as Hans had never heard any bird sing before. It was its death-song. Ever fainter and weaker grew the notes; its graceful throat bowed forward, and slowly it sank downwards, till at last it fell dead at their feet.

'See what magnificent wings the creature has!' observed the stranger; 'so large and white! They are well worth having; I will take them with me. Now, you can see, Hans,' added he, as with one stroke he severed the wings from the dead swan, 'that this sabre is some use to me.'

They continued their wanderings over the mountains for many, many leagues, till at last they saw a large city lying beneath them with more than a hundred towers and cupolas glistening like silver in the sunshine. From the very heart of this city rose a stately marble palace, its roofs overlaid with red gold and here dwelt the King of the country.

Our two travellers did not go straight into the city; they turned into a little wayside inn to shake the dust off their clothes and tidy themselves up before they went into the town. Here the innkeeper began to talk to them about the King, how he was such a kind, good-hearted old man, and had never done an ill turn to anyone all his life and how his daughter, the Princess was a very wicked lady. She had no lack of beauty, for a fairer maiden could scarcely be found, but she was a sorceress and through her malignant arts many a handsome young Prince had lost his life.

She had given all men leave to come and be her suitors—anyone might come whether he was a prince or a tailor, it was all the same to her. She made him play with her at, 'What am I thinking about?' and if he could guess her thoughts three times, then she promised to give him her hand and make him King over the whole country when her father died. But if he could not guess right all the three times (and no one had ever done so yet) she always had him put to death. Sometimes he was hanged, sometimes beheaded—so wantonly wicked and bloodthirsty was this Princess. Her father, the good old King, was cut to the quick by her cruelty and perversity, but he could not interfere for he had once promised that he would have nothing to do with her love affairs and she might do exactly as she pleased. So every time that a young prince came to play at this fatal game with her and failed, he was either hanged or beheaded. It was not of any use to warn him beforehand—the Princess could always infatuate the people when she chose. The innkeeper went on to say that the old King was so much afflicted by all the misery this brought upon the land that he and all his soldiers spent one day every year in fasting and prayer, praying that the Princess's cruel heart might relent; but relent she never would.

'The hateful Princess!' exclaimed Hans, when the innkeeper had finished his story. 'To think of her bewitching people's hearts in this manner! I should never be such a fool, however charming she was; I should hate her rather than love her!' Just as he spoke a loud cheering from the people in the road made him hurry to the window. The Princess herself was riding past, and she was so beautiful that people invariably forgot all her cruelty in their admiration and always burst into a loud cry of joy whenever she appeared among them.

Twelve fair young girls, clad in white silk robes and each bearing a golden tulip in her hand, rode on coal-black steeds beside her. The Princess herself had a snow-white horse, very richly caparisoned. Her riding-habit was of cloth of gold, sewn with rubies and diamonds; the whip which she held in her hand glittered like a sunbeam; the gold crown that weighed down her rich dark hair seemed made of stars, and the light, gauze-like mantle that robed her shoulders was composed of as many thousand hues as butterflies' wings. Yet all this splendour was nothing compared with the sunshine of her smile, the piercing light that flashed from her dark eyes and her majestic brow.

As soon as Hans beheld her the blood rushed to his face, and he could not utter a single word. Indeed, the Princess looked the very same as the fair maiden wearing the golden crown whom he had seen in his dream on the night of his father's death. He had not imagined any mortal maiden to be so beautiful and he could not help loving her with all his heart. The tale he had heard of her being a hard, cruel sorceress who would have people hanged or beheaded when they could not guess her thoughts could not be true. 'Everyone has leave to become her suitor, even the poorest. I will go up to the palace and woo her, for I feel I cannot live without her.'

They all tried to persuade him to give up this idea, assuring him that he would fare no better than the suitors who had been before him. His travelling-companion especially entreated him not to go up to the palace on any account. But Hans would not listen to these friendly warnings. He cleaned his clothes carefully, brushed his shoes till they were quite bright, washed his hands and face, combed his long fair hair, and set out through the city, straight for the marble palace. 'Come in,' said the King when Hans knocked at the door. He went in and the good old King came forward to meet him, wearing his dressing-gown and embroidered slippers, yet with his gold crown upon his head, and bearing the sceptre and the orb, the symbols of kingly power. As

soon as he heard that Hans came as a suitor to his daughter, he began to weep so bitterly that sceptre and orb rolled down on the floor and he had to dry his eyes on his dressing-gown. The poor old King! 'Don't consider it!' he implored; 'it will be the same with you as with all the rest. Come and look here.'

And he led Hans out into the Princess's pleasure garden, and a ghastly sight awaited him. On many of the trees hung the wasted skeletons of three or four Princes who had wooed the

Princess but had not succeeded in guessing what she was thinking about. Every time the wind rustled the foliage of the trees the dry skeletons rattled and clattered together. The sight and sound was so horrible that the birds had all been scared away, for they dared not rest their wings in this grove of death. The flowers were tied up to human bones instead of sticks, and grisly skulls grinned from behind every flower-pot or every plant that needed shelter from the winds.

'Here you can see,' said the old King to Hans, 'what your fate will be. Give up the mad idea, I beseech you! Think, too, how unhappy it will make me. Have pity on me, if not on yourself!' The Princess herself, returning from her excursion, came riding into the court of the palace with all her ladies. The King and Hans went up to her and said 'good morning,' and she was so gracious and friendly. She offered her hand to Hans and he loved her more passionately than ever and could less than ever persuade himself that she was really the wicked sorceress that people took her to be.

They returned to the hall and a troop of prettily dressed little pages came in and handed round sweetmeats and gingerbread nuts to everyone—the King and Princess, her ladies and Hans. But the old King was so sad and downcast that he couldn't enjoy anything, and the gingerbread nuts were too hard for his teeth.

It was agreed that Hans should come up to the palace again next morning, and that the judges and the whole assembled council were to be present as witnesses to the Princess's game. If he guessed right this first time, he was to come again on the two following days, although hitherto not one of the suitors had survived the first day of the trial.

Hans did not lose confidence in the least; on the contrary, his spirits rose more and more and he thought only of the beautiful Princess, and would not believe he might fail. Almost dancing with joy, he made his way back to the roadside inn where his companion was waiting for him. He could never be weary of telling how kind and gracious the Princess had been towards him and of praising her incredible beauty. He longed for the morning when he might again go back to the palace.

But his companion shook his head sadly. 'I am so fond of you,' he said, 'and we might have stayed together a long while, and now I must lose you! My poor, dear Hans! But I won't disturb your happiness on what is perhaps the last evening that we spend together. We will be gay, really gay; tomorrow, when you are gone, I shall have time enough to weep.'

By this time all the people in the city had heard of the arrival of a new suitor to the Princess and there was general mourning in consequence, for it was thought impossible that Hans could do any better than the suitors that had come before him. That evening the stranger ordered a large bowl of punch to be brought in, and told Hans that he must drink the Princess's health. But no sooner had Hans emptied his first glass than he felt his eyelids grow so heavy that he could no longer hold them up; he sank back in his chair and fell into a sound sleep. His companion lifted him gently into bed, and as it was now night and quite dark, he took out the large wings that he had cut from the dead swan and fastened them on to his shoulders. Then, taking the bundles of ferns the old woman had given them, he opened the window and flew out of the city straight to the marble palace, where he concealed himself in the corner of a bow-window belonging to the Princess's sleeping-room.

Perfect stillness reigned throughout the city. At last the clock struck a quarter to twelve, whereupon the Princess's window opened, and the Princess herself clad in a loose white mantle, and borne up by long black wings, flew out. She flew over the town and towards a high mountain in the distance; but Hans's companion instantly made himself invisible and followed through the air close behind her. He waved his bundle of ferns three times in the air, muttering, 'Blow, winds, blow—north, south, east and west!' and the four winds arose and struggled in the air, beat in the Princess's face, and took hold of her white cloak and kept it fluttering to and fro till it spread out like a

wide sail on either side of her.

'How cold it is! how dreadfully cold, and how windy!' sighed the Princess. At last she reached the mountain and tapped it with her hand, so a deep rumbling, like thunder, was heard from within, and the mountain yawned widely. The Princess entered and Hans' companion followed her.

They went through a long wide passage whose walls glistened strangely, for more than a thousand red-hot spiders were running up and down them. The passage led into a large hall built of silver and gold. Flowers—some red, some blue, and all as large as sunflowers—glistened from the walls, but if anyone had been so far deluded as to try to pluck them, he would have discovered that their green twisted stalks were really poisonous snakes, and that the false flowers themselves were formed by the red and blue fire that issued from the venomous mouths of the reptiles. The ceiling was sewn with glow-worms and bats, which flapped their thin bluish wings to and fro incessantly. In the centre of the hall stood a throne built upon four horse-skeletons harnessed with the web of the fiery-red spiders; the throne itself was of milk-white glass, and the cushions inside it were supplied by little black mice who were continually snapping and biting at one another's tails. Above it was a canopy of crimson spiders' webs, studded with the prettiest little green flies, all glittering like precious stones. On the throne sat an aged troll wearing a crown on his ugly head and holding a sceptre in his hand. He kissed the

Princess on the forehead and bade her sit down on the throne beside him. Then the band struck up. Great black grasshoppers played their jews' harps, and the owl with his 'Tu-whit, tu-whoo!' was chief singer. Little black goblins with will-o'-the-wisp on their caps, danced round and round the hall. The other people at the troll's court certainly entered the hall with a very grand air and did their best to keep up the dignity suitable for their rich dress. Our stranger stationed himself close behind the throne so that he saw and heard everything, though no one could see him and he could see clearly what shams they were. In reality they were nothing but broomsticks with cabbage heads, which the troll had bewitched into some sort of life, and to which he had given gaily embroidered costumes. They just served to keep up appearances, and what more did he want?

After the dancing had gone on for some time, the Princess told the troll that she had a new suitor and asked what she should think of next morning when he came up to the palace to guess her thoughts.

'Listen, I'll tell you,' replied the troll. 'Choose something very easy and simple, and he will be the less likely to guess it. Think of your own shoe; he will never think of that. Then you can have his head cut off; but mind, don't forget to bring me his eyes tomorrow night; I will have them, or I will have your own. Remember our compact!'

The Princess bowed very low and promised not to forget. Presently the troll repeated some magic words which made the mountain groan and yawn asunder, and the Princess flew out again. Hans's companion followed her, swift as thought, and with his wizard ferns conjured up the four winds to blow more strongly than before so that the Princess sighed heavily over the cold and windy weather and made all possible haste to get back to the bow-window of her sleeping-room. And the stranger, who was tired after his night exercise, flew quickly back to the room where Hans was asleep, took off his wings, and laid himself down to rest.

It was quite early in the morning when Hans awoke. He got up and his companion arose also. He did not tell Hans of his adventure during the night, but, without making any mention of the mountain troll, he begged Hans to ask the Princess if she had not thought of her own shoe when he went up to the palace.

'I may as well guess that as anything,' was Hans's reply; 'and I believe the angels may have whispered it to you during the night my friend, for I hope and trust they are on my side. But now let us bid each other good-bye, for if I do not guess right, I shall not see you again.

So Hans went on his way to the palace. The assembly-hall was crowded with people. The councillors sat in large easy-chairs with cushions of eider-down to lean their heads upon, because they all had headaches with having so many hard questions to think about. The old King rose up when Hans came in, and began drying his eyes with a white pocket-handkerchief. Presently the Princess entered. She looked even lovelier than yesterday, and greeted the whole assembly with a most winning smile; but to Hans she held out her hand, saying, 'Good morning, my friend.'

And now the game began: 'What am I thinking about?' asked the Princess, and she looked at Hans archly as she spoke. But no sooner did she hear him bring out the single word 'Shoe,' in answer than she turned pale, and all her limbs began to tremble. It did no good; she could not deny that he had guessed right.

Gracious! how glad the old king was. He jumped up and kicked his slippers in the air for joy and the spectators all clapped their hands, some to applaud the King and some to show how pleased they were at Hans's victory—for victory it was for this one day at least.

His comrade too was well pleased when he heard of his success; but as for Hans himself, he folded his hands in quiet thankfulness that he had been saved for one day from the peril of death. The very next day he must undergo his second trial.

The evening passed just like the one before. As soon as Hans was asleep, his comrade flew out and followed the Princess to the strange mountain. This time, however, he took one of the willow-twigs as well as the old woman's fern-bundle and called up a storm, not only of wind, but of rain. It poured upon the poor Princess in torrents and she was really thankful to reach the shelter of the mountains. No one noticed the stranger but he was there, nevertheless, and heard and saw everything that went on. This time it was arranged that the Princess should think of her glove. Hans was duly instructed and could not but guess aright.

The whole court cut capers when they heard it, just as they had seen the King do on the former occasion: but as for the Princess, she threw herself down upon a sofa and would not speak a single word.

And then Hans had to guess only once more. If he succeeded on the third day too the beautiful Princess, whom he loved so passionately, would become his bride, and he should be king over the whole country after her old father's death. If he guessed wrong, then, alas! he must lose his life, and his bright blue eyes would be carried as a tribute to the wicked mountain troll.

Hans went to bed earlier than usual that evening and soon fell into a sound and peaceful slumber. His companion then fastened the swan-wings on his shoulders, buckled the sabre to his belt, took all three wizard wands in his hand and flew off to the marble palace.

The night was pitch dark and the wind had already risen when the traveller had waved each of his wands three times, stirring up the threefold powers of wind, rain, and hail. The trees in the garden of skeletons bowed like reeds to the blast; it lightened every moment, and the thunder rolled on continuously as though it would never cease the whole night long. The bow-window opened, and the Princess fluttered out into the wild atmosphere. She was pale as death—not that she was afraid of tempests, for she used to enjoy them—but this night, when her white mantle spread out around her like a sail unfurled by the wind, when the rain streamed pitilessly on her face and the hailstones pelted her on all sides, she hovered on slowly and with pain, and her wings could scarcely bear her up. She expected to sink to the ground every instant. At last she reached the strange mountain.

'There's such a hail-storm outside!' said she, on entering; 'I never knew such bad weather.'

'One may have too much, even of a good thing,' replied the troll.

Then she told him, shivering with fear and dread, that Hans had inexplicably guessed right the second time. If he should win the third trial, the game would be his indeed and she might never come to the mountain again, never again pay tribute to the troll as she had sworn to do. And she wept most bitterly. 'Never fear! he won't guess this time!' replied the troll. 'I will find something he has never thought of in his life, unless he is really a greater magician than I am. But now let us be merry!' And he took the Princess by the hand, and danced with her all round the hall. The goblins and will-o'-the wisp danced too, and the red spiders jumped gaily up and down the glistening walls. The owl tu-whitted with all his might, the crickets chirped and the black grasshoppers blew the jews' harps. They had danced till they were tired and the Princess said she must hasten home in case she was missed. The troll said he would keep her company, so that they might have more time together.

So they flew away through the storm, the traveller waving his three wands close behind them. Never had the troll been out in such a hurricane. When they arrived at the palace he bade the Princess farewell, and at the same moment whispered to her, 'Think of my head!' But Hans's companion overheard what he said and while the Princess was slipping into her room through the window, and just as the troll was about to turn round and fly back to his mountain, he seized him by his long black beard and, drawing his sabre, cut off his huge demon head. He threw his body into the sea for the fishes to eat, but the head he wrapped up in his silk handkerchief, and took it with him to the inn.

Next morning he gave the bundle to Hans, telling him not to untie it until the Princess asked him to declare what she was thinking of.

There was such a crowd in the King's hall that day that the people pressed one against another, like radishes tied up in a bunch, and every man trod on his neighbour's toes. The judges and councillors sat again in their easy-chairs, with the soft eider-down cushions to lean their heads on, and the old King had on an entirely new suit of clothes. His gold crown and his sceptre, too, had been freshly polished and glittered marvellously; but the Princess was very pale and was clad in black.

'What am I thinking about?' she asked Hans for the third time, and immediately he untied the handkerchief. He started back with horror and amazement when he saw the hideous head and a shudder ran through all the bystanders. The princess sat mute and motionless as a statue and could not say anything. At last she rose from her seat and held out her snow-white hand to Hans in token that he had guessed rightly and had won the game. Looking neither at him nor at anyone present, her eyes still riveted on the misshapen head in the handkerchief, she sighed heavily and said, 'Now you are my lord and master! Our wedding must be celebrated tonight.' And the whole assembly burst into a prolonged cheer.

The band was called out to play in the streets and the church-bells were all set ringing, for mourning was changed into joy. Three oxen were roasted whole in the market-place, besides fowls and ducks in endless quantities, so that everyone who wanted could come and have dinner. The fountains flowed with wine instead of water, and if you went into the baker's shop to buy a penny roll, he gave you six buns into the bargain—with currants in them, too. In the evening the whole city was illuminated. The soldiers fired their guns, the little boys ran about letting off crackers; in the palace there was eating and drinking, dancing and singing among all the fair ladies and gallant cavaliers of the court—no end to the rejoicings.

But in all this gaiety the Princess remained pale and sad. Hans at last went in despair to his companion to ask his advice on how to win his bride's love and to entice a smile from her. The stranger gave him a little vial filled with a colourless liquid like water and three feathers from the swan-wings, bidding him steep each of the three feathers in the liquid and then sprinkle the Princess's forehead with the drops clinging to the feathers. Three times must he sprinkle her with each of the three feathers, and then she would be free from her enchantment.

Hans did exactly as his companion had counselled him. He sprinkled the Princess' brow three times with the first feather, and she uttered a loud shriek and was transformed into a coal-black swan with fiery-red eyes. He sprinkled the black swan with the second feather, whereupon it became pure white, excepting one black ring encircling its slender throat. He dipped the third feather in the liquid and shook the drops three times over the white swan's head, and immediately the swan vanished and his own beloved Princess stood in its place, looking a thousand times lovelier than ever. Her cheeks glowed, her eyes sparkled brightly and she shed tears of joy and thankfulness.

Then she told him that a few years ago she had been wandering alone near the strange mountain in the evening. There evil spirits hold their sway and she was surprised by the mountain troll. He cast his wicked spell upon her to make her serve his cruel purposes, and so potent were those spells that not even the death of the troll could entirely release her. Again and again she thanked Hans for having freed her from his hateful enchantments.

Presently Hans's companion came to the palace with his wandering-staff in his hand, and his knapsack on his back. Hans embraced him very eagerly, entreating him to stay with him and share in his great happiness. But his companion shook his head, saying, very gently, 'No, that cannot be; my time is up. I have now paid my debt. Do you remember the dead man whom his evil-minded creditors would not let rest in his coffin? You gave all your fortune to secure him rest and peace. I am that dead man!'

And in the same moment he vanished.

The wedding feast lasted for a whole month. Hans and his fair Princess loved each other dearly, and the good old King lived through many happy days and delighted in nothing so much as in his tiny grandchildren, who used to play with his bright sceptre, and 'ride-a-cock-horse to Banbury Cross' on his knees. But Hans, in the course of time, ruled over the whole country, and became a great and powerful monarch.

The Garden of Paradise

There was once a king's son. No one had so many beautiful books as he where he could read about everything that had ever happened in the world and see pictures of it too. There was only one thing which no book could tell him, and that was where he could find the Garden of Paradise. He wanted to know this most of all.

When the Prince was a very little boy, just beginning to go to school, his grandmother told him that every flower in the Garden of Paradise tasted like the sweetest cake, and the pistils like the choicest of wines. On one plant there grew History, on another Geography, on a third the German Language. Whoever ate the flower immediately knew his lesson, so the more he ate the more he learned of History, Geography, or German.

The Prince believed all this but, by and by when he had grown bigger and wiser, he saw plainly that the beauty of the Garden of Paradise must be something quite different.

'Oh, why did Eve take the fruit from the Tree of Knowledge? Why did Adam eat the forbidden fruit? If I had been in his place it would never have happened—then sin wouldn't have come into the world.' He said this when he was a child and he was still saying it when he was seventeen. The Garden of Paradise occupied all his thoughts.

One day he went into the wood alone, for wandering about

like this was his favourite pastime. Evening approached, the clouds gathered, the rain poured down like a river; it was as dark as the bottom of the deepest well. The Prince slipped on the wet grass and stumbled over bare rocks on the stonier ground. Everything was dripping wet and the poor Prince was soaked to the skin. His strength was just failing him when he heard a strange rushing sound and saw a large lighted cavern in front of him. A huge fire was burning in the centre and a fine stag was being roasted on it. An old woman, as tall and strong as if she were a man in disguise, sat and tossed pieces of wood into the blaze. 'Come nearer,' she said, 'sit down by the fire and dry your clothes.'

'There is a terrible draught here,' said the Prince, as he sat down on the ground.

'It will be still worse when my sons come home,' answered the woman. 'You are now in the Cavern of the Winds and my sons are the four Winds of the World. Do you understand me?'

'Where are your sons?' asked the Prince.

'It's no use answering stupid questions,' said the woman. 'My sons do as they please; they play skittles with the clouds up there,' and she pointed up into the sky.

'Indeed,' said the Prince. 'You speak roughly, and don't seem nearly as gentle as the women I am accustomed to see around me.'

'Yes, they have nothing else to do. I must be harsh if I am to control my boys. However, I can control them, although they're pretty obstinate. D'you see those four sacks hanging by the wall? They have as much respect for them as you used to have for the birch rod behind the looking-glass. I pick them up and push them into the sacks. There they sit, and they don't get out till it pleases me. And here comes one of them!'

It was the North Wind. He brought an icy blast with him; large hailstones danced on the ground and flakes of snow flew round him. He was dressed in a jacket and trousers of bear's skin, a seal-skin cap was pulled over his ears, long icicles hung from his beard and hailstones fell one after another from under the collar of his jacket.

'Don't go straight to the fire,' said the Prince, 'you may perhaps get your face and hands frost-bitten.'

'Frost-bitten!' repeated the North Wind, and he laughed loudly. 'Frost is my greatest delight! But what sort of weak-kneed boy are you? How did you get into the Cavern of the Winds?'

'He's my guest,' said the old woman; 'and if you are not satisfied with this explanation, you shall go into the sack. So now you know.'

This was quite enough. Then the North Wind related whence he came, and how he had spent the last month.

'I come from the Arctic Ocean,' said he. 'I have been on the Bear's Island, along with the Russian whalers. It's a glorious place! The ground seems made for dancing, it's flat as a plate. It's made of half-melted snow overgrown with moss; sharp stones, and the skeletons of whalers and polar bears are strewn about it looking like gigantic limbs. They are covered with musty green and you would think the sun never shone on them. I blew a little into the mist so that one could see a hut built from a wreck and covered with the skin of a whale. A polar bear sat growling on the roof. I walked on the shore, peeped into the birds' nests, looked at the poor naked young ones squeaking with their beaks wide open; I blew down their throats and taught them to be quiet.

'Great walruses with swine-like heads, and teeth an ell long, rolled beneath the waters. And then the hunting began; the harpoon thrust into their breasts and a stream of blood shot up like a fountain and splattered the ice. Then I remembered my part in the game; I made my ships, the icebergs, surround the boats. Oh! how all the crew shouted with fear. But I roared louder than they. They had to unload all the dead whales and walrus and throw them out on the ice. I shook snowflakes over them, and drove them southwards in their battered ships. They will never come back to Bear's Island!'

'Then you have done mischief!' said the mother of the Winds.

'Others can tell you the good I have done,' said he. 'But here comes my brother of the West. I love him the best of all; he smells of the sea and has a really healthy coldness about him.'

'Can that be the little Zephyr?' asked the Prince.

'Yes, it is certainly Zephyr,' said the old woman; 'but he isn't little any longer. He used to be a pretty boy, but that's a long time ago now.'

The West Wind looked like a wild man and he had on a sort of padded hat so he shouldn't get hurt. In his hand he held a club of mahogany wood he had hewn in the American forests.

'Where have you been?' said the mother.

'In those wild forests,' he said, 'where the thorny lianas weave between the trees, where the water-snake rests in the damp grass and men would be quite out of place.'

'What did you do there?'

'I looked at the deep river, saw how it hurled itself from the rocks and flew like dust towards the clouds, making a bright rainbow. I saw a buffalo swim down the river and the stream carry him away. A flock of wild geese were swimming too; they flew away when the water plunged down a precipice, but the buffalo must have gone with it. Then I raised such a storm that the ancient trees crashed to the ground, broken in splinters.'

'And have you done nothing else?' said the old woman.

'I have turned somersaults in the Savannahs; I have ridden wild horses, and shaken cocoa-nut trees—ah, yes, I have great stories to tell! But one mustn't tell all one knows, my old mother!' And he kissed his mother so roughly that she almost fell. He was a wild fellow!

Now came the South Wind in his turban and floating Bedouin cloak.

'It is very cold here,' he said, as he threw wood on the fire; 'I can see that the North Wind has arrived before me.'

'It is so hot that a polar bear could be roasted in here,' growled the North Wind.

'You're a polar bear yourself,' said the South Wind.

'Do you want to go into the sack both of you?' asked the old woman. 'Sit down and tell me where you have been.'

'In Africa, mother,' he answered. 'I have been hunting lions in the land of the Kaffirs. Such beautiful grass grows on those plains, green as olives! The gnu danced there and the ostrich ran races with me, but I am swifter than he. I came to the yellow sands of the desert where one might think oneself at the bottom of the sea. I met with a caravan; they had just killed their last camel, in hopes of getting water to drink but they did not find much. The sun was burning over their heads, the sands roasting beneath their feet. There seemed no end to the desert. I rolled myself up in fine loose sand and whirled it up in immense pillars. What a famous dance it did! You should have seen how puzzled the dromedary looked and how the merchant threw his caftan over his head. He flung himself down before me as he used to do before Allah. There they are all buried and a pyramid of sand stands over them. If I blow it away one day the sun will bleach their bones and travellers will see that human beings have passed that way before them.'

'Then you have only done evil,' said the mother. 'Get into the sack.' And before he was aware of it, the South Wind was seized and shut in the sack. It rolled about on the floor until the mother sat down on it and then he was obliged to lie still.

'These are desperately wild fellows,' said the Prince.

'Yes, indeed they are,' replied she, 'but they have to obey me in the end. Here is the fourth.'

This was the East Wind, who was dressed like a Chinaman.

'So you've come from that corner of the world,' said the mother. 'I thought you had been to the Garden of Paradise?'

'I shall go there tomorrow,' said the East Wind; 'it's a hundred years tomorrow since I was there. I have just come from China, where I danced round the porcelain tower so that all the bells began to ring. In the street below some officials were being flogged till the bamboo canes broke upon their shoulders. Yet they were well-to-do people from the first to the ninth grade. They cried out, "Thanks, thanks, my fatherly benefactor," but they didn't mean what they said. I clinked the bells and sang, "Tsing, tsang, tsu!"'

'You are a wild boy,' said the mother; 'it is just as well that you are going to the Garden of Paradise tomorrow. Your visits there always improve you. Remember to drink plentifully from the source of wisdom, and bring me a little flask filled with it.'

'Very well,' said the East Wind. 'But why have you put my brother of the South into the sack? Let him come out. I want him to tell me all about the bird called the phoenix; the Princess in the Garden of Paradise always asks me about him. Open the sack, dearest mother, and I will give you two cups full of tea, as fresh and green as when I plucked it.'

'Well, then, for the sake of the tea and because you are my darling, I will open the sack.' She did so, and the South Wind crept out; but he looked very much ashamed because the stranger Prince had seen his disgrace.

'Here is a palm leaf for the Princess,' said the South Wind; 'it was given to me by the old phoenix, the only one in the world. He has written the history of his life on it with his beak; the Princess can read it herself. I saw the Phoenix set fire to his own nest; I saw him as he sat in it and was burnt up like a Hindoo wife. How the dry branches crackled, and how sweet was the smell that rose from the burning nest! At last everything was burnt by the flames; the old phoenix was in ashes but his egg lay glowing in the fire. It broke open with a loud noise and the young one flew out. He is now king over all the birds and the only phoenix in the world. He has bitten a hole in the leaf I gave you; that is his greeting to the Princess.'

'Well, let's have something to eat,' said the mother of the Winds, and so they all sat down to eat the roasted stag. The Prince sat next to the East Wind and they soon became good friends.

'Which Princess is it whom I heard so much about,' said the Prince, 'and where is the Garden of Paradise?'

'Ah!' said the East Wind, 'do you want to go there? Well, come with me tomorrow; but I warn you that no human being has been there since Adam and Eve's time. When they were driven out, the Garden of Paradise sank under the earth though it still retained its warm sunshine, its balmy air and all its beauty. The queen of the fairies makes her home there, and there also is the Island of Bliss where death never comes and where life is so beautiful! If you sit on my back tomorrow, I will take you there; I think that would be allowed. But don't talk any longer now, for I want to sleep.'

And so they all went to sleep. The Prince woke early in the

morning, and was not a little surprised to find himself already far above the clouds. He was sitting on the back of the East Wind who kept tight hold of him, and they flew so high that woods and meadows, river and seas, looked like a large coloured map.

'Good morning,' said the East Wind. 'You may as well sleep a little longer, for there is not much to see on the flat surface beneath us unless you enjoy counting churches; they stand out like little bits of chalk on a green board down there.' What he called the green board were fields and meadows.

'It was rude to leave without saying good-bye to your mother and brothers,' said the Prince.

'That's forgiven as you were asleep,' said the East Wind.

They went faster than ever—so fast that the tops of the trees, the branches and leaves, rustled as they passed them by. As they crossed the seas and lakes, the waves rose higher and large ships bowed low like swans in the water. In the evening, when it was dark, the large towns had a most curious appearance. Lights burnt here and there and it was just like watching the sparks on a burnt piece of paper as they vanish one after another. The Prince clapped his hands with joy, but the East Wind begged him to be quiet and to hold fast, as otherwise he might fall off and get caught on the top of a church spire.

'Now you can see the Himalayan mountains,' said the East Wind; they are the highest in Asia. We shall soon come to the Garden of Paradise.' So they turned more towards the south, and straightway smelt the fragrance of spices and flowers. Figs and pomegranates were growing wild; red and white grapes hung from the vines. Here they descended and stretched themselves on the soft grass while the flowers nodded to the Wind, as if they wished to say, 'Welcome, welcome!'

'Are we in the Garden of Paradise?' asked the Prince.

'No, not yet,' said the East Wind, 'but we shall soon be there. Do you see that rock and the large cave with the vine branches hanging in front like large green curtains? We must go through that. Wrap your cloak round you; the sun is shining here but take a step farther and you will find it as cold as ice. The bird that is flying past the cave has one wing warm as summer and the other cold as winter.'

'So this is the way to the Garden of Paradise!' said the Prince.

They went into the cave. Oh, how cold it was there! They did not stay long for the East Wind spread out his wings which shone like the purest flame. What a cavern! large blocks of stone hung in the strangest forms above them, water trickled down and the cave was sometimes as high and broad as the sky, sometimes so narrow that they had to creep along on their hands and feet.

'Surely we are going by the path of Death, to the Garden of Paradise,' said the Prince but the East Wind didn't answer him. Instead he pointed to the loveliest blue light which gleamed ahead. The rocks above them became more and more like mists, and at last became as clear and bright as a white cloud in the moonlight. The travellers breathed the softest air, fresh as the mountains, fragrant as the roses of the valley. A river flowed by which was as clear as the atmosphere itself. Gold and silver fishes swam in it; purple eels, which sent out blue sparks with every movement, were playing beneath the surface and the broad leaves of the water-lily shone with all the colours of the rainbow. A bridge of marble led over the water to the Island of Bliss and the Garden of Paradise, and it shone like a delicately carved pearl.

The East Wind bore the Prince over. The flowers and leaves sang the sweetest songs about his childhood in supple tones which no human voice could imitate. The Prince had never before seen trees so large and full of sap, and he didn't know if they were palm trees or gigantic water plants. The most wonderful creepers hung about them in long wreaths as they do in the margins of illuminated manuscripts when, fold in fold, they twine their way among the initial letters. Close to them in the grass stood a flock of peacocks with their bright tails spread out; but when the Prince touched them, he found they were not birds but plants: they were large plantain-leaves that sparkled with a thousand stars. Lions and tigers sprang cat-like over green and sweet-smelling hedges, and they were quite tame. The timid wood-pigeon with her pearly plumage flapped her wings against the lion's mane, and the shy antelope stood by and nodded his head as if he wanted to play with them too.

Then the Fairy of Paradise approached them. Her garments shone like the sun and her countenance was as gentle as that of a happy mother rejoicing over her child. She was very young and very beautiful and the fairest of maidens followed her, each with a star shining in her hair. The East Wind gave her the leaf from the phoenix and her eyes shone with joy. She took the Prince by the hand and led him in to her palace, whose walls were bright like a splendid tulip-petal held up to the sun. The dome was like one single bright flower and the longer you looked into it, the deeper the cup appeared to be. The Prince walked to the window and looked out of one of the panes. There he saw the Tree of Knowledge, with the Serpent and Adam and Eve standing by its side. 'Weren't they driven out?' he asked. The Fairy smiled and explained to him that Time had formed a picture on every pane, but they were not ordinary pictures; they had a life of their own for the leaves of the tree moved, and men came and went, as in a mirror. He looked through another pane, and there he saw Jacob's dream. Soon he found that everything which had happened in the world lived and moved in these panes of glass. Only Time could have made such cunning pictures.

The Fairy smiled and led the Prince into a high spacious hall, whose walls seemed covered with portraits and where each face seemed more lovely than the last. They were millions of blessed spirits, who smiled and sang. And in the middle of the hall stood a large tree with luxurious branches where golden apples, of different sizes, hung like oranges among the green leaves. This was the Tree of Knowledge, whose fruit Adam and Eve had eaten. A bright red drop of dew hung from every leaf so it seemed as though the tree wept tears of blood.

'Let us go in the boat,' said the Fairy, 'we shall find it so refreshing. It rocks on the waves without moving from its mooring place, but you will see all the countries in the world go gliding by us.'

It was wonderful to see all the coast moving past. First came the high, snow-covered Alps, with their clouds and dark fir-trees; the horn's deep tones were sounded in the hills and the herdsmen sang merrily in the valley below. Then banyan-trees trailed their long, hanging branches over the boat, coal-black swans sailed on the water and the strangest-looking animals and flowers were to be seen on the shore. This was New Holland, which had succeeded the high, blue Alps. And then came the hymns of priests, the dance of savages, accompanied by the noise of drums and the wooden tuba. Egypt's lofty pyramids, fallen pillars, and sphinxes half buried in the sand, sailed by. The northern lights shone over the icy mountains of the north; fireworks which no mortal could imitate. The Prince was delighted and he saw a hundred times more than we have related here.

'And may I stay here always?' he asked.

'That depends on you!' answered the Fairy. 'If you don't disobey our rules as Adam and Eve did, then you may stay here for ever.'

'I will never touch the apple on the Tree of Knowledge,' said the Prince; 'there are a thousand fruits here quite as beautiful.'

'Think about it carefully. If you are not strong enough go

back with the East Wind who brought you, for he is just going to fly back and will not return for a hundred years. The time will pass away here as if it were only a hundred hours, but even that is a long time for temptation and sin. Every evening when I leave you, I must tempt you to come with me. I must beckon to you, but beware of listening to my call. Do not come, for each step will only increase the temptation. You will come into the hall where the Tree of Knowledge stands and I shall be sleeping under its fragrant branches. You will bend over me and if you touch me, Paradise will sink beneath the earth and be lost to you. The sharp wind of the desert will whistle round, the cold rain will drip from your hair and sorrow and care will be your inheritance.'

'I will stay here,' said the Prince. And the East Wind kissed his forehead, and said, 'Be strong, and we shall see each other again after a hundred years. Farewell, farewell!' And then he spread out his great wings, which shone like lightning in harvest-time or the northern lights in winter. 'Farewell, farewell!' echoed from the trees and flowers. Storks and pelicans flew with him in a long ribbon to the boundary of the garden.

'Now we will begin our dancing,' said the Fairy, 'and while I am dancing with you and the sun is sinking I will beckon you and say, "Come with me". For a hundred years I must repeat this call to you every evening but every day your strength will increase until you do not even want to follow. This evening will be the first time—I have warned you.'

The Fairy then led him into a large hall made of white lilies whose yellow stamens formed little golden harps, sending forth clear sweet tones resembling those of the flute.

The sun was setting and the whole sky was like pure gold. The lilies shone like the loveliest roses amid the purple gleam. The farthest wall of the hall parted slowly and the Prince saw the Tree of Knowledge in a splendour that dazzled his eyes. He heard someone singing with a soft and gentle voice and it seemed as though she was saying, 'My darling, my child, my darling.'

Then the Fairy beckoned, saying, 'Come with me, come with me,' and he ran up to her, forgetting his promise even on that first evening.

The spicy smell became stronger, the harps sounded more sweetly and it seemed as though the million smiling faces in the hall where the Tree was growing, nodded and sang, 'We must know everything. Man is Lord of the earth.' Instead of tears of blood, red sparkling stars were dropping from the leaves of the Tree—or so it appeared to him.

The haunting song came again and the Fairy parted the branches and in another moment was hidden behind them.

'I have not sinned yet,' said the Prince, 'nor will I.' He flung aside the boughs where she was sleeping—beautiful as only the Fairy of the Garden of Paradise could be. She smiled as she slept; he bent over her, and saw tears tremble behind her eyelashes. 'Are you weeping for me?' he whispered. 'Don't cry, my beautiful one!' And he kissed the tears from her eyes. There was a fearful clap of thunder, the loudest and deepest that had ever been heard. In the tumult the Fairy vanished, the verdant Paradise sank deep into the ground; the Prince felt it melt in the darkness; it glimmered in the distance like a star. A deadly coldness shot through his limbs; his eyes closed and he lay for some time apparently dead.

When he regained consciousness the cold rain was beating on his face, the sharp wind chilled his body.

'What have I done?' said he. 'I have sinned like Adam; I have sinned, and Paradise has sunk far beneath the earth.' And he opened his eyes and saw the star in the distance, the star which sparkled like his lost Paradise; it was the morning-star in Heaven.

He stood upright, and found himself in the wood near the Cavern of the Winds; the mother of the winds sat by his side; she looked very angry and raised her hand.

'Already, on the first evening!' said she, 'Well, I expected it. If you were my son you should go straight into the sack.'

'He shall go there anyway,' said Death. He was a strong old

man, with a scythe and large black wings. 'He shall die, but not yet. I shall watch him and will let him wander for a little while on the earth, and repent of his sin. He may improve, he may grow good. I shall come back one day when he least expects it and lay him in the black coffin. If his head and heart are still full of sin, he will sink even lower than the Garden of Paradise sank; but if he has become good and holy, I shall put the coffin on my head and fly to yonder star, for the Garden of Paradise is there also. He shall live in the star, that bright sparkling star, for ever.'

The Little Mermaid

Far out in the wide sea, where the water is as blue
as the loveliest cornflower and as clear as the purest crystal, where
it is so deep that many church-spires would have to be balanced
on one another to reach from the lowest depth to the surface
above, dwell the Mer-people.

The palace of the Mer-king stands where the water is deepest.
The walls of this palace are made of coral, and the high, pointed
windows are of amber while the roof is composed of mussel-
shells, which, as the billows pass over them, are continually
opening and shutting. This looks exceedingly pretty, especially
as each of these mussel-shells contains a number of bright, glittering pearls, any one of which would be considered a most costly
ornament in the upper world.

The Mer-king who lived in this palace had been a widower
for many years and his old mother managed the household
affairs for him. She was, on the whole, a sensible sort of lady but
she was extremely proud of her high birth and station, so she
wore twelve oysters on her tail while the other great people of
the sea were allowed only six. In every other respect she deserved
unlimited praise, especially for the affection she showed to the
six little princesses, her granddaughters. These were all very
beautiful children. The youngest, however, was the most lovely.
Her skin was as soft and delicate as a rose-petal; her eyes were as

blue as the deepest sea, but like all other mermaids, she had no feet and her body ended in a fishes' tail.

The whole day long the children used to play in the large rooms of the palace where beautiful flowers grew out of the walls around them. When the great amber windows were opened, fish would swim in as swallows fly into our rooms. But the fish were bolder than the swallows; they swam straight up to the little princesses, ate from their hands and allowed themselves to be caressed.

In front of the palace there was a large garden, full of fiery red and dark blue trees whose fruit glittered like gold and whose flowers resembled the bright, burning sun. The sand which formed the soil of the garden was also a bright blue colour—something like flames of sulphur—and a strange, blue glow spread over everything, so that one might have thought oneself in the middle of the sky instead of at the bottom of the sea. When the waters were quite still and one looked upwards the sun appeared like a purple flower which streamed with light.

Each of the little princesses had her own plot in the garden where she might plant and sow as she pleased. One had hers made in the shape of a whale, another chose the figure of a mermaid, but the youngest had hers quite round like the sun and she planted only flowers that were the colour of the sun itself.

She was certainly a singular child, very quiet and thoughtful.

Once when her sisters were dressing themselves up with all sorts of gay things that had come out of a wreck, she asked for nothing but a beautiful white marble statue of a boy which had been found in it. She put the statue in her garden, and planted a red weeping willow by its side and let its long branches fall so that restless violet shadows entwined on the blue ground.

Nothing pleased the little princess more than to hear about the world of human beings living above the sea. She made her old grandmother tell her everything she knew about ships, towns, men, and land animals, and was particularly pleased when she heard that the flowers of the upper world had a pleasant smell (for the flowers of the sea are scentless), and that the woods were green, and that the fish fluttering among the branches were of various gay colours, and could sing with a loud clear voice. The old lady meant birds, but she called them fish because her grandchildren, having never seen a bird, would not have understood her otherwise.

'When you are fifteen,' she added, 'you will be allowed to go up to the surface of the sea. Then you will sit by moonlight in the clefts of the rocks, see the ships sail by and learn what towns and men are.'

The next year the eldest of the sisters reached this age and she promised to tell the others of everything she saw, for their grandmother could never tell them enough and there was so much that they wanted to hear about. But none of the sisters longed so much for her fifteenth birthday as the youngest—she who had longest to wait, and was so quiet and thoughtful. Many a night she stood by the open window, looking up through the clear blue water. She could see the sun and the moon. If a shadow passed over them, she knew it must be either a whale or a ship, sailing by full of human beings who little thought that, far beneath them, a little mermaiden was stretching her white hands longingly towards the keel of their ship.

When the eldest sister returned from her first visit she had a thousand things to relate. Her chief pleasure had been to sit on a sandbank in the moonlight looking at the large town which lay on the coast, where lights were beaming like stars, and where music was playing. She had heard the distant noise of men and carriages, had seen the high church-towers, and listened to the bells ringing. How attentively her youngest sister listened to her words! The next time she stood by her open window, gazing upward through the blue waters, she thought so intensely about the great noisy city that she imagined she could hear the church-bells ringing.

Next year the second sister had permission to swim wherever she pleased. She rose to the surface of the sea just when the sun was setting, and this sight so delighted her that she declared it to be more beautiful than anything else she had seen above the waters.

'The whole sky seemed tinged with gold,' she said, 'and I cannot describe the beauty of the clouds. Now red, now violet, they glided over me and a flock of white swans swept over the water just where the sun was setting. I gazed after them until the sun sank out of sight and the bright rosy light on the surface of the sea, and on the edges of the clouds, gradually disappeared.'

The third sister was the boldest and when her turn to visit the upper world arrived, she ventured up a river. There she saw green hills covered with woods and vineyards with houses and castles among them. She heard the birds singing, and the sun shone so hot that she had to keep plunging below in order to cool her burning face. In a little bay she came upon a number of children who were bathing and jumping about. She would have joined in their games but they fled back to the land in great terror, and a little black animal barked at her in such a manner that she too was frightened and swam back to the sea. She could not forget the green woods, the verdant hills, and the pretty children who were swimming about in the river so fearlessly although they had no tails.

The fourth sister was not so bold; she remained in the open sea and said on her return home she thought nothing could be more beautiful. She had seen ships sailing by, so far off that they looked like sea-gulls, she had watched the dolphins gambolling in the water, and the enormous whales spouting water from their nostrils so that it looked as though there were fountains all round her.

The fifth sister's birthday was in the winter, so when she rose to the surface she found the sea was a green colour and immense icebergs were floating on it. These, she said, looked like huge pearls although they were much larger than church towers. She sat down on one of them and let the wind play with her hair and all the sailing ships changed course hurriedly when they saw her. Towards evening a great storm arose and as the icebergs were tossed up and down by the waves they reflected the reddish glare in the sky. Lightning tore through the clouds and the thunder rolled on, peal after peal. The ships furled all their sails and pandemonium reigned on board, but the little princess sat quietly on her iceberg and watched the forked blue flashes dart into the sea.

On her first visit to the upper world each of these sisters was quite enchanted at the sight of so many new and beautiful objects, but the novelty was soon over, and it was not long before her own home appeared the most attractive of all. Still, many an evening the five sisters rose hand in hand from the depths of the ocean. Their voices were far sweeter than any human voice and when a storm was coming they would swim in front of the ships and sing—how sweetly they sung—describing the happiness of those who lived at the bottom of the sea and entreating the sailors not to be afraid, but to come down to them. The mariners, however, did not understand their words and thought the song was only the whistling of the wind.

While her sisters were swimming at evening-time, the youngest daughter remained motionless in her father's palace, looking up after them. She would have wept, but mermaids cannot weep and consequently when they are troubled they suffer infinitely more than human beings do.

'Oh! if I were only fifteen!' she sighed. 'I know I should love the upper world and its inhabitants so much.'

At last the time she had so longed for arrived.

'Well, now it is your turn,' said the grandmother. 'Come here and I will dress you up like your sisters.' And she wound a wreath of white lilies round her hair and commanded eight large oysters to fasten themselves to the princess's tail, in token of her high rank.

'But it is very uncomfortable!' said the little princess.

'One must not mind slight inconveniences when one wishes to look well,' said the old lady.

The princess would willingly have given up all this splendour and exchanged the heavy crown for the red flowers of her garden, which were so much more becoming to her, but she dared not do so. 'Good-bye,' she said and swam away as lightly as a speck of foam.

When she reached the surface the sun had just sunk below the horizon but the clouds still shone with golden and rosy hues. The evening star was gleaming in the pale western sky and the air was mild and refreshing. A large ship with three masts lay on the still waters. Innumerable flags were fluttering from the masts but only one sail was unfurled; not a breath was stirring, and the sailors were sitting quietly on the spars and rigging. Music and song resounded from the deck and after it grew dark hundreds of lamps suddenly burst forth into light.

The little mermaid swam close up to the captain's cabin and looked through the clear window-panes. She saw many richly dressed men within. The handsomest among them was a young prince with large black eyes. He was just sixteen years old and everyone on board was celebrating his birthday with a grand festival. The crew were dancing on deck and when the young prince appeared among them a hundred rockets were sent up into the air, turning night into day, and so terrifying the little mermaid that she plunged deep into the water. She soon peered out again, however, and it seemed as if all the stars were falling down on her. She had never seen fireworks before, never heard that men possessed such wonderful powers. Large suns revolved around her, fiery fish swam in the air and everything was reflected perfectly on the clear surface of the sea. It was so light in the ship that everything could be seen distinctly. How handsome the young prince was! He shook hands with the sailors and laughed and jested with them, whilst sweet notes of music mingled with the silence of night.

It was late, but the little mermaid could not tear herself away from the ship and the handsome young prince. She stayed looking through the cabin window, rocked to and fro by the waves. A foaming and boiling began slowly in the depths beneath, and the ship moved on and the sails were spread. Then the waves rose high, thick clouds gathered over the sky, the noise of distant thunder was heard and the sailors, seeing that a storm was coming on, furled the sails again. The great vessel was tossed about on the tempestuous ocean like a light boat and the waves rose like black mountains above it. The ship dived into the valleys of the sea like a swan and then was lifted on high again. This seemed delightful to the little mermaid but the ship's crew thought very differently. The timbers cracked, the stout masts broke under the violence of the sea and water rushed into the hold. The little mermaid realized that the people on the ship were in danger, for she herself had to keep dodging the beams and splinters torn from the vessel and floating about on the waves. At one moment it was so dark she could see nothing, the next a sudden flash of lightning would make the whole scene as clear as day. She looked for the young prince and when the ship split open she saw him sink into the sea. She thought happily that he would come down to her palace and then she remembered that a man cannot live in the sea. 'No, no, he must not die!' She swam through the

wreckage regardless of danger and at last found the prince, who could scarcely swim any longer. He had already closed his eyes and would have been drowned had not the little mermaid come to his rescue. She seized hold of him and kept him above water, letting the current bear them on together. When morning came the storm had passed but there no trace of the ship remained. The red sun came up out of the water and his rays seemed to bring back some colour into the prince's face, though his eyes were still closed. The mermaid pushed his wet hair back from his forehead and thought how he looked like the statue in her garden. She kissed him gently and hoped he might live.

Soon she saw land with its snow-covered mountains. A green wood stretched along the coast and at the edge of the wood stood a chapel or convent, she could not be sure which. Citron and lemon trees grew in the garden surrounding it and an avenue of tall palm trees led up to the door. The sea formed a little bay where the water was smooth but very deep and under the cliffs there were dry, firm sands. The little mermaid swam there with the prince. She laid him upon the warm sand and took care to place his head high and to turn his face to the sun.

Then all the bells began to ring in the large white building near by and a number of young girls came out to walk in the garden. The mermaid swam a little out from the shore, hid herself between the rocks, covered her head with foam so that her little face could not be seen and watched the prince. It was not long before one of the young girls approached. She was frightened at finding the prince in this state but she soon recovered herself and ran back to call her sisters. The little mermaid saw that the prince revived and that all around smiled kindly and joyfully upon him. But he did not look for *her*, he did not know that it was she who had saved him. And when the prince was taken into the house, she felt so sad that she immediately plunged into the water and returned to her father's palace.

If she had been quiet and thoughtful before, she now grew still more so. Her sisters asked her what she had seen in the upper world, but she made no answer. Many an evening she rose to the place where she had left the prince. She saw the snow on the mountains melt, the fruit in the garden ripen, but she never saw him so she always returned home sorrowful. Her only pleasure was to sit in her little garden gazing at the beautiful statue that was so like him. She no longer cared for her flowers; they grew up in wild luxuriance, covered the steps and twisted their long stems and tendrils among the branches of the trees until it became quite dark there.

At last she could endure it no longer and told the whole story to her sisters. Soon others heard of it and among them was a mermaid who remembered the prince for she, too, had seen the festival on the ship. She knew what country he lived in and the name of its king.

'Come, little sister,' said the princesses, and, linking their arms together, they rose in a long row out of the water just in front of the prince's palace.

This palace was built of bright yellow stones and a flight of white marble steps led down to the sea. A gilded cupola crowned the building and white marble figures, which might almost have been taken for real men and women, were placed among the pillars surrounding it. Through the clear glass of the high windows one could look into the magnificent rooms hung with silk curtains and adorned with beautiful paintings. The mermaids gazed through the windows of one of the largest rooms and saw a fountain playing in the centre. The waters sprang up to reach the glittering cupola above and the sunbeams fell dancing on the water and brightened the pretty plants which grew round it.

The little mermaid now knew where her beloved prince dwelt and afterwards she went there almost every evening. She often approached nearer the land than her sisters dared, and even swam up the narrow channel that flowed under the marble balcony. Here on bright moonlight nights she would watch the young prince when he believed himself to be alone. Sometimes she saw him sailing on the water in a gaily painted boat with many coloured flags waving above him. She would hide among the green reeds that grew on the banks and listen to his voice. Many a night when the fishermen were casting their nets by torch light she heard them talking about the prince and relating the noble deeds he had done. Then she was very happy, thinking how she had saved his life and remembering how his head had rested on her bosom, and how she had kissed him. But he knew nothing about it and could never even dream of her.

Human beings became dearer and dearer to her every day until she wished that she were one of them. Their world seemed to her much larger than that of the Mer-people. They could sail over the ocean in their ships or climb to the summits of the high mountains that rose above the clouds, and their wooded domains extended much farther than her eye could see. There were many things that she wanted to know but her sisters could not give her any satisfactory answer. So she asked the old queen-mother, who knew more than anyone about the upper world, which she used to call 'the country above the sea'.

'If men are not drowned do they live for ever?' she asked one day. 'Don't they die as we do down here?'

'Yes,' was the grandmother's reply, 'they too must die, and their life is much shorter than ours. We live to the age of three hundred years yet when we die we become foam on the sea and are not allowed a grave among those that are dear to us. We have no immortal soul, we can never live again and are like the grass which, once cut down, is withered for ever. Human beings, on the contrary, have souls that continue to live when their bodies become dust and as we rise out of the water to the abode of man, so they ascend to glorious unknown dwellings in the skies, which we can never see.'

'Why haven't *we* immortal souls?' asked the little mermaid. 'I would willingly give up my three hundred years for just one day of being human, if I might thus enter the heavenly world above.'

'You mustn't think about that,' answered her grandmother; 'it is much better as it is. We live longer and are far happier than human beings.'

'So I must die and be dashed as foam over the sea, never to rise and hear the gentle murmur of the ocean, never to see the beautiful flowers and the bright sun! Tell me, dear grandmother, is there no way I could get an immortal soul?'

'No,' replied the old lady. 'It is true that if a human being loved you with all his heart, and promised to be faithful to you, his soul would flow into your body and you could share human happiness. But that can never be, for although we think the most beautiful part of our body is the tail, the inhabitants of the earth think it hideous; they cannot bear it. To appear handsome to them the body must have two clumsy props which they call legs.'

The little mermaid sighed and looked mournfully at the scaly part of her body which was otherwise so fair and delicate.

'We are happy,' added the old lady; 'we may jump and swim about merrily for three hundred years. That is a long time and afterwards we shall rest peacefully in death. This evening we have a court ball.'

The ball of which the queen-mother spoke was far more splendid than any which earth has ever seen. The walls of the hall were of crystal, very thick, but very clear. Hundreds of large mussel-shells were planted in rows along them, some of rose-colour, some green as grass, but all sending out a bright light which not only illuminated the whole room but also shone through the glassy walls into the waters around. They made the scales of the numberless fish, great and small, crimson and purple, silver and gold-coloured, appear more brilliant than ever. Through the centre of the ballroom flowed a bright clear stream, on the surface of which mermen and mermaids danced to the sound of their own voices.

The little princess sang more sweetly than anyone else and they clapped their hands and applauded her. She was pleased at this for she knew that there was no more beautiful voice than hers, on earth or in the sea. But her thoughts soon returned to the world above; she could not forget the handsome prince, she could not control her sorrow at not having an immortal soul. She stole away from her father's palace and while all was joy within, she sat in her little neglected garden lost in thought. Suddenly she heard the sound of horns resounding over the water far away in the distance, and she said to herself, 'He is going out to hunt, he whom I love more than my father and mother. I will risk everything to win him—and an immortal soul. While my sisters are still dancing in the palace I will go to the sorceress I have always been so frightened of, but who is the only person who can advise and help me.'

So the little mermaid left the garden and went to the foaming whirlpool where the sorceress dwelt. She had never been this way before. No flowers or sea-grass bloomed along her path; she had to cross an expanse of bare grey sand before she reached the whirlpool, whose waters were eddying and whirling like mill-wheels, rushing along with everything they had seized into the abyss below. Then she had to pass through a boiling, slimy bog, which the sorceress called her turf-moor. Her house stood in a wood beyond this and a strange place it was. All the trees and bushes around were polypi, looking like hundred-headed serpents shooting up out of the ground, their branches were long slimy arms with fingers of worms waving on every side. Whatever they seized, they fastened upon so that it could not loosen itself from their grasp. The little mermaid stood still for a minute looking at this horrible wood and her heart beat with fear. She would certainly have turned back had she not remembered the prince—and immortality. The thought gave her new courage so she bound up her long waving hair so that the polypi might not catch hold of it, crossed her arms over her bosom and, swifter than a fish can glide through the water, she slipped through these terrible trees which vainly stretched their eager arms after her. She saw how almost every polypus had something in his grasp, held as firmly by a thousand little arms as if enclosed by iron bands. There were whitened skeletons of human beings, helmets, chests, skeletons of land animals and even a little mermaid whom they had seized and strangled. This seemed the worst sight of all to our poor little heroine.

Soon she came to a marshy place where immense, fat snails were crawling about and in the middle of it stood a house built of the bones of unfortunate people who had been shipwrecked. Here the witch sat caressing a toad in the same manner as some people would a pet bird. She called the ugly fat snails her chickens, and she let them crawl all over her.

'I know exactly what you are going to ask me,' said she to the little princess. 'Your wish is foolish, yet it shall be fulfilled though it is sure to bring misfortune on you, my fairest princess. You have come just at the right time' continued she; 'had you come after sunset I wouldn't have been able to help you for another year. You must swim to land and sit down on the shore and swallow a drink which I will prepare for you. Your tail will then fall and shrink into the things which men call legs. This transformation will be very painful for you will feel as though a sharp knife passed through your body. All who look on you will say

that you are the loveliest child they have ever seen. You will keep all your graceful movements and no dancer will move so lightly, but every step you take will cause you unbearable pain: it will be as though you were walking on the sharp edges of swords and your blood will flow. Can you endure all this suffering? If so, I will grant your request.'

'Yes, I can,' answered the princess, with a faltering voice; for she remembered her dear prince and the immortal soul which her suffering might win.

'Remember,' said the witch, 'that you can never become a mermaid again once you have received human form. You may never return to your sisters and your father's palace and unless you shall win the prince's love to such a degree that he shall leave father and mother for you, that you shall be part of all his thoughts and wishes, and unless the priest join your hands so that you become man and wife, you will never obtain the immortality you seek. Sould he marry another you will die on the following day for your heart will break with sorrow and you will be changed to foam on the sea.'

'Still I will do it!' said the little mermaid, pale and trembling as a dying person.

'Besides all this, I must be paid; and it is no little thing I ask for my trouble. You have the sweetest voice of all the dwellers in the sea and you think it will charm the prince; this voice, however, I demand as my reward. I need the best thing you possess in exchange for my magic drink, for I shall have to sacrifice my own blood so the draught may be as sharp as a two-edged sword.'

'But if you take my voice from me,' said the princess, 'what will I have left to charm the prince?'

'Your graceful body,' replied the witch; 'your modest movements and your eloquent eyes. With these it will be easy to infatuate a vain human heart. Well now, have you lost courage? Put out your little tongue, so I can cut it off and take it in return for my magic drink.'

'Be it so!' said the princess, and the witch took up her cauldron in order to mix her portion. 'Cleanliness is a good thing,' she remarked as she began to scrub out the cauldron with a handful of toads and snails. Then she scratched her bosom and let the black blood trickle down into the cauldron. She threw in new ingredients, the smoke from the ingredients assumed horrible forms, and a moaning and groaning proceeded from it. The magic drink at length became clear and transparent as pure water; it was ready.

'Here it is!' said the witch to the princess, cutting off her tongue at the same moment. The poor little mermaid was now completely dumb for she could neither sing nor speak.

'If the polypi should try to seize you as you pass through my little grove,' said the witch, 'you have only to sprinkle some of this magic drink over them and their arms will burst into a thousand pieces.' But the princess had no need of this counsel for the polypi drew hastily back as soon as they perceived the bright phial that glittered in her hand like a star, so she passed safely through the formidable wood, over the moor and across the foaming stream.

The sun had not yet risen when she arrived at the prince's palace and those well-known marble steps. The moon still shone in the sky as she drank off the wonderful liquid contained in her phial. She felt it run through her like a sharp knife and she fell down in a swoon. When the sun rose, she awoke and felt a burning pain in all her limbs and when she opened her eyes she found the handsome prince was bending over her. Full of shame, she looked down and saw that, instead of the long fish-like tail she had hitherto borne, she had two slender legs. But she was quite naked and she tried in vain to cover herself with her long thick hair. The prince asked who she was, and how she had got there and in reply she smiled and gazed at him with her bright blue eyes, for alas! she could not speak. He led her by the hand into the palace and as she went she felt as though she were walking on the edges of sharp swords, but she bore the pain willingly. On she passed, light as a zephyr and all who saw her wondered at her light undulating movements.

When she entered the palace, rich clothes of muslin and silk were brought to her. She was lovelier than anyone else who lived there, but she could neither speak nor sing. Some female slaves, gaily dressed in silk and gold brocade, sang before the prince and his royal parents and one of them had a very clear, sweet voice. The prince applauded her by clapping his hands and this made the little mermaid very sad, for she knew that she used to sing far better than the young slave. 'Alas!' she thought, 'if only he knew that I have given away my voice for his sake.'

The slaves began to dance. Then the lovely little mermaiden stood up and, stretching out her delicate white arms, glided about the room. Every movement displayed the perfect symmetry and elegance of her figure, and the expression which shone in her eyes touched the hearts of the spectators far more than the song of the slaves. Everybody was enchanted, especially the young prince, who called her his dear little foundling. She danced again and again, although every step cost her excessive pain, and the prince then said that she should always be with him and he had a sleeping-place prepared for her on velvet cushions in the ante-room of his own apartment.

The prince ordered a suit of men's clothes to be made for her so that she could accompany him in his rides. So together they traversed the fragrant woods, where green boughs brushed against their shoulders, and the birds sang merrily among the fresh leaves. She climbed up steep mountains and although her tender feet bled, she only smiled and followed her dear prince to the heights where they could see the clouds chasing each other beneath them, like a flock of birds migrating to other countries.

During the night when all the palace was at rest, she used to walk down the marble steps in order to cool her burning feet in the deep waters and she would think then of her family under the waves. One night her sisters swam together to the spot, arm in arm and singing, but alas! very sadly. She beckoned to them and they immediately recognized her and told her how greatly they mourned for her in her father's house. After this they visited her every night and once they brought their old grandmother with them, who had not seen the upper world for a great many years. They also brought their father, the Mer-king, with his crown on his head, but these two old people did not venture near enough the land to speak to her.

The little mermaiden became dearer and dearer to the prince every day but he only looked upon her as a sweet, gentle child, and the thought of making her his wife never entered his head. And yet she would have to be his wife before she could receive an immortal soul, she would have to be his wife or she would change into foam and be driven restlessly over the billows of the sea.

'Do you not love me above all others?' her eyes asked, as he caught her fondly in his arms and kissed her lovely brow.

'Yes,' the prince would say, 'you are dearer to me than any

other, for no one is as good as you are. You love me so much and you are so like a young maiden whom I saw once and may never see again. I was on board a ship which was wrecked by a sudden tempest and the waves threw me on the shore near a holy temple. A young girl found me on the shore and saved my life. I only saw her once, but her image is vividly impressed upon my memory and her alone can I love. But she belongs to the holy temple and you, who resemble her so much, have been given to me for consolation. We will never be parted!'

'Alas! he does not know that it was I who saved his life,' thought the little mermaiden, sighing deeply.

'The prince is going to be married to the beautiful daughter of the neighbouring king,' said the courtiers; 'that is why he is having that splendid ship fitted out. It is given out that he wishes to travel, but in reality he is going to see the princess.' The little mermaiden smiled at these and similar conjectures, for she knew the prince's intentions better than anyone else.

'I must go,' he said to her. 'I must see the beautiful princess as my parents ask me to do so, but they will not compel me to marry her and bring her home as my bride. And it is quite impossible for me to love her for she cannot be so like the beautiful girl in the temple as you are, and if I had to choose, I should prefer you, my little silent foundling with the eloquent eyes.' And he kissed her rosy lips and folded her in his arms, so that a sweet vision of human happiness and immortal bliss arose in her heart.

'You are not afraid of the sea, are you, my sweet, silent child?' he asked tenderly, as they stood together in the splendid ship which was to take them to the country of the neighbouring king. And then he told her of the storms that sometimes agitate the waters, of the strange fishes that inhabit the deep, and of the wonderful things seen by divers. But she smiled at his words, for she knew better than he what went on in the depths of the ocean.

At night, when the moon shone brightly and when all on board were fast asleep, she sat in the ship's gallery, looking down into the sea. It seemed to her that she saw her father's palace and her grandmother's silver crown. She saw her sisters rise out of the water, looking sorrowful and stretching out their hands towards

her. She nodded to them, smiled, and would have explained that everything was going on quite according to her wishes but just then the cabin-boy approached and the sisters plunged beneath the water, but so suddenly that the boy thought what he had seen on the waves was nothing but foam.

The next morning the ship entered the harbour of the king's splendid capital. Bells were rung, trumpets sounded and soldiers marched in procession through the city, with waving banners and glittering bayonets. Every day saw some new entertainments; balls and parties followed each other. The princess, however, was not yet in the town for she had been sent to a distant convent for education, where she had been taught every royal virtue. At last she arrived at the palace.

'It is she!' exclaimed the prince when they met; 'it is she who saved my life when I lay like a corpse on the seashore,' and he pressed his bride to his beating heart.

'Oh, I am all too happy!' said he to his dumb foundling. 'What I never dared to hope for has come to pass. You must rejoice in my happiness, for you love me more than all others who surround me.' And the little mermaid kissed his hand and it seemed to her that her heart was broken.

The church-bells rang, and the bride and bridegroom joined hands and received the bishop's blessing. The little mermaid, clad in silk and cloth of gold, stood behind the princess and held the train of the bridal dress but she heard nothing of the solemn music and her eyes saw nothing of the holy ceremony. She remembered her approaching death and what she had lost both in this world and the next. That very same evening bride and bridegroom went on board ship, cannons were fired and flags waved in the breeze. In the centre of the deck stood a magnificent pavilion of purple and cloth of gold with the richest and softest couches where the royal pair were to spend the night. A favourable wind swelled the sails and the ship glided lightly over the blue waters.

As soon as it was dark, coloured lamps were hung out and dancing began on the deck. The little mermaid was reminded of what she had seen the first time she rose to the upper world and the present scene was just as splendid. She was obliged to join in the dancing and everybody praised her for never had she danced with more enchanting grace. Her little feet suffered extremely, but she no longer felt the pain for the anguish her heart suffered was much greater. It was the last evening she would see the man for whose sake she had forsaken her home and all her family, had given away her beautiful voice, and daily suffered the most terrible pain. It was the last evening she would breathe the same air as he, or watch the deep blue sea and the starry sky. An eternal night, in which she might neither think nor dream, awaited her. Her heart was filled with thoughts of death, yet she smiled and danced with the others till past midnight when the prince kissed his lovely bride, and arm in arm they went into the magnificent tent to sleep.

All was now still; only the steersman stood at the ship's helm.
The little mermaid leaned her white arms on the bulwark and
looked towards the east, waiting for the dawn and the first
sunbeam which would kill her. She saw her sisters rise out of the
sea. They were deathly pale and their long hair no longer waved
over their shoulders: it had all been cut off.

'We gave it to the witch,' they said, 'to persuade her to help
you so you do not die. Here is a knife she has given us. Before
the sun rises you must plunge it into the prince's heart and when
his warm blood trickles down on to your feet they will again
be changed to a fish's tail. Once more you will be a mermaid
and will live your full three hundred years before you change to
foam on the sea. But hurry, either he or you must die before
sunrise! In a few minutes the sun will rise and then you must die.'
With these words they sighed deeply and disappeared into the
sea.

The little mermaid drew aside the purple curtains of the prince's tent. She bent over him and kissed his forehead and then, glancing at the sky, she saw that the light was growing stronger every moment. The prince's lips murmured the name of his bride—he was dreaming of her, and her only—and the knife trembled in the hand of the unhappy mermaid. All at once, she threw the knife far out into the sea and, with eyes fast becoming dim, she turned and plunged into the sea, and felt her body slowly dissolving into foam.

The sun rose and his rays fell so gently on her she was scarcely sensible of dying. A host of ethereal beings seemed to be flying about her head, and their voices sang so sweet and soothing a melody that no human could have caught the sound. They hovered round her, borne by their own lightness through the air, and the little mermaid suddenly found she had a frame as transparent as theirs and that she was rising gradually out of the foam.

'Where are you taking me?' she asked.

'To the daughters of the air,' came the answer. 'A mermaid has no immortal soul, and can only acquire one by winning the love of one of the sons of men. The daughters of air do not have immortal souls, but they can acquire them by their own good deeds. We fly to hot countries, where the children of earth are sinking under sultry breezes and our fresh, cooling breath revives them. We diffuse ourselves through the atmosphere, we perfume it with fragrant flowers and thus spread delight and well-being over the earth. By doing good in this way for three hundred years, we win immortality and share the eternal bliss of human beings. And you, poor little mermaid, who, following the impulse of your own heart, have done and suffered so much, you have been raised to the world of spirits so that by performing deeds of kindness for three hundred years you may receive an immortal soul.'

The little mermaid stretched out her arms to the sun and, for the first time in her life, tears moistened her eyes.

By this time all were awake and rejoicing in the ship. She

saw the prince with his pretty bride; they had missed her and they looked sorrowfully down on the foamy sea as if they knew she had plunged in. Unseen she kissed the bridegroom's forehead, smiled upon him and then, with the rest of the children of the air, soared high above a rosy cloud which was sailing peacefully over the ship.

'After three hundred years we shall fly to the kingdom of heaven.'

'We may arrive there even sooner,' whispered one of her new sisters. 'We fly unseen through men's dwellings and whenever we find a good child, who gives pleasure to his parents and deserves their love, a year is struck off our three hundred. But when we see a rude, naughty child, we weep bitter tears and every tear we shed adds a day to our time of trial.'